RISE OF THE GORGON

Visit us at www.boldstrokesbooks.com

By the Author

Sacred Fire

Rise of the Gorgon

RISE OF THE GORGON

by
Tanai Walker

2015

RISE OF THE GORGON
© 2015 By Tanai Walker. All Rights Reserved.

ISBN 13: 978-1-62639-367-7

This Trade Paperback Original Is Published By
Bold Strokes Books, Inc.
P.O. Box 249
Valley Falls, NY 12185

First Edition: August 2015

Credits
Editor: Cindy Cresap
Production Design: Susan Ramundo
Cover Design By Sheri (graphicartist2020@hotmail.com)

Acknowledgments

A tremendous thanks to Sandra Lowe who saw so much more potential in this story and its characters, than its oblivious creator. Much respect and admiration to Cindy Cresap, Super-Editor. A special thanks to my sister, Tianna, the real life inspiration for the character Tammy Crockett.

Dedication

To Janette, my best friend, lover, partner, and hopefully soon, my wife. Next time, keep up with your peanut butter cups.

CHAPTER ONE

Austin, Texas

There was no point in arguing with Anne Humphries when some right-wing pundit got under her skin. When Elle arrived, she was sitting in her car, lips pursed tightly as she listened to the radio broadcast of Phil Whitman's morning show out of Dallas. The man was an internationally known asshole, beloved by his followers, hated by just about everyone else. He flaunted his conservative views and enjoyed vilifying smaller, left-wing journalists.

Elle didn't have a fancy satellite radio in her car, and so she quickly climbed out of her car and into Anne's. Whitman was in the middle of a rant about the new wave of Internet journalists and bloggers.

"As I said earlier, Marv, they all want to be like Anne Humphries and Elle Pharell. They want the big dollars. They want the bleeding heart hippie corporations to budget the spread of their anti-American sentiment."

Elle chuckled ruefully. "Really?"

Anne shushed her with a finger. "He said that I'm no Molly Ivins."

Elle winced. "That was a low blow."

On the radio, Phil asked, "Wasn't Pharell once a student of Anne Humphries? It seems she would have taught her a little bit more about journalism with integrity instead of how to capitalize on sensationalism and conspiracy."

Elle and Anne let out a collective snort.

Anne shook her silvery-blond curls. "He's been going on like this for the past fifteen minutes."

"He's just jealous," Elle said. "Our little blog has blown up."

"I should call in," Anne said decisively.

"You promised to stop doing that."

"He's talking shit about us. In the same time zone."

"That's exactly what he wants, Anne. He's goading you to put some life into his boring ass show."

She sat back in her seat. "Well, maybe I should give the old buzzard what he wants."

Elle laughed. "No. He'll piss you off and you'll say something off-color."

Anne titled her head as if to get a better look at her. "When did you become so wise?"

Elle reached over the middle console and patted her hand. Anne, in turn, gripped it in her own with Elle's on top. Mahogany over ivory. Separated by race and nearly thirty years, they were unlikely work partners. The respect and admiration they had for each other transcended the superficial.

"You're still wiser than me," Elle said. "Phil Whitman just happens to be your number one weakness."

"These are the kind of people we are going to have to watch out for fellow Texans," Phil ranted. "Liberal lesbians shoving their LGBT-feminist agenda down our throats."

Elle raised her hands in mock fear. Anne laughed.

"Speaking of Pharell. She's also the daughter of Georgia Democratic Congresswoman Regina Pharell," Phil said and gave a chuckle. "That's right, folks. The apple doesn't fall far from the tree. Anne Humphries's little cohort is on a campaign to uncover the lack of treatment for veterans—"

Anne snapped off the radio. "Let's get to work."

"What did he say about my mother?" Elle asked.

"Oh, are we calling in now?"

"No," Elle said reluctantly. "Let's get to work."

She went back to her car for her purse and laptop bag. Anne waited for her so they could walk into the building together. They had met during Elle's first year in the graduate journalism program at the University of Texas. She had been excited to study under Anne Humphries, the infamous out lesbian reporter with the Mississippian drawl that she refused to clip.

Anne had just retired from her own thirty-year career in journalism, which she referred to as her hell-raising phase. She saw teaching as a cushy job. She passed the mediocre students through and pushed hard on the few she thought had potential. She made Elle's first semester hell. Devastated, Elle pressed on, determined to astound her idol.

What she didn't know was that the little blog she had been working on since her sophomore year had drawn more than a few curious glances. She called the blog the *Green Patriot* and wrote pieces on stories that received little to no attention from the media. Anne Humphries was a fan of her work and secretly didn't mind when a new blog post came out and Elle's assignments were late. The professor she wanted so hard to impress was already quite amazed.

As Elle's studies progressed, their student-professor relationship became one of mentorship and friendship. Together they took the *Green Patriot* from a blog with a few hundred readers to an Internet news magazine with articles and videos. They owned a renovated office building that served as their headquarters/studio. Eventually, they came to employ nearly fifty people.

"We've come a long way to be annoying guys like Whitman," Elle said as they approached the *Green Patriot*'s headquarters.

"It still irks me," Anne said.

As they entered the lobby, the receptionist, Paula, stood, self-consciously smoothing her skirt, a worried look on her face. Her eyes darted to Rob Loera.

He stood slowly. "Hey, Elle."

"He's been here since we opened the building," Paula said.

"You should have called me," Elle said and looked to Rob. "You should have called me."

He was dressed in a black T-shirt and baggy carpenter pants with a camouflage print. His long, broad face was pale; the whites around his dark eyes were red.

"I didn't think," he said. "I've been…you know—"

Elle nodded sympathetically. She knew his problems well and did her best to help whenever she could. "I know, Rob. Come on up so we can talk."

They went to the elevator and filed in. Elle hit the button on the elevator for the third floor. Rob usually towered over them, but he stood with his shoulders hunched forward like a man triple his age.

"How have you been, Rob?" Anne asked.

"Not so good," he said, his usual baritone a hoarse whisper. "Not sleeping much. Not eating."

Anne glanced at Elle, worry shading her periwinkle eyes a darker hue.

Elle placed her hand on Rob's forearm, her fingers brushing the lightning bolt tattoo there. He was shaking. When she looked into his eyes, she saw fear.

She had struck up a conversation with Rob at a rally for veterans in DC in front of the Capitol building. At twenty-five, he had just finished his third tour in Afghanistan. Several injuries to his knee and a gunshot blast to the shoulder forced him out of the army on medical discharge. His leg and shoulder healed, but there were other wounds that ran deeper. After his return stateside, Rob began to suffer signs of PTSD. What the government offered in the way of therapy and drugs didn't do a thing to relieve him. When Elle met him, Rob was unemployed and homeless, often spending nights in his truck.

She led him to her private space. She could hardly call it an office. It was barely big enough to hold a desk, a filing cabinet, a couple of chairs. She had squeezed in a shelf for knickknacks after winning a National Association of Black Journalists award.

Rob took his usual seat across from her desk.

"I needed to talk to you," he said. "I really needed to talk to you."

She combed her hand through her short, spiked hair. "I'm here, Rob. You know that. You've had it harder than this."

"I'm tired, Elle," he said. "It's like something's building up inside me."

"You said you haven't been sleeping," she said. "Aren't you taking your new meds?"

"They don't work," he said and looked away worriedly, mumbling, "It's like they're not letting me sleep."

Elle straightened in her seat. "The medicine?"

"My dreams, the things I see when I close my eyes. That's why I can't sleep."

"What do you see?" Elle asked and watched his face crumple as if he were about to start sobbing. She knew it was bad when Rob tried holding back his feelings.

"It's not stuff from the war." He wiped his eyes with the back of his hands. "It's new things I haven't seen until now."

"Bad dreams," she said as if trying to help him fill in the blanks of his sleepless nights.

"No, not bad dreams," he shouted, startling her. "I'm seeing these fucking hajis." He paused. "I know you don't like that word, Elle. I'm sorry. I've been seeing this town and people staggering around like zombies, wallowing in their own filth, eating each other."

"They're just dreams, Rob."

"No, it's not." He stood up. "When I worked for that contract company, ZIS. I think that's when it happened."

Elle frowned. He had never mentioned his short-term stint with the security company in much detail, just as a side job he did before he came back to the States after his discharge.

"So you're saying these dreams are memories?"

"Yes, things I wasn't supposed to remember."

Elle's first thought was to get Anne in the room, because she had a way of knowing when someone was absolutely nuts or telling the complete truth, or even a little bit of both. Elle let her emotions get in the way, her favorite being self-righteousness.

"What do you mean?" she asked. "What were you not supposed to remember?"

"I don't know," he said. "But I hurt a lot of innocent people, and I don't know why."

There was a rising panic in his voice. He'd never seemed delusional before. Rob suffered from extreme anxiety and depression that made it hard for him to adjust to life away from the war.

"You need sleep," she said. "I can get you a room at one of those places."

"What about my place?" he asked.

"You know I'll look after it," she said. "When was the last time you slept?"

"Seven days," he mumbled.

Elle sighed. The last time she saw Rob had been a week ago. They discussed an upcoming television appearance over lunch. He had seemed himself that afternoon. She stood, walked around the desk, and touched his shoulder.

"I'll get you some place good. You go and don't worry about your place or work. I'll take care of it all."

He shook his head. "No."

"Rob," she said softly. "You haven't slept in seven days. We have to treat this like an emergency."

He jumped out of his seat, startling her. "No more *places*, no more hospitals, not for me. Not anymore."

"You don't mean that."

He lifted his shirt, reached into his waistband, and removed a large black handgun. Elle stepped back, fear gripping her heart. Her mind reasoned with the situation. This was Rob; they had shared meals together and eased each other's nerves before television appearances. He would not kill her.

Determined to remain calm, she slowly stretched her arms out to Rob.

"Whatever is going on, there's no need for guns."

"I keep seeing 'em, Elle. Whenever I close my eyes."

"Rob, what happened to the people?"

"I don't know," he said. "I guess we were rounding them up into trailers, packing them in like you wouldn't even pack cattle. And they were like, oblivious to what was going on. Some of them struggled and we Tasered them and tossed them in the trailer right on top of the other."

Elle edged closer, half focused on his words, half focused on the gun. She wanted to scream, but who would come running? Anne? One of the interns? None of them was a match for a combat-trained soldier and his big black gun.

"We can fix this, Rob," she said. "You're safe here. You know that."

"You don't understand. We weren't much better than those people were. We were fucked up too. It can't be reversed. It will only get worse."

He pressed the muzzle to his temple.

She screamed his name.

He looked into her eyes one last time. "I'm sorry."

She saw his finger pull the trigger. Then she turned her head at the deafening sound of the gun's thunder. The splatter of blood, bone, and brain was faster than her hands. She felt the spray on her cheek like a blast from a high-powered hose.

She screamed, but this time she didn't hear herself. She felt her lungs burning with the effort of her alarm and anguish. She looked back at Rob. He lay there on the floor of her office, a quickly spreading pool of blood around what remained of his head.

Anne burst through the door. She saw Rob on the floor, and her face contorted with grief. She stepped over him and crossed the distance between them to put her arms around Elle. She pulled away and checked her for injuries. She was speaking, but Elle couldn't hear her. The interns were at the doorway, terror in their eyes.

Anne grabbed Elle's shoulders and shook her sternly. Her face was red, and she looked just as terrified as the interns. Elle could hear her a bit. She sounded so far away. She could hear something else too. She thought it was a siren until she realized how out of breath she was, and how much her throat burned.

Looking around at the haunted faces of Anne and her co-workers, Elle realized then that she'd never stopped screaming.

❖

They kept her in the conference room for the rest of the day, trying their best to shield her from the investigation going on down the hall in her office. After the paramedics came in to check her vitals, no one but staff, interns, or Anne entered to bring information about the world beyond the wooden door. The press was outside the building, and police were all over the place inside and out. No one gave her many details other than the obvious. No one spoke of what happened. No one mentioned him. Still, she knew the exact moment the medical examiners moved Rob's body out of the building; a hush fell throughout the halls in a wave.

Anne broke the silence by presenting her with the workout clothes that she kept for days when she went to the gym from the office, and she changed right there in the conference room.

Everything felt so surreal. She felt detached from them all. She kept seeing Rob's head give way to a gunshot and turn into a red blur.

Someone brought her baked potato soup, but she just couldn't bring herself to eat it.

The police came to speak with her, and she calmly answered the questions they asked. They wanted to know the nature of her and Rob's relationship. They wanted to know if there was some romantic element. She felt so numb that she forgave them their idiotic questions. She simply told them no, and then told them about the dreams Rob said plagued him, how he claimed not to have slept for seven days. She told them about the state of his mental health since his discharge from the military.

When she met Rob, he was in a bad place. His anxiety kept him from working a full-time job and he was on the verge of homelessness. After some coaxing, he spoke to her about his tours and the horrors he had seen. The death. He wanted to bring awareness to his plight and tell the world what other soldiers experienced upon return from service. She wrote a blog about him that became popular with vets as well as civilians. She brought him into the studio for an interview and video piece, which went viral within a day. After that, a big network invited them to a round table discussion on a national news show.

The exposure got Rob a position as a delivery driver with benefits that could cover his mental and physical health costs. The attention made Rob uneasy at first. Not everyone was supportive, namely his family. After a year, he seemed to have settled into his job. He bought a small plot of land out in the country. He saw his therapist regularly. They kept in touch, and Elle liked to think they were friends. He seemed to be on the right path.

"Until this morning," she said.

"What was that?" Anne asked.

Elle looked around and noticed that the police were gone. The door to the conference room was open. The offices beyond were dark.

Elle blinked. "What time is it?"

"A little after eight," Anne said. She moved close and took her hand. "How are you feeling?"

She blinked back tears. "Lost."

Anne embraced her. "I'm sorry this happened, Elle."

She nodded, overcome with tears.

"It was no one's fault," Anne said.

"He came to see me," Elle said. "He killed himself in my office."

"Rob was very ill."

"He'd been doing so well. Why didn't I see that he was having a hard time?"

Anne lifted her shoulders in a small shrug. "I'm going to get you out of here. Your parents called and they want to talk to you right away. Your mother chewed me out for not taking you to a hospital."

"Thank you," Elle said. Her parents had always been a little overprotective.

"You would have done the same for me." Anne stood and helped her to her feet. "One of the local anchorwomen is outside. I told her to stick around just in case you wanted to give a statement."

"I can't—"

"I'll get rid of her. You're staying with me tonight. No arguments."

Elle smiled wanly. "You'll get none from me."

They left through the back entrance. A cold front had blown in sometime during the afternoon bringing chilly winds. Anne's car waited near the door. A patrol car sat close by. In the distance, Elle could see a news van and the spotlight from a camera. Anne hustled her into the passenger seat of her car and scrambled around the car into the driver's side.

They drove away quickly. Anne asked if she wanted to stop for dinner.

"I'm not hungry," Elle said.

"You weren't hungry at lunch, though I don't blame you," Anne said. "Now is the time for you to get something in your stomach."

"I just want to lie down in a dark room," Elle said. "I want to close my eyes, but I don't think I'll be able to. I'm afraid of what I might see."

She thought of her final conversation with Rob. He'd been afraid to sleep, haunted by dreams he claimed were memories. Through the haze of the day, she had asked Anne to check with the company he mentioned. ZIS, or Ziggurat International Securities, was a contract military firm that had expanded during the conflicts in the Middle East during the 90s and 00s.

"Did you get in touch with the Ziggurat people?" Elle asked.

"Yes," she said. "My brain didn't make the connection at first, but I remember hearing about them way back in the late eighties. They're a major private military contractor. They've worked with all the heavy hitters. The CIA, NSA, and the DOD."

"What do they have to say about Rob?"

"Well, they're denying him."

Elle straightened in her seat. "What do you mean?"

"I called them up, and they're saying he was never on their payroll."

Elle felt her brow furrow. "Rob wouldn't lie about something like that."

"He obviously wasn't in his right mind."

"He was never delusional—"

"Not that you know of."

"Then what?" Elle shouted. "You're saying that he all of a sudden became delusional?"

"I'm trying to understand what drove him to the edge," Anne said. "I know you cared for the guy, and that you looked after him. I'm sorry he's gone, Elle, but he doesn't need you to look after him anymore. He doesn't need you to make more of his death than what it is."

Elle stared at her in disbelief. Anne was usually on her side about such things. They disagreed often on hot button issues, but this was different. This was someone they knew.

She couldn't let it go. "He remembered something that freaked him out, that made him so guilty he couldn't go on anymore."

"So he just forgot? Or something so traumatizing happened that he blocked it?" Anne asked. "That still doesn't count for the fact that they don't seem to remember him."

"Maybe they don't want to remember him," Elle said. "Maybe they helped the process along a bit."

"We can't do this anymore," she said. "We're becoming a respected news source. We can't afford to chase conspiracy theories. We'll lose credibility if we run something like this."

"Is that what you're worried about? The *Green Patriot*?"

"Someone has to," Anne grumbled.

"A man is dead."

"You did what you could. It's over."

They drove a few minutes in silence.

"Take me home," Elle said.

Anne cursed under her breath. "No. Out of the question. You shouldn't be alone tonight."

"I'm serious," Elle said. "Where's my phone? Where's my car?"

"I had Paula and one of the interns drive your car back to your place," Anne said. "I'm not taking you home. God knows what you'll get up to left to your own devices."

"Stop the car, Anne."

"Absolutely not."

More silence.

"Take me to Rob's place."

Anne gave her a pointed look. "Hell no."

"I have to get there before the cops or his family start snooping around," Elle said. "He gave me a key to his trailer months ago. It's in my purse."

Anne looked to her and frowned. "Why do you have a key to Rob Loera's house?"

"He trusted me, Anne. He tried to tell me before he took his life. Something drove him to it, and I'm going to find out what it was."

Anne pulled into a strip mall and sighed. They stared at each other for a moment. They had shared in almost every facet of each other's life over the past twelve years. They had shared great success and great losses along the way. Elle trusted that there was no one else in the world who knew her as well as Anne. She was sure Anne knew she wouldn't rest until she knew why Rob Loera put a gun to his head. Elle knew Anne cared more about the truth than sponsorships or the respect of assholes like Phil Whitman.

Anne pointed to the GPS in her dash. "Get that damned thing to tell us how to get there."

❖

Rob's trailer was on a piece of land on the outskirts of town. He had invited Elle over to check out the property before he purchased it. She liked the place instantly, especially the sprawling mulberry tree in the front yard. In the spring, the smell of the fruit, new, ripe, and rotting, perfumed the breeze. They had talked of making wine from the berries, or at least some jam or pie filling.

In the dark of night, the mulberry tree looked like a fearsome creature. Anne propped the screen door open as they stood on the cement steps beneath a buzzing light that illuminated the entire yard. Elle slid the key into the gold colored bolt and turned it. The door opened revealing the darkened interior of the house.

Anne left the door open, allowing the light from the outside to enter. Elle fumbled around until she found a lamp and snapped it on.

The living room was immaculate. A couch, a small television, and a stand for the television were the only furnishings. There was a small desk as well. On it were various repairs in progress. The motor for some small appliance and some fishing lures cluttered the desktop. There was also a small caliber handgun, the cylinder open and the chamber empty of bullets.

Elle found she couldn't take her eyes from the gun. Anne noticed.

"Let's not touch anything," she said. "The last thing we need is the cops on our asses."

Elle agreed. She would gladly answer any more questions the cops had for her, and now that she was in a better frame of mind, she could raise some of her own. She peered into the kitchenette. It looked clean and well organized.

"Someone's been crashing on the couch?" Anne asked. She pointed to several bed pillows covered in white cases that had been left propped against a rolled up blanket.

Elle shrugged. It made her hopeful to think Rob had spent his final days with someone who could shed light on the events of his final days, an old army buddy or a relative.

They moved to the kitchen. It was just as clean. There was one clean bowl, one clean spoon, and one clean plastic tumbler on a towel next to the sink.

"Well?" Anne asked.

"What?" Elle asked.

"What are we looking for?"

"I don't know," Elle said. "Let's check the back."

They moved through the living room to the short hall. Behind the first door was the bathroom. It was just as pristine as the kitchen. Even the wastebasket was empty.

"Whoever is crashing on the couch is a tidy houseguest."

"Another military guy?" Anne asked.

She moved to the last door. The bedroom. She turned the knob. She could sense the disorder of the room before the light from the hall could reveal it. The bed had been dismantled. Its mattress leaned against one wall with sheets draping the top corners. In the center of the mattress was a crude crucifix painted onto the white quilted fabric in a rusted red color.

Dead candles covered the rest of the furniture, mixed in were figures and icons from various religions. Elle saw several statues of Indian deities, a totem pole, and some plaster saints. There were several articles pinned on the walls of various tragedies in the Middle East. She saw pictures of bodies after bombings on the Gaza strip, and of alleged terrorists being tortured at the hands of American soldiers at Abu Ghraib. She spotted a map marked in topographic rings. It was definitely military. A neon pink yard sale price sticker marked a spot on the map. There were coordinates written in small, neat writing.

"We should go," Anne said close behind her. "We should get out of here."

Elle turned to point out the spot on the map and saw photos of her own face over Anne's shoulder on the opposite wall. They were photos, snatched from the galleries of Internet search engines, stills from her newscasts and various events. She gasped and walked toward them. Around the cluster of photos were painted black lightning bolts, and there was Rob's dress jacket on a makeshift stand. There were splashes of the same red paint on the sleeves.

She felt light-headed and regretted not eating the food those interns had offered earlier. The air was suddenly too heavy and she had to leave. She stumbled past Anne and out of the trailer. She welcomed the cold, wanted desperately to feel it cleansing her of the grim sights in the back bedroom. She heard the screen door slam and Anne's footsteps behind her.

She stood in front of Elle and touched her face with warm hands.

"Are you okay?"

"I don't know," Elle gasped. "What was that?"

"Just breathe," Anne said.

They sank down on their knees on the cold grass. Elle felt Anne's comforting touch between her shoulders.

"Why?" she asked.

"I can't say. I suppose it turns out he was a very sick man."

"He was doing better. I swear he was."

"Then he had an episode that he couldn't recover from."

"Something drove him over the edge. It was the work he did for Ziggurat."

Anne sighed. "I'm going back to lock up—"

"I'm coming with you."

"Elle. Don't be so difficult."

"No," she insisted. "I want to take pictures. I want to be able to understand why Rob did what he did. You just have to go with me on this, Anne."

She took a moment before she nodded. "Well, let's hurry."

They stood carefully and turned back to the trailer.

CHAPTER TWO

Prague, Czech Republic

The customers of Legiobanka went about their business as usual on an early Thursday afternoon. The air in the wood and marble paneled lobby had the same muffled quietness of a church or a library, unchecked by the shuffle of feet, low voices, and Brahms on the loudspeaker.

A stout security guard stood at his post at the entrance. When he saw the first man in the Albert Einstein mask, he stepped forward dutifully, his hand on his radio. A customer on his right, whom he had only moments ago chatted with him about the weather, jabbed a stun gun to the girth at his middle. He let out a short scream and fell to the polished wood.

"Nobody move," the stun-gun wielding patron announced. "This is an aggravated protest."

A group of nine more men entered the bank. They all wore identical latex masks with the visage of the great genius with the characteristic white mustache and cheap, wispy, gray costume hair. Uncharacteristic of the real Einstein, they each carried small submachine guns in one hand and duffel bags in the other. They menaced the bank customers with the snub-nosed weapons as they walked to the area in front of the main counter where they dropped the duffels in a semicircle.

The last Einstein dropped to his knees and began to open each bag. He pulled out a strange type of equipment. The devices were of a matte black metal and sized the same but differed in shape. Most were boxy while others were smooth and cylindrical. Thin blue wires cascaded from various openings.

The unmasked bandit used zip ties to bind the guard's ankles and wrists. One of the Einsteins handed him an Uzi. He vaulted to the top of the front counter, an open trench coat with a tartan-patterned lining flowing behind him like a cape. He shouted in Czech for everyone to remain calm. He had dusky skin and a plain, long face. Gold-rimmed glasses rested across the bridge of his nose. He watched the Einsteins work. Two of them minded the strange equipment while another pair dragged the trussed up guard away from the entrance. The remainder of the Einsteins separated the customers from the employees. He checked his watch.

"My friends," he announced. "I don't mean anyone harm. There is something you as citizens of this great country and patrons of this bank should know. Legiobanka is corrupt. They house the dirty secrets of the most notorious corporation in the world."

He paused and looked down at the customers and employees. They were frightened, clutching each other and looking to the entrance for help. He raised his gun and fired a short blast. The people shrieked and cowered.

"I need all of you to listen," he said. "These are dangerous times that we live in, but not because of some foreign dictator with a nuclear weapon or some bearded brown-skinned man with bombs strapped to his chest. No. The danger is the people who rule in the shadows, the people our governments have sold their sovereignty to."

He paced the counter, his boots kicking aside pens and forms. "These people are creating weapons that can kill without bullets or gas. Weapons that can displace entire city blocks with the push of a button. My colleagues and I have brought such a weapon today."

He paused as if to gauge their reactions.

"You are all free to go. Remember what will happen here today, and don't let the media or the government convince you otherwise."

The men in the Einstein masks ordered the employees and the patrons to stand up. They began to herd them toward the entrance. The people looked confused and relieved to be free to leave the bank.

"Yes," he assured them as he smiled benevolently. "All of you."

His eyes focused in the direction of a thin woman with graying hair pulled back into a severe bun. She clutched the arm of a fellow employee, a fat man with a yellow polka dot bow tie.

"Not you," he said. "I need you to stay."

"I won't go without her," the fat man said.

He paced the counter and regarded the smartly dressed man in shiny wing tips. He stooped and very gently placed the muzzle of the gun in the soft place of Bow Tie's stomach just below his sternum.

"She won't be harmed, I assure you. If you stay I cannot promise you the same."

Bow Tie swallowed so hard that the dots seemed to rattle.

The woman with the bun touched his arms. "It will be fine, Heinrik."

He shut his eyes vigorously and nodded. Heinrik took his place with the others as they filed out. He looked back over his shoulder once.

"Thief," the woman said. "Mad man. Good people work here and good people patronize this bank. You are wrong to come here."

He remained in his crouching stance on the counter. "Do you know what I had to go through to get possession of this weapon?" he asked. "The kinds of people I came in contact with? I learned a few things from them. One thing I learned is that any fool can wave a gun around, and an even bigger fool can pull a trigger—"

"Please," the woman said evenly. "I have a family."

"And you will see them soon," he said. "The sooner you help me the faster you can leave this. It depends. What type of fool do you take me for?"

"I don't have access to anything. I swear to you."

He raised the gun and belted the woman across the face. She fell to her knees and began to sob. He jumped from the counter and landed next to her. He kneeled.

"It was not my wish to strike you," he said. "To harm an old woman."

She straightened, facing him, a hard look in her eyes. "You are a bully."

"If you knew what I knew, you would understand."

She looked away from him defiantly. "Which box do you need access to?"

A slow, cold smile spread across his face. "Dr. Peter Geist."

She nodded. "Allow me to show you the way."

He tilted his head solemnly. "You are a wise woman. A brave woman."

She led them up a staircase trimmed with an ornate iron banister with brass railing to the second floor. They stopped inside a small office. He stood behind her as she searched a database for the box she needed. She pointed to a number on the screen with a stiff arm.

"You won't get into trouble for this," he said.

"I've worked here for sixteen years," she said. "Nearly two decades of tireless service. I have a spotless record. I would never break the law or steal. Don't worry yourself with my record."

He studied her for a moment.

"I'm not just a common thug," he said. "I have come here for what is rightfully mine. In the wrong hands, it could hurt many people. Your patron, Geist, he is the thug. He is the thief."

She handed him a keycard without a word. There was shame in her eyes, and he knew that her silence was the only power she had left. He felt sorry for the old woman. He didn't want to frighten her, and yet he couldn't be soft.

"If you could be so kind as to show me the location of the boxes."

She led him down a white tiled corridor. The short, blocky heels of her sensible shoes seemed to ring out her reluctance with each step.

He patted her plump shoulder once he returned her to the lobby. He watched as his colleagues showed her to the door. Once she was gone, he waved the card triumphantly at his accomplices.

"The police will be here soon."

"Good." He smiled. "Let them come."

Whistling, he walked to the safety deposit box storage room. He slid the card into the reader mounted to a wall. The reader beeped, and the door clicked as the deadbolt deactivated. He pushed the door open. There were hundreds of aisles of shelves, each labeled with a sequence of numbers and a color code. He found the section he was looking for, and was rounding the first shelf when he realized that he was not alone.

A woman stood before an open drawer. She held a slender white tube about four feet long. She was, for a lack of better word, beautiful. She was not shapely, but tall with long, spidery limbs. In a black motorcycle jacket, jeans, and black ankle boots, she certainly wasn't dressed like a bank employee. She smiled at him and used her hip to slowly slide the drawer closed.

"That wouldn't happen to be Dr. Geist's blueprint?" he asked nervously.

She tossed her blond head.

"Who are you?" he asked.

"I represent someone invested in the work of Dr. Geist."

"No one could be as invested as me and my colleagues. We helped Geist create the device, and now that he is dead it belongs to us."

The woman took a step forward, and he raised the gun. She stopped. Her eyes were a steely hazel, and they didn't waver as they gazed into his. She extended the tube.

When he reached for it, she snatched the tube away. He stumbled forward and raised the gun again. He made the decision that he would shoot her if she continued to goad him.

"This isn't a game," he said.

"You aren't a killer," she said. "You're a scientist and a scholar."

He shook the gun. "I'm prepared. I knew I might have to use this."

"You're not a killer," she insisted. "I am a killer. A real one. It was irresponsible for you to bring what you've brought here. Because of that you will not leave this building alive."

The intention in her voice frightened him. She was not a soft man in a bow tie or an old woman. Her eyes were cold and deadly. The gun he held didn't intimidate her. He took a step back. The plans were his life's work. He would shoot the bitch and that would be the end of it.

Her strike was as sudden and savage as a cobra. She used the tube to crack the knuckles of his hand that held the gun. He heard it clatter to the tiles as another perfectly aimed fist crashed into the bridge of his nose. He felt the crunch of the cartilage as it gave way.

He stumbled backward, his heel kicking his gun under one of the shelves. He cupped his bloody nose with one hand and used the other to signal his surrender. He blinked rapidly and swayed on his feet as he struggled with consciousness.

"We have money," he managed. "We can triple what you're being paid. Who do you work for?"

"I don't know," she answered quietly. "I don't know who I work for."

Before he could say another word, she surged forward. She rushed behind him and buckled an arm across his neck. He straightened hoping to weaken her grip. He felt her arms constrict, and his pulse began to sound in his head. Unable to take air into his lungs, he panicked. He flailed his arms and legs in an attempt to break from his attacker. His vision blurred and blackened.

❖

She released her grip on the man. His knees sagged, and he fell at her feet in a lifeless heap. She stepped over him and retrieved the tube that had fallen during the scuffle. She left the storage room and headed for the entrance of the bank.

The leader of the heist on Legiobanka had asked whom she worked for. Her truthful answer had come before she could think of it. She didn't know. She didn't recall anything before entering the bank in the early morning hours and waiting in an abandoned office. The purpose of her being there, what she was to do, was clear to her.

Failure was not a concern. She was not afraid, and it occurred to her that death was favorable over capture.

She had sat for several hours turned away from the door in a high backed executive chair. The owner was away on holiday, his life on display on the desk. A wife. Two small children in one picture, a few years older in another. A small bottle of schnapps in the bottom drawer and a glass paperweight on top of several threatening loan delinquency notices.

She had a bit of the liquor and listened. At first, there were the sounds of the old building creaking and groaning as the city around it stirred awake. Then she could hear people. She couldn't make out what they were saying of course. Her ears were not that keen. She could hear their thoughts though.

The average person, bombarded with television psychics, would describe her gift as a psychic one. Instead of vague impressions and emotive visions, her brain was constantly tapped into the frequency of human brain waves. She could hear them like static, punctuated by a pulse much like a heartbeat but more erratic. Fear, happiness, arousal, anxiety—each created a different pattern to her ears.

When confronted by the man among the safety deposit boxes, she could hear his nervousness and uncertainty as a high-pitched warped buzz. She could hear him make up his mind to attack, not in words or visions, but as the pulse.

She left him dead on the floor and went on to find the others. They knew too much. What they knew was no concern of hers, but she figured her employer's desire for their demise had to do with the tech they had brought to the bank. She knew that she must protect the tech at all cost.

As she neared the lobby, she could hear their pulses intermingling into a chorus like radio interference, a steady static hiss that permeated the air. Each differed from the other slightly, but their thoughts were clear. They were anxious and afraid.

She slipped into the lobby and hid behind a marbled pillar. The masked men were absorbed in their tasks of checking the equipment and watching the door. She could hear sirens in the distance. Her time was running out.

She stepped into view, and the Einstein checking the devices looked up from his task. His eyes searched her for a bank employee nametag. The static of his brainwaves shifted with his confusion.

"We have a lost lamb here," he announced to the others.

The Einsteins exchanged glances.

"She must have been on the second floor," one of them said.

"No one was supposed to be on the second floor at this time," another said.

"Who are you?" a third asked.

The Einsteins moved in closer.

"Just send her this way," the fourth said. "Phillipe wants all the civilians out."

One of the Einsteins posted at the door motioned for her. "Don't be afraid now. We mean you no harm. You don't want to linger here."

She didn't move or say a word.

The Einstein nearest her, the one who seemed to be in charge of the tech, turned his attention away from a cylindrical device covered in wires.

"Go on, sweetheart," he said in English. "The man's got a gun."

She turned to him and slid the baton from her sleeve. He straightened.

"Who the hell are you?"

His pulse punctuated the air in bursts like some kind of SOS. She lunged using the baton to belt him across his face. He fell to the floor, scrambling for a weapon. She kicked him in the side.

They began to fire at her then, rattling raucous tattoo that splinted the wood paneled wall above her head as she ducked, scooping up the gun the Einstein had reached for so desperately. She ran for cover and slid on her knees across the marbled floor to the safety of an ancient wooden desk used for storing bank slips.

The shooting stopped, and the Einsteins began to argue among themselves as they scrambled for safety. Their collective pulse was a chorus of blips and droning buzz with an alternating high-pitched whine.

"She has a gun."

"Did anyone hit her?"

"Nadal. The device," one of them called. "Are you hurt?"

The Einstein she had knocked to the ground stood cautiously and began to limp toward his colleagues.

"What are you doing?" an Einstein asked. "The device."

"Screw it," Nadal answered. "Phillipe said nothing about mercenaries."

"Mercenary?" another Einstein posited. "She is only one woman."

"Nonetheless, my nose is broken," Nadal groaned. "Where the hell is Phillipe?"

She peeked around the side of the desk. Several of the Einsteins had taken cover behind the front counter, Nadal and another Einstein posted behind a wood and brass pillar. The rest were scattered to the far side of the bank cowering behind various pieces of overturned furniture.

They shouted at each other from their hiding spots.

Beneath her, the floor began to thrum. She looked to the devices still arranged in a semi-circle like some kind of contemporary set of standing stones. She reached into her pocket and removed what appeared to be a roll of a popular brand of candied mints. She pulled back the wrapper revealing a row of what looked to be just as the package suggested, white, plump disc-shaped mints but with a silvery sheen. She dumped three-fourths of the contents into her hand and dropped them to the floor.

Each "mint" landed on its side, lined up as they had rested in the package. They began to roll along the floor, picking up speed as they crossed the distance between her and the devices. As they neared the equipment, the mints leapt from the floor and clung to the metallic bodies.

The floor was vibrating now. It wouldn't be long. She pressed her thumb over the top of what remained of the package of mints. It depressed with a click, and she stood with the tube from the safe deposit box in one hand, the Uzi in the other. She turned away from the devices and began to sprint toward the exit.

The Einsteins raised their guns and fired at the path of her flight. The grumble and roar of nine simultaneous explosions drowned out the staccato beat of automatic fire. She felt the rush of hot wind and debris at her back. She didn't have to look back to know the trajectory of the explosion obliterated the middle of the front desk and disintegrated the devices. A special compound would render whatever pieces remained unrecognizable to authorities.

She ran to the pillar and shot Nadal and the Einstein with him. She took shelter there from a crossfire of bullets from the Einsteins behind what remained of the front desk. Dusty smoke from the explosions filled the lobby. She squinted against the grit floating in the air. She could hear footsteps pounding just outside the entrance and raised voices. The police were outside.

She walked toward the crumbled front desk. The Einsteins rose as one and fired on her. She aimed the gun at them and swept her arm as the bullets flew. They fell one after the other. She moved in close and saw them lying in a heap, their pulses reduced to a faint hiss as their life force began to fade.

She jogged to the opposite side of the bank. There were three Einsteins left, and they had decided on surrender. She felt something she guessed to be pity as they emerged from their hiding spaces weaponless, their hands raised. They lived in a world where there were rules of combat. One of the three Einsteins stepped forward uneasily, his pulse a sharp, steady ring. He was defeated and frightened, but hopeful.

She envied him that hope.

"Please," he said. "It's over. Arrest us."

She raised the gun and squeezed the trigger. His body seized and jerked as he fell. He crumpled at her feet. Strangely, the other two stood rooted in place. She could hear confusion and shock in their pulses.

"Are you not police?" the Einstein on her right asked. "Interpol?"

"No," she answered. She knew that speaking to them was not part of her directive, but she still felt compelled to answer them before she killed them.

"Who are you?"

"I am the Gorgon."

She squeezed the trigger again and the gun rattled in her hands. She stepped over them and out a side service entrance that led to an alleyway. A small motorbike waited partially hidden behind some trashcans. The sleek, silvery piece of machinery was like nothing available on the market or off. She knew that someone had made it especially for her. There was a place to secure the white tube she carried.

She mounted and settled in the long black saddle. The wheels on the bike were shorter and wider than average, setting the body inches from the ground. A gyro sensor kept the bike stable. She could see police at the mouth of the alley trying to control the pandemonium.

She started the bike, and its engine hummed to life. She rolled out of the alley into a crowd of bystanders bundled in their coats against the winter chill. She nosed through the gathering, passing a few police officers as she went. One of them spied her and planted himself in her path.

"Did you just come from that way?" he asked in Czech as he pointed toward the alley.

"I don't speak Czech," she said.

"Yes," he said slowly in English. "Please wait."

She continued to roll forward and he grabbed her throttle hand. She flipped her wrist and grabbed hold of his wrist. She sat up and pulled him forward, slamming her other fist into his face. Her throttle hand freed, she twisted the accelerator and sailed forward, clearing the mob. She shifted into full speed.

In the rearview, she saw a small car with blue sirens followed by a second and a third. She gunned the engine as she neared a line of traffic. She zipped through the cars and over tram rails, handling the bike against the icy air as if it were an extension of her body.

She escaped the traffic and skirted through a park, startling several cyclists and a dog walker. She jumped a curb, crossed over a brick-paved walkway, and hit the street. She sped through the entrance of one of the thirteen bridges that crossed over the Vltava

River. The traffic was moderate, and she slowed her pace and joined in with the commuters.

She could still hear sirens in the distance and knew that the police were not far off her trail. Halfway across the bridge, she spotted a Hummer with flashing lights on its roof. She pulled the brakes and slowed the bike to a stop. She turned the bike into the opposite lane, crossing the tram tracks. The tires spun in place as she gunned the engine. The bike jumped forward, gaining speed in a matter of seconds.

From the other end of the bridge, two more police cars pulled ahead of traffic. Once again, she slowed to a stop. The chase was over. She abandoned the bike, collected the white tube, and ran to the guardrail. She looked over her shoulder at the bike. Smoke poured from the engine, and soon flames would engulf it leaving nothing for the authorities to puzzle over.

The Hummer arrived on the scene, and blue uniformed officers leapt from the open doors, their hands on their guns. She could hear their shouts for her surrender.

She leapt onto the rail and jumped. Once airborne, she tucked her arms close and pointed her toes downward. Forty-three feet and the freezing, choppy Vltava River seemed to rush up to meet her.

She hit the water hard. The impact made her world go black. The shock of the landing paralyzed her body. Her brain flickered as if it were a light bulb partially screwed into its fixture. She could only feel herself sinking into the cold depths of the river.

It was the sudden pain that brought her to her senses. Her limbs began to struggle against the current and the ache in her ribs. She opened her eyes and saw the murky water swirling around her.

She didn't panic and attempt to breathe and fill her lungs with the freezing gray water. She fought the urge to move toward the light of day. They would be looking for her.

She sank. Despite the cold and the pain. It was a moment of peace. It was a moment that was her own far from the static of other people's pulses. She began to kick her legs and propel herself forward using her arms. The current of the river helped her move.

The peace had passed. She swam, mindless to all except the directive to deliver the contents of the white tube.

When she opened her eyes, two identical gray-haired men in black suits waited on the muddy bank with a woman in a burgundy fur trimmed jacket. She knew the woman as Thora Hunt. The identity of the twins she didn't know. They stood over her in a semicircle, shifting on the uneven ground. One of the men held an oversized black umbrella in his black gloved hand. The other held a flashlight. Above, the sky was dark and starless.

"Gentlemen," Thora said in her calm, cultured voice. "May I present the Gorgon."

As she spoke, she stooped and retrieved the tube and handed it to the men.

"Get up now," she said. "We cannot linger here."

The Gorgon rolled over onto her side and groaned at the stiffness in her legs and the white-hot sting in her arms. She managed to get to her knees.

"Quickly now," Thora said.

She stood on wobbly legs, and Thora placed a warm hand on her cheek. The beam of the flashlight illuminated her silver hair. Thora removed her hand and placed an inoculation device at her neck, administering something that burned like venom.

The Gorgon gasped and fell to her knees. Thora reminded her to breathe. After a quarter of a minute, she felt her pain melt away. She straightened again and followed the men and Thora up the bank. They crossed a narrow, icy field that ended in a long black road.

Two sleek black sedans purred on the rocky shoulder. Thora opened the trunk of one of the cars and removed a bundle of clothes.

"Change into these so you'll be warm."

She did as Thora instructed. The men watched her appreciatively through the dark and drizzle. She kept her own eyes on Thora. The spray of light mist of rain felt cold against her skin, but there was a pleasantness about water from the sky misting her. She focused on that.

When she was dressed, Thora stepped close, holding the yoke. The sight of the black plastic collar with its flashing blue light further calmed her. She bowed her head and Thora clasped the yoke around the neck and inserted the metal prong into the skin at the base of her neck. She winced a bit at the sting of the probe as it penetrated her spine. She pulled the collar of her fleece jacket up and over the yoke.

"Car," Thora said.

She left them, grateful to be away from the men. She slid into the backseat of the warm car. The driver at the wheel said nothing to her, and she didn't speak to him. She knew there would be food in the compartment of the middle console. She helped herself to a sandwich wrapped in fine paper and tied with string. It was cold lamb and veggies. She had devoured the first half when Thora entered the car bringing the cold and wet in with her. She settled in with a sigh.

The driver pulled away from the scene.

She finished her sandwich. Thora removed the paper and string from her lap and handed her a bottle of water.

"Drink this and rest," she said. "We're headed home."

The Gorgon drained the bottle. She rested her head on the back of the seat. Thora reached over and touched her face.

"You did very well today," she said. "It won't be long before they all recognize your gifts."

"Yes," the Gorgon said.

"Geist thought he could hide from us in death," she said. "If his students had their way, one of our major nests would have been exposed by a six point earthquake in the middle of Central Europe."

She nodded, glad that Thora was pleased with her work.

"You don't know," she said, reaching over to pet her damp hair. "But we have been at this for some time."

"Those men back there, were they good?"

Thora frowned. "Good? What a thing to ask."

"The men at the bank said they worked on those blueprints and Geist took the credit."

"Those *boys* at the bank are not meant to be a part of the changes coming to the world," Thora said. "Now the men we gave those plans to, and you and I are the future."

The Gorgon pondered these words as she sipped at a second bottle of water.

"One day," Thora said, "I will open your eyes. You will be the integral instrument by which Olympus ushers in a new world."

The Gorgon nodded. Olympus. She didn't know much more about them. She only knew Thora who guided her.

She patted her lap. "Come and rest now."

The Gorgon curled up on the seat and laid her head on Thora's wool trousers. She closed her eyes and dreamt of floating adrift in the cold current of the river.

CHAPTER THREE

Anne's brow furrowed as she negotiated the traffic around the San Marcos church where Rob Loera had been baptized as a baby. They passed a barricade guarded by police. On the other side of the barricade, a fanatical religious group famous for picketing the funerals of soldiers waved their multi-colored signs with the most hateful things Elle had ever seen in print.

"Assholes," Anne murmured under her breath.

Elle settled back in her seat as they passed the creeps. She sighed and tried to steel herself for Rob's funeral. Seeing his mourning relatives, friends, and colleagues would bring all of those feelings of guilt to the surface. Since his death, she had hardly been able to sleep, eat, or do much of anything else. She found herself researching Ziggurat's past. Anne of course thought it a waste of time. She seemed annoyed by Rob's death.

"It's not good for us right now," Anne had said the morning after they saw the macabre display in Rob's bedroom. They were hiding away from the world in Anne's kitchenette eating and drinking things that were not meant for breakfast.

"I need you to go ahead and make a vanilla statement and mourn your friend in private."

Elle understood that it was best to make a public statement as soon as possible and not allow too long for speculation. Elle steered clear of her personal and the *Green Patriot*'s social media accounts for fear of what she would see on the Internet.

"I'll make a statement, but it won't be my last on the subject," she had said.

"This isn't what I want us to be known for," Anne argued. "It'll set us up as one of those sensational rags and we won't be taken serious ever again."

"If I find out that Ziggurat in any way," Elle said. "I'll—"

"You'll what?" Anne asked. "Take them on in court? Go Rambo and beat them all up?"

Elle shot her a disdainful look. "You're being ridiculous. I'll expose them for his death, and everyone will see how they take advantage of discharged soldiers looking to make a quick buck."

Anne shook her head. "And people will think about it for a few minutes and move on. After that, we'll be on the Discovery Channel chasing Bigfoot and UFOs"

Elle studied her shrewdly. "Why is it so farfetched for you to believe that Rob was telling the truth?"

Her eyes widened. "He shot himself in front of you, in your place of work, like he wanted to spite us."

They hadn't spoken much on the subject since that morning. Elle had made her statement, and she and Anne did their best to handle the aftermath of Rob's death. Things were tepid between them and cooling rapidly. She was surprised when Anne offered to go to the funeral with her. They hardly talked over breakfast, and the car ride hadn't been a picnic either.

A man in a green vest directed Anne to a makeshift parking lot in a field of low-cut grass a few blocks from the church.

Anne turned to her. "Are you ready for this, Elle?"

"No," she admitted and smiled. "But when has that ever stopped me?"

Anne chuckled. "Almost never."

They stepped out into the chilly January morning. She was glad she settled on a black suit instead of a skirt for the funeral. Anne took her hand and they fell in line with the many people walking toward the church. Elle spotted several green dress uniforms as they walked.

They filed into the church, and Elle could see the coffin at the front draped with an American flag. Half of the lid was open.

Her heart froze, and her legs nearly followed suit. Anne sensed her hesitation and squeezed her hand. They exchanged looks.

"Excuse me."

An older man approached. He leaned heavily on a cane. His face was red with the effort of walking and grief. It was Joseph Loera, Rob's father.

"You're not welcome here, Ms. Pharell."

She felt her own face flush with anger and shame. "Mr. Loera, with all due respect, I—"

"No," he said, his voice rising, catching the attention of those around them. "He was sick. But you made it worse, having him parade around the country. He lost himself mixing in with you and your type."

"My type?" Elle asked, glancing at Anne who was definitely pissed.

"Mr. Loera, we came to pay our respects," Anne said. "Your son's funeral is hardly the time for this."

Two guys in Army dress uniforms approached. They were Rob's younger brothers, and they looked as pissed off as their daddy.

"You heard him the first time," one of them said. "Get out of here before our mother sees you. She's been through enough as it is."

Without another word, Elle turned away from them and faced the accusing looks of the people behind them waiting to take their seats in the pews. She walked quickly out of the church, her eyes stinging with tears. She hurried back in the direction of the car. Anne followed, and called for her.

She caught hold of Elle's jacket sleeve as they neared the car. "Don't let that upset you. They're just a grieving family right now. They don't know better."

"Please don't tell me what to get upset about right now," Elle snapped. Her tears fell freely as she paced in front of the car.

"Where the fuck were they when he was damned near homeless? They turned their backs on him because of his mental illness. They didn't want to deal with it. I was the one who stepped up and helped him."

"Elle," Anne said. "Let's just get in the car and get out of here."

She shook her head and started to sob. "I didn't want the last time I saw him to be that morning in my office..."

Anne stepped forward and embraced her. "I'm sorry things turned out like this."

Elle moved away and climbed into the car. Anne followed.

"Are you okay?" she asked.

"They need to know the truth," Elle said.

Anne sighed. "Who needs to know the truth about what?" Though she knew very well what Elle meant.

"The Loeras need to know that it wasn't the Army or me that drove Rob to the brink," she said. "It was Ziggurat."

"Have they suddenly changed their minds about denying that he ever worked for them?" Anne asked roughly.

"So fucking what?" Elle said. "They're liars."

Anne started the car and backed out of the makeshift parking lot. "You're worrying me with this, Elle. I know it's personal, but you can't let that cloud your judgment. If you rub Ziggurat the wrong way it could be bad for the *Green Patriot*."

"I don't plan on breathing a word about this in a public arena until I have all the ammunition I need."

"Don't let this consume you, Elle. I need you around, you know."

She smiled wanly. "I know."

Anne's car rolled past the protesting zealots. Elle looked out the window at their self-righteous, angry faces below the signs.

"You have to be grateful for them," Anne said.

Elle frowned. "Yeah, they give us all a common enemy."

As they drove back to Austin, Elle thought about the institutions Rob had trusted—the Church, the Army, his family, and Ziggurat. They had all turned on him when he was no longer useful, denied him, or betrayed him. Rob must have thought that she too would ultimately fail him, and at the moment, she felt helpless enough to agree.

❖

Elle sat in the coffee house in front of a steaming cup of black coffee with a shot of espresso. The strong taste made her not feel so numb. Normally, she felt stoked to meet up with Tammy Crockett, editor and founder of *Lower Frequencies*, a conspiracy theory magazine. She was an excellent drinking buddy.

She entered the coffee shop and scanned the place for Elle. She was tall and stout. A massive afro added to her bulk. She wore a shirt with the *Les Miserables* playbill on the front.

Elle waved her over and she smiled.

They hugged and exchanged greetings before settling into their chairs again. A waitress came by to take Tammy's order.

"So how's it been going?" she asked.

"Anne is hovering, and I may be going insane," Elle said.

"After what happened, I would be too."

Elle shrugged. "How about you? I heard you're writing a book."

"Tame shit," Tammy said. "A collection of urban legends."

"Sounds like fun," Elle said.

The waitress brought her a mug topped with foam drizzled with caramel.

"And your current project?" Tammy asked. "You're really going through the looking glass here, lady."

"I'm not afraid of Ziggurat," Elle said. "And I'm surprised the great Tammy Crockett would be afraid of a faceless corporation."

"I'm pretty attached to my family, and I'm totally allergic to black masks shoved over my head."

She took a sip of her coffee and realized how awful it tasted. Tammy's drink looked much more appetizing. "You're over exaggerating."

"These guys play footsy with the NSA. They already don't like people like us."

"People like us?" Elle asked. "You mean big-mouthed black broads?"

"You know it," Tammy agreed.

"So what have you found out?"

"The first record of the company starts when they were contracted by the White House for that whole war on drugs fiasco.

Ziggurat got outed for torturing some South Americans who happened to live around a coca plantation. Since then, they've either been on the straight and narrow or they've learned how to keep their dirt swept under the rug."

Elle frowned, intrigued. "And when did they venture to the Middle East?"

"During the Gulf War," Tammy said. "They set up shop in Kuwait when the dust settled. It was as if they somehow knew they were in it for the long haul."

"Damn," Elle said.

Tammy sipped her drink and wiped her lip with a napkin. "I haven't been able to dig up any ex-employees in my network."

Elle nodded. "But you were able to find someone who knows the area on the map I showed you."

Tammy didn't answer, only regarded her with large solemn eyes. "I don't know, Elle."

"What don't you know?"

"You just can't go traipsing around Kuwait."

"It's a relatively safe zone."

"So is America, but there are still places sane people don't venture."

"Listen to yourself. You've gone soft."

"Hey, it's one thing writing articles from the safety of my office in a pocket of progressivism in the middle of the Bible Belt, but it's another thing to go snooping in a foreign country that has a past of not being so welcoming to Americans."

"I have to try," Elle said.

Tammy rolled her eyes. "Anne is going to kill me."

"Let me deal with Anne."

Tammy sighed and leaned over the table. "I know a guy who knows a guy who knows the area. What Loera had circled is a rural desert area probably inhabited by nomadic shepherds."

"Can your guy get me out there?"

"Yes. He'll get a small entourage together, a translator, and some security. You'll have to cover the expenses. Most of these people are ex-mercenaries from various countries, or lone freelance contractors. They're the type of people who make money from conflict and political strife. I'm talking the fucking dregs of society."

Elle pondered her words. "I understand."

"My contact assures me that this guy is a saint," Tammy explained. "His name is Alexander Mo'moh. He's Afro-French so he is a brother, sort of. He made a name for himself fighting off Somali pirates, but now he's the muscle for some hardcore humanitarian efforts."

Elle raised her eyebrows. "I'm impressed."

"He's a big fan of yours as well," Tammy said. "Please try not to break his heart on the first day."

She grinned. "Check."

"This is the only favor I've earned so far, Elle. I had to ask for it. Now I have to come through for someone."

"Thank you, Tammy," Elle said. "If I can help you in any way."

"Don't worry. You'll be the first person I'll think of. Just don't go over there and get yourself into some deep shit."

"I'll go about things as low-key as possible. I'll go to the village and ask questions," Elle said. "I'll take Rob's picture to see if any of the natives recognize him."

"And if someone does?" Tammy asked. "He wasn't out there doing missionary work."

"I'll figure it out."

Tammy checked her phone. "I've got to dash then. I've got a deadline."

Elle smiled. "Look at you, all grown up."

Tammy smiled back. "I'll get back with you when I have more details from Mo'moh. Good luck telling Anne what you're up to."

Elle narrowed her eyes. "She is not the boss of me."

She sat in the café for an hour after Tammy left. She ordered what Tammy had sipped on during their meeting. It didn't taste much better than the coffee. She pondered what she could say to Anne to keep her from going completely insane.

Elle returned to the *Green Patriot* headquarters and found Anne at the office in the studio at the news desk. She sat with Marco, the junior correspondent. He was taking Elle's place while she took some time off. Anne peered over his shoulder and pointed out something in his notes while the two discussed the lines.

Anne looked up from her work and smiled. "I wasn't expecting you today."

Elle shrugged. "I got bored. I wanted to check up on things. Hi, Marco."

"Good to see you up and about," he said.

"I second that," Anne said. "Marco is doing a great job here, but people are flooding the website looking for you."

"I wanted to talk to you about that," Elle said.

She walked around the counter and paused. "I'm getting a bad feeling about this."

"Can we maybe talk about it first?" Elle asked.

Anne came close and linked their arms. They walked to the elevator. Once the doors closed, she turned to Elle.

"You are not going to Kuwait."

"Wait? What?"

"I know you, and the most insane course of action is usually what you go for."

"That's not true."

Anne folded her arms and leaned against the wall.

"Hurricane Katrina," she said.

Elle narrowed her eyes. "Oh my God, that was not the same."

The elevator stopped, and Anne speed-walked toward her office with Elle close behind. A few of her co-workers said hello and she waved to them. Their smiles quickly thinned out when they noticed the matching annoyed expressions on Elle and Anne's faces. They had witnessed their disagreements before, and no one wanted a part of it.

Elle closed the door softly behind her.

"I've already decided and that's that."

"I don't believe you," Anne said. "You'd risk your life, and what we've built together to chase ghosts on the other side of the world?"

"This is just something I have to do," Elle said. "Tammy is in contact with a guy who knows the area."

"Oh Lord." Anne tossed her head back and straightened. "You've enlisted the help of a conspiracy theorist—"

"You like Tammy," Elle said. "She's good at what she does."

"I'm not doubting her integrity," Anne said. "She's a kid. What kind of contacts can she possibly have?"

"Young people can't have contacts?" Elle asked.

"Okay, fine," Anne said. "Tammy is going to hook you up with some paranoid screwball and the two of you are going to poke around that spot on the map a crazy man circled."

"Rob wasn't crazy," Elle said. "Something happened there and I'm going to find out."

Anne stared at her. "You won't. You won't find anything and you'll come back to Austin and you'll blame yourself some more."

"At least I'd have tried."

Anne turned away from her. "I won't support this," she said. "I will not stand for it."

"I don't need your approval."

"Goddamnit, Elle." Anne turned back to her. "What about the *Patriot*? People want to know your side of what happened with Loera. Is that what you're afraid of? Facing the public?"

Elle folded her arms. Anne knew her too well. She sighed and moved close. Anne touched her shoulder. "It wasn't your fault."

"I know that," Elle snapped.

"Then why send yourself on this ridiculous quest?"

"For Rob."

"And your job?"

Elle felt her anger surge at the question. How could her friend and mentor, her colleague, her partner, threaten what they had built together?

"We're doing something big here, Elle. We've got sponsors, people who are going to wonder where you are. They didn't fucking sign on for Marco. They signed on for you."

"If they pull out there will be more."

"We've got too much overhead to lose sponsors. We employ good people I don't want to lose. I need you back in one week, Elle.

That's all I'm giving you. If you're not back to put things back to normal…"

"What?"

"Then it'll be the end of the *Green Patriot*."

"Come on. You're being ridiculous."

"That's it, Elle, one week for you to return to the land of the living."

She searched Anne's face for some telltale emotion. She didn't want to hurt Anne or make her feel abandoned. In that moment, she toyed with dropping the Kuwait trip. She would never speak of Ziggurat again. Then she saw Rob's face as he apologized to her before he pulled the trigger.

"I could have helped him," she said. "Why didn't he open up to me?"

She shook her head. "I can't tell you that, Elle."

"I have to do this," she said. "I know you don't understand—"

"I never said I didn't," Anne said.

She'd made a video thanking the Green Patriot staff and announcing her sabbatical from broadcasting. She could only hope that Anne would understand.

CHAPTER FOUR

The first thing she was aware of was a distant music, a heavily stringed piece that echoed around her muffled by some barrier. The next thing she became aware of was the darkness. It was a calm, humid, black air that swaddled her limbs close. The light came gradually, glowing against the lids of her eyes. The music came at her unhindered. She opened her eyes and saw the silhouette of a woman. The woman spoke, and she knew her voice the way she knew the sound of the instruments that played the music.

The warmth began to seep away, and she felt the watery, clear, bluish gel all around her, clouding her vision, in her mouth, and down her throat. She was submerged in it. Her lungs began to burn as the sensation of choking claimed her body.

The woman above her spoke again and stooped close. She felt the woman's hands close around her shoulders and lift her up and into the world.

She choked and sputtered the gel from her lungs and sinuses. The woman kneeled beside her. She patted her back and said soothing things.

Once her breathing leveled out she was able to look at the white-haired woman. The angular features and full lips were familiar. Her face was wrinkled and kind; her eyes were a clear blue like the gel.

"Do you know who I am?" she asked.

"Thora," she said.

"Do you know who you are?"

"I am the Gorgon."

"Do you know what day it is?"

She shook her head.

"What is your last memory of?"

"You," she answered.

"Where were we?"

"I don't know."

"What did we speak of the last time you saw me?"

"I don't remember," she said. She glanced at her surroundings. She was sitting up, but she had been lying in a long container of hard plastic full of gel. There was a lid that opened in two sections like a coffin. The bottom half remained closed over her legs. The room beyond was furnished with steel counters with pristine white tops.

"I only remember your face and voice."

"Very good," Thora stated. She reached up and began to remove the electrodes attached to her temples. She then stood and stretched out her arm. "You can stand now."

She stood on shaky legs, her feet slipping in the gel. She stepped out of the pod. Thora draped a large towel around her shoulders and used another to wipe away the wet globs. She helped her remove the soggy black underwear and tank top she wore.

Thora led her out of the room to another room, this one with a large wooden desk and a fireplace. There were folded clothes in a chair. She began to dress in cargo pants and a blue thermal T-shirt. The fire had a crisp scent as if something burned along with it. She sat cross-legged in front of the dancing flames. The sight of them soothed her.

Thora brought a silver tray on wheels. There was a porcelain tea service and a plate with a sandwich and a bowl of steaming reddish broth.

"Cold lamb." She smiled. "Your favorite. Eat up now."

Thora made them both a cup of tea. She took her own cup to a chair close by where she perched and sipped while she stared at the fire.

She watched Thora as she finished the food. The room around her was familiar, a place she had gone to many times, just like the tiled room and the pod where she had lain. Was she ill? Was Thora her nurse?

"Who am I?" she asked.

"You are the Gorgon," she said. "In private, I call you Cassandra."

She nearly gasped upon hearing that name. It was like a lifeline among the torrent of questions that filled her mind. She didn't know where the line would lead, but she grasped it.

"You chose that name for yourself some time ago," Thora said. "The Greek princess who would have the gift of prophecy from Apollo. She spurned the Sun God, and in return he made it so no one would ever believe her predictions."

"She foresaw the fall of Troy," she said.

"Yes," Thora said.

"Why don't I remember anything? Am I sick?"

"You are quite well, my dear. You don't remember specifics from your past because it's too dangerous," Thora said. "Knowing too much makes one a target in our line of business."

"Business?"

Thora went to her desk and returned with a tablet. She handed it to Cassandra who peered at the pictures on the screen curiously. She saw a smiling woman with dark brown skin. She held a small trophy. Her dark hair was short and stylishly tousled. She wore a black sparkling dress that revealed her petite build accentuated by the curve of her hips. Another picture showed the same woman with a microphone. A thick crowd of people milled behind her. The picture began to move, and the throng jostled the woman who seemed too focused on the camera and the words she spoke to notice. The people behind her waved signs calling for the rise of the ninety-nine percent and the occupation of Wall Street.

Though there was no sound, Cassandra could tell that the woman spoke with intent.

"Easy on the eyes isn't she?" Thora asked.

Cassandra felt her flush and wasn't sure how to answer the question.

"Her name is Elle Pharell. She's a reporter with the *Green Patriot*, a progressive news website. She's gotten herself mixed up in some business with Ziggurat. It seems one of their grunts popped and shot himself in front of her. Unfortunately, he remembered one of the missions Ziggurat unsuccessfully washed from his memory."

She returned to her chair and her tea and looked into the fire. "I have complained for years about the clumsy techniques of those amateurs. Their employees don't seem to have very long shelf lives, especially once they're let loose into the world."

Cassandra scrolled through the dossier. There were more pictures of the reporter, Elle Pharell, as well as the Ziggurat grunt, Rob Loera, who had trained in the army before working with the security firm.

"They're not exactly known around the world for their humanitarian efforts, and now of course the reporter is making her way to Kuwait. I've set you up to go in as a translator. You're to hamper her little investigation."

Thora sipped her tea. "It should be very simple for you. Enjoy yourself. The reporter is very gregarious. She's American of course, and privileged. Her mother is a Congresswoman in Georgia. Her father is a professor of theology. She's smart and most likely intuitive. Stay tuned in to her pulse and make sure she doesn't connect the dots between Ziggurat, her soldier friend, and Olympicorp."

"And if she does?"

"You'll have to make sure she disappears," Thora said simply. "It's a dirty business, and she is as innocent as they come, but…"

"She's expendable."

She looked back down at the pictures on the tablet. Any other questions she had about her life until that moment were forgotten.

Later in the evening, Cassandra lay in a bed in a room that Thora said belonged to her. She wondered where Elle Pharell slept each night. Most likely, the reporter slept in familiar places and she knew the story of how her bed came to be there. She had actually gone out and purchased the rug.

She wondered how she had come to know of such things like rugs being purchased, and didn't know about other things.

She slipped out of bed and left the room. The house beyond was grand and stately with wood paneling on the walls and lush tapestries. There was an indoor pool, and she could see the night beyond through a wall of glass panes. She removed her clothes and donned a black swimsuit waiting on top of a stack of towels. She dived into the crystal clear water. It was blessedly familiar. She liked to swim below the surface. The water seemed to cradle her and she darted effortlessly from one end of the pool to the other.

Thora was there when she exited the pool. She wore a long black satin robe belted at the waist. She smiled and handed her a towel.

"I do enjoy watching you swim," she said. "It's a testament to the power within you."

"And what power would that be?" Cassandra asked moodily.

"Your strength and your will," Thora said. "You have been trained extensively, your brain rewired to withstand more than an average human being. Your power is a hardwired instinct."

She turned away from Thora and looked down at the pool ruefully. The water still rippled from her swim.

"What if that reporter rejects me?" she asked. "What if she knows what I am?"

Thora gave a dry chuckle. "There is no way she'll know exactly who you are."

She walked around Cassandra and placed a hand on her chest. "Those people out there are scurrying ants. That reporter you're already so enamored with will never know how close she has come to true greatness when she lays eyes on you."

"I am not enamored with her," Cassandra said.

Thora smiled. "Of course not, how silly of me. If this is going to be difficult for you—"

"It's nothing," she said. "Like you said, she is expendable."

Thora threaded her fingers through Cassandra's wet hair. The hand that had rested on her chest traveled up to her throat and cupped the side of her face. Thora pulled her close and nuzzled her cheek.

"My darling," she whispered. "Let me ease your doubts."

Cassandra's breathing quickened. Her hands found the warmth of Thora's body beneath the satin robe. She pulled at the sash and slid her hands to her waist clad in more of the silken material.

Thora gasped at the contact and found her lips with her own. As they kissed, Thora dragged the straps of the suit from her shoulders and over her breasts. She cupped them in her hands and circled her nipples with her thumbs.

"Is this familiar to you, my darling?"

"Yes," Cassandra answered.

She guided them to a cushioned chaise lounge. She lay there and lifted the gown beneath her robe over her hips revealing pale thighs and a mons covered with auburn hair.

Cassandra stood over her for a moment. For all of her grand talk Thora wasn't much for building up the moment. She looked back up, her eyes slits of lust, her chest flushed with desire all the way up to her throat. Thora reached for her.

Yes, this was familiar to her. She bent before Thora and parted her legs, waited for the short moan of anticipation.

"Quickly. Now."

Cassandra lowered her head and tasted her slowly. She knew that Thora liked her to finish her off quickly, but she took her time earning distasteful grunts from Thora. Thora's pulse told Cassandra when she was most aroused.

"Quickly," Thora reminded her in a raspy voice as she grabbed a handful of her hair at the scalp.

She redoubled her efforts, reaching up to grab a still pleasantly firm thigh; the muscles there battled with her hand. Thora shivered and Cassandra pressed her face there, feeling the reaction of her body to the orgasm.

Thora straightened soon after and moved away from her. She touched the side of Cassandra's face as she belted her robe.

"Off to bed with you now. You need plenty of rest."

In the privacy of her own quarters, she showered the smell of chlorine and Thora from her hands and face. She climbed into bed and, as she had been ordered, slept a dreamless sleep.

CHAPTER FIVE

Elle met Alexander Mo'moh just five minutes after her plane landed. Before she could clear the gate, she was hustled through the security check and off to some back room. Elle was sure her trip would end before it could begin. After five minutes, more security officers returned and escorted her along a narrow hall where she came face to face with her guide.

He grinned broadly. "Ms. Pharell, I am Alexander Mo'moh."

When he saw the look of terror on her face, his grin faltered.

"My apologies," he said. "I didn't mean to unnerve you."

"Elle," she said and extended her hand. "You've practically kidnapped me so I think we should be on a first name basis."

The broad grin returned. "Yes, of course. Alexander."

She followed him out to a gated lot of parked cars.

"Everything is in place," he explained. "We just have one small hiccup."

Elle tilted her head. "What is it?"

"The translator, Abqurah, dropped out at the last minute and sent this girl in his place," Alexander said.

"So?" Elle asked. "We still have a translator."

"The problem is Zahavi, our muscle. He only works with people he knows, and he's very upset that this stranger has joined us."

As they rounded a row of cars, Elle saw them, a tall, bearded bear, of a man in a black T-shirt and baggy camo pants. Standing next to him was a trim blonde squinting her eyes in the sun. She wore jeans, military style boots, and a khaki jacket.

As Elle and Alexander neared them, the big man became very animated and trudged their way in great strides.

"What took you so long?" he asked. "Have you discussed what we are going to do about Charlie's Angel?"

The woman he spoke of hung back. She leaned on a white Suburban, her hands in the pockets of her jacket and a slight smile on her face as if she found the situation amusing. Elle peered at her across the distance between them.

"You're being rude to our employer, Ms. Pharell," Alexander said.

"Yes, of course. I am Eitan Zahavi. I was a captain in the 900th Kfir Brigade when you were in grammar school."

Alexander interjected. "Do you have any sense of tact, man?"

"That's fine," Elle said and extended her hand. "I can appreciate someone of Mr. Zahavi's experience, and I can certainly understand his concerns."

"You see?" he asked Mo'moh. "A very smart woman. Yes."

Alexander muttered something in French. "Elle, you must understand that sometimes in our business we broker jobs out to other people. Abqurah found someone willing to take the job for nearly nothing so that he could keep more of the cash himself. Perhaps his gambling has gotten bad again."

Elle looked to Zahavi who shrugged.

Behind them, the blonde strode forward purposefully. She had remarkable bearing. A purposeful stride. Elle noticed and admonished herself for noticing such a thing. Still, she couldn't help but wonder if the woman had been an athlete in the past.

Zahavi turned and noticed her approach. He frowned. "I've never heard anything of this woman. It makes me nervous, as it should make you nervous, Ms. Pharell."

"Cassandra Hunt," she said and offered her hand.

Elle smiled and introduced herself. "I'm sorry for the confusion—"

"I know over thirty languages," Cassandra said quickly. "Most of them I learned by being in the country of their origins. Since 2001, I have come in contact with every Arabic dialect from Egypt to Iran…"

The next phrase she spoke must have been in Hebrew because Zahavi's face reddened and he turned on Cassandra Hunt, roaring a retort in his native tongue.

Alexander stood between them shouting at Zahavi to back down. Cassandra stood calmly, and continued to speak calmly in the language that so incensed the big man. She didn't shrink away or step one inch backward.

"Enough," Elle told them. "I came here to find out why my friend, an American soldier, felt he had to take his own life. I didn't travel across the world for my plans to be ruined by a pissing match."

Zahavi settled down. "This is dishonorable. She insults me."

"Get over it," Elle said. "You're a big boy. I'm sure you've been through worse."

He muttered something in English about American woman.

"And I can do without the misogynistic bullshit," Elle said.

Alexander stepped forward. "Are you in?"

"Fine," Zahavi said and gave a smile that was more of a snarl. "Money is money."

He walked away from the group, and Alexander followed, seemingly determined to help smooth his ruffled feathers.

Cassandra once again offered her hand. This time, Elle was able to take it.

"That was impressive, Ms. Pharell," she said. Her eyes were a steely hazel and hooded by her sandy brow.

"Call me Elle, please," she said. "What did you say to piss him off?"

She grinned sheepishly and put her hand to the back of her head. "I'm sorry. I've had to deal with his complaining all afternoon. It sent me over the edge to see him try to convince you that I'm not good enough for this job."

"I never doubted that you were," Elle said.

Alexander returned. "Ladies, whenever you're ready."

Elle nodded. "I have reservations for us at the Al Mansar. Do you know the way?"

He grinned. "Of course."

Elle followed them to the Suburban dusted with a fine coating of sand. Cassandra helped load her things into the back.

"It was chillier in Texas when I left," Elle remarked of the weather.

She chose to sit in the backseat next to Cassandra. How could she resist?

"We've had a string of fair days," she said to Elle. "Very nice."

"Have you been here a while?"

"A few weeks," Cassandra said. "I just finished a job with Amacorp."

Up front, Zahavi made a rude noise. "Did you wear a suit and tie?"

Cassandra and Elle exchanged glances. Elle wondered if he would be this ornery for the entire journey. She looked to Cassandra who didn't seem to be bothered. She was probably used to men being pricks. Elle knew the game well. She shuddered to think of how women were treated away from Western ideals.

"How was your flight?" Cassandra asked.

"Long. Boring."

"Sounds like you're glad to be on solid ground."

"I was until Alexander made me think I was about to be subjected to all the horrors of an airport security check," Elle said.

He laughed from the driver's seat. "Airports make me nervous."

Elle watched Kuwait unfold before her. After the Gulf War conflict, Kuwait rebuilt itself into a viable country with cities and sprawling suburbs. Once they reached the city limits, she found herself marveling at the shops and restaurants.

"It used to be bad here," Alexander said. "The Iraqis laid waste to the place."

"Were you around then?"

"No, I was in Rwanda helping to clean up the mess there."

They pulled in front of the entrance of the hotel. Everyone removed their luggage and followed Elle to the front desk. They milled around the lobby while Elle checked in. She handed them their room keys.

"Nice," Cassandra said as Elle handed her a keycard. Her eyes were a cool gray indoors, and Elle could have fallen into an old-fashioned swoon at that sheepish half smile.

Her phone chirped and she checked it to see a text from Anne: *Call me when you get settled*

"We'll all meet down here for dinner so you can brief me on what the trip will look like," she said to her companions.

She found her room to be nice enough. She sat on the edge of the bed and checked her phone. It was two o'clock in Kuwait City. That meant it was about three a.m. in Texas. Anne Humphries never slept through the night so Elle dialed her.

"There you are," she said in greeting.

"Hey, Anne. I made it."

"Good," she said. "By morning there should be a traveler's check waiting for you in the lobby from a good friend of mine. I told him about your plight and he wanted to donate something to help you out."

"Thanks," Elle said. "That means a lot."

"And I am still pissed at you," Anne said.

"I figured that," Elle said. "I was hoping you weren't by some miracle."

"Nope," Anne assured her. "But how's this for a miracle? I called your mother."

Elle straightened. Her mother blamed Anne for influencing her to join what she called the dark side of journalism.

"You what?"

"Bye," Anne said sweetly and disconnected.

"Goddamnit," Elle whispered. "That was low."

She took a nap, and when she woke up, she went down to the restaurant. Cassandra was already there, her hair tied back into a ponytail.

"Hey," she said. "Should we get a table?"

Elle nodded. "I wish alcohol was allowed here in Kuwait. I desperately need a drink. My mother is looking for me."

Cassandra laughed. "She doesn't know where you are?"

"She has an idea now." Elle sighed. "I'll have to call her."

"Moms," Cassandra said.

"What about yours?" Elle asked.

"We traveled a lot, and I learned I have a knack for learning different languages. My parents were in the army."

A waiter showed them to their table and took their drink orders. Elle ordered a sparkling water, her thoughts on a nice bottle of sweet red wine. Kuwait's alcohol ban was killing her already.

"That must have been interesting," Elle said. "Moving around a lot."

She nodded thoughtfully. "I had fun. Got into trouble."

Elle laughed. "What kind of trouble?"

"Let's just say, I left a lasting impression everywhere I went."

Elle didn't doubt that and once again admonished herself for allowing the translator to distract her from her mission. She thought of Tammy Crockett's warning about mercenaries and the dregs of society that roamed the Middle East doing odd jobs.

"I read about what happened with that soldier," Cassandra said. "What do you hope to find out?"

Elle thought about Rob wincing as he put the gun to his head.

"Someone hurt him and I want to find out why. He was my friend."

She couldn't help the tears that came to her eyes. She daubed them away with a dinner napkin. Cassandra touched her elbow, and Elle looked away shyly.

"There was a map at his house, and he told me about people who were not right in the head, about rounding them up like cattle. He said he had no memories of the event until recently."

"No memories?" Cassandra asked.

"As if he repressed them," Elle said. "It gets stranger. The company he says he worked for at the time claims to have never heard of him."

"What do you think?"

"I don't want to jump to conclusions," Elle said. "Everyone has been trying to convince me I'm off on a wild goose chase."

"I've found that those are the best chases."

Their eyes met, and Cassandra gave her that same half smile from earlier. Elle couldn't tell if she was flirting or trying to reassure her. Elle broke the contact and looked at the menu.

"What looks good, Cass?"

When she didn't answer, Elle looked up to see a quizzical look on Cassandra's face.

"Why do you call me Cass?"

"I'm sorry," Elle said. "I didn't ask if it was okay."

"Oh, it's okay." She smiled. "It's nice."

Elle let out a short laugh. "Has no one ever called you Cass before?"

She shook her head.

"Ever? You're pulling my leg."

Cassandra looked worried suddenly. Elle took her hand and squeezed it. "Don't mind me. I'm being slow-witted. Of course no one has ever called you Cass."

Alexander and Zahavi showed up at that exact moment and caught her holding hands with Cass. She loosened her grasp and removed her hand slowly in an attempt to be casual about the situation. She felt her face burn as Zahavi raised his eyebrows.

"You girls don't waste any time do you?" he asked.

Alexander cleared his throat. "Excuse my friend. He has no manners or tact."

Cass smiled. "No worries."

The two men sat and the waitress took their orders for drinks. During the distraction, Elle took the time to admonish herself. She wasn't on any ordinary assignment and out on the town for some fun. She had come out to Kuwait for Rob. She couldn't allow herself to fall into anything or anyone that could prove to be a distraction from the task at hand.

Cass glanced up from her menu. Their eyes met. She smiled sheepishly and Elle could have died on the spot.

"I thought we were going to go over the maps?" Elle asked.

"After dinner," Alexander said. "There are many people in Kuwait who are less than trustworthy. Call it a stink in the atmosphere that never cleared."

"And never will," Zahavi chimed in. "But how can you ever explain such a thing to Americans—"

"There are plenty of us who understand perfectly fine," Elle said.

"Not the ones with the power," Zahavi said. "Not the ones who count."

She listened to Zahavi and Alexander talk of occupations by various governments and their theories. Between the two of them, they had seen a lot of action in nearly every part of the world. Soon, the conversation dissolved into war stories and comparing of scars. Elle broke the party up before the men started to strip over the remnants of their dinner.

They went up to Alexander's room where he rolled out several maps on the small breakfast table. Elle crowded around with the others as Alexander pointed out their route and explained what to expect.

"There will be checkpoints at the usual places," he said, focusing his attention on Elle. "They're looking for illegal immigrants. As we get farther out there is the possibility of locals posing as police setting up phony checkpoints. Most of the time they want some cash. Cassandra will negotiate for us, and if things get ugly, we'll let Zahavi loose."

At the mention of his name, Zahavi gave a good-natured growl.

"I called around and asked some questions about the area," Alexander said. "Now is the time for us to compare notes, as you Americans say. What are you looking for out in the desert, Elle Pharell?"

She told them how she tried to help Rob with his problems. She told them about the morning he showed up at her office and killed himself. She went on to tell them Rob's last words and about the maps she found in his trailer.

"So we're here because of some crazy man?" Zahavi asked.

"He wasn't crazy," Elle insisted. "He worked for a company called Ziggurat. I believe something happened that traumatized him."

She couldn't help but look to Cass who smiled sympathetically. She looked to Alexander.

"What intel do you have?"

"There is a village out there. I spoke with a man who says that the place is a ghost town."

Elle straightened in her seat. "Then that's it, just like Rob said."

Alexander sighed. "The village is supposedly cursed by the devil himself."

Elle chuckled. "You don't actually believe that."

Zahavi muttered something in Hebrew.

"It's just talk," Elle said. "Some backwoods explanation for what happened."

"I don't believe the place is cursed," Alexander said. "I won't, however, fool myself to think that the answer will be right out there in the open with a bow on it. You're paying us to take you to the town. After that, we'll come back to Kuwait City."

Elle looked around at the three of them. "I didn't expect more than that, of course."

"So you'll be satisfied with a ghost town?"

"I'll have to be," Elle said. She felt more than a little saddened by the revelation that she might not find the answers she had come to Kuwait in search of. She glanced over at Cassandra who watched her intently, her brow knitted in sympathy.

"We should get some sleep," Alexander said. "We'll depart early."

Elle stood and said good night to her companions. She slipped out of the room, followed by Cassandra and Zahavi. She went to her room and debated calling Anne. Back home it was seven a.m., and Anne was more than likely on her way to work.

Elle decided on a bath instead. The tub in her room was short but deep. She didn't need much legroom, so it was more than adequate. She turned on the faucet and went for her travel sized bath oil.

As she dug around her suitcase, there was a knock at the door. She spied through the peephole and saw Cassandra waving small bottles. Elle tried not to throw the door open too enthusiastically.

"Get in here," she gasped.

The smile on Cassandra's face as she sauntered into the room, hit Elle with a wave of intoxication stronger than anything the three bottles in her hand could provide.

"I thought you might like a nightcap."

Elle grinned. "You are my new best friend."

They sat at a table the same style as the one in Alexander's room. Except it was the two of them. Alone.

"Are you running a bath?" Cassandra asked.

Elle hopped up and went to turn off her water. She returned to find Cassandra pouring straight vodka onto ice cubes. She topped the drinks off with orange juice.

"How illegal is this?"

Cassandra chuckled. "Very. Just be cool."

"Of course." Elle lifted her glass in a salute.

"To Rob," Cassandra said.

She attempted a smile. "To Rob."

They sipped their drinks in silence each regarding the other with a courteous curiosity.

"This is good," Elle said. "I was wondering how I would get through this trip without cocktails."

Cassandra laughed. "I'm glad I can be of service."

Elle grinned. She could think of another way she could be of service. She took a quick gulp of her vodka.

"So what are you doing so far away from home?" Elle asked.

She shrugged. "I've never stayed in one place for too long."

"Never?" Elle asked.

"There is so much of the world to see," Cassandra said. "So many cultures and customs and languages."

Elle nodded in agreement. "It all sounds very adventurous. I've traveled but not as extensively as I dreamed as a kid."

"Why not?"

"There was college, and the ink wasn't dry on my degree before I started the *Green Patriot* with Anne."

"What is that like?"

Cassandra propped her elbow on the table and rested her chin in her palm. Her eyes were a little glassy, and Elle laughed despite herself.

"It's very busy," Elle said. "And lately it's become chic among the big journalists to have us on their show, you know, the way, way left perspective. Anne and I take turns. I still don't have the hang of it yet."

"I think you're fabulous," Cassandra said. "I mean, you're well-spoken and you know your facts. You're not just blowing steam."

Elle smiled. "I'm glad you think so."

She stood. "We should get some rest."

"Yeah," she said. "Thanks for the cocktail."

"Good night, Elle."

"Good night, Cassandra."

She smiled. "Call me Cass. I like it."

Elle smiled back. "Okay, Cass. Good night."

CHAPTER SIX

They drove down the empty highway surrounded on either side by miles of desert and sparse vegetation. The wind lifted sand from the dusty shoulders and chased it alongside the path of the Suburban.

Alexander sat in the driver's seat. His pulse was steady with very little deviation. It signified his strength and confidence. Next to him, in the passenger seat was Zahavi. He tossed a knife from one hand to the other. A shard of light reflected from the blade and bounced on the ceiling of the Suburban. Static clouded his pulse. He wasn't as strong or resilient as Alexander.

Elle, on the other hand, was fast asleep. She had leaned over in her sleep five minutes ago and rested her head on Cassandra's shoulder. Elle had the most unique pulse she believed she had ever come across. The woman practically thrummed like a tuning fork, radiating a pleasant hum Cassandra could feel against the skin on the backs of her hands and on her face when they were sitting so close. Of course, there was static too, more than Alexander.

Elle's pulse shifted suddenly into a series of rapid strains like strings in the soundtrack of a horror movie. Her static rose to a roar, and her body stiffened. Before she could react, Elle sat up blinking, her eyes fogged with confusion.

Without thinking, Cassandra placed her hand over Elle's. They peered into each other's eyes, and she could feel Elle's brain relax along with her body. Cassandra could see the fearful sleep that clouded her mind dissipate like a fog.

When she had shaken the nightmare, Elle moved her hand, and her eyes darted around the car at Alexander, then to Zahavi, and out the window, and finally back to Cassandra.

"Where are we?" she asked groggily.

"About fifty miles out," Alexander said.

Elle stifled a yawn with her hand and glanced over at her. "I'm sorry I fell asleep. I must seem like a real amateur."

"You are," Zahavi said.

"But we don't hold that against you," Alexander added. "You had a long flight."

Elle looked to Cassandra. "I hate long drives."

"You get used to it." She wondered what exactly had haunted Elle's dreams. Had the death of the soldier been so traumatic? She couldn't imagine death haunting her, and she was sure that many had met their ends at her hands, either directly or indirectly. Thanks to Thora and Olympus, she would never worry about ever remembering any of her deeds, at least not in exact detail. She occasionally saw glimpses of her previous missions, but she never felt the need to dwell on the visions.

Of course, she never told Thora. Cassandra didn't want her to tighten the bolts on her mind-washing procedure. It was all her own little secret.

As for Elle, her mind retained every detail of the soldier Loera's death. What else would drive her so far away from home and the job she loved so much?

Elle turned her head to look at Cassandra, her brow bent slightly.

"I'm okay," she whispered.

Cassandra smiled and gave a quick, short nod. When she met Elle in person the day before she never expected to be so taken by her. It was that strange pulse and those shining eyes along with that lovely smile.

At the moment, Elle was pensive. She used a tablet to type a few notes. Mostly, she stared out the window. What she or the others didn't know was that their destination was closer than any of them thought. Loera had been off in his coordinates, and Alexander's contact was just as clueless.

Cassandra enjoyed the passing scenery, for what it was worth. The sky was blue and wide and streaked with thin, wispy cirrus clouds. Elle was next to her giving off the lovely pulse. She wished they were alone together.

After an hour and a half of driving around the desert, Alexander stopped the car under the pretense of stretching his legs. Elle gladly slipped out of the car to stretch like a cat. Cassandra kept her eyes on Alexander. He checked his precisely charted map and cursed under his breath in French.

Zahavi sauntered past her, yawning. "Now comes the real fun," he whispered. He walked a couple of feet over the shoulder before unzipping his fly and proceeding to take a long, noisy piss against a large rock.

She turned to Alexander. "What's up?"

"There should have been a road about thirty miles back," he said absentmindedly and looked up at her. "According to my source."

"Where did he get his info?" Cassandra asked.

"Old US satellite imagery. Gulf War stuff."

She nodded. "Any ideas?"

"Mark out a fifty mile radius, circle this spot, perhaps we'll catch a glimpse of the place we're looking for," he said.

"And then?"

"You'll have the honor of explaining to our employer that she's come all this way for nothing," he said and raised one eyebrow rakishly. "I am sure you can soften the blow."

Cassandra took a step back. She expected such macho bullshit out of Zahavi, but not Alexander who had seemed so mild.

Elle joined them. She turned a circle, her hands on her hips as she surveyed the desert around them. She looked to Cassandra.

"We're lost aren't we?" she asked.

"It seems this village is harder to pinpoint than we expected," Alexander said. "I'm trying to figure out a solution."

Elle looked at the map. "So Rob's coordinates were wrong."

"It's hard to get this stuff right when you are under extreme psychological duress," Alexander said. "Like I told you, we'll keep looking, but there is only so much we can do."

He made a show of sending a pointed look at Cassandra, and Elle looked to her.

"You don't think we'll find it, do you?" she asked. "Is that what you two were whispering about?"

"We'll keep looking," Cassandra said.

"Don't sugarcoat things for me," Elle said. Her eyes flashed intently, and a metallic edge appeared in her wonderful pulse, signaling her anger. "The whole thing was a bust. I knew there was the possibility."

A sharp whistle drew their attention to Zahavi. He stood in the vicinity of his makeshift urinal with a pair of binoculars. Once he had their attention, he turned and looked out at the desert before him.

Elle led the way, jumping from the dusty shoulder to the rocky soil and made her way to Zahavi. He handed her the binoculars and she peered in the direction he pointed. Cass joined them and spotted the bleached bones of a goat. Looking in the distance, she saw the faint outline of a few scant buildings.

Elle passed her the binoculars, and she handed them to Alexander.

"Is that it?" she asked him.

"We will soon find out," he replied.

They returned to the Suburban and took their respective places. It was a rough and bumpy ride to the small group of buildings. Elle leaned forward and peered between the two front seats as if they were approaching Cibola itself.

Cassandra felt an unsettling feeling in her stomach. She hadn't known much of apprehension until that moment. It felt bittersweet.

Alexander stopped the Suburban about fifty feet from a squat building with walls of stone and a roof made of sheet metal. Elle jumped out of the truck, camera ready. Cassandra hurried after her along with Alexander. The village, on closer inspection, was a scattering of small stone buildings or tents that leaned or totally collapsed. Shoes and sandals waited lined up outside a few of the structures nearly covered with dust.

Cassandra stood behind Elle watching her survey the place. A lone breeze stirred the sandy pathways between the unkempt structures as if to punctuate the desolation. Elle turned back to look at her companions. She didn't say a word, but the corners of her mouth pulled themselves down.

Cassandra wanted to say something helpful, but delegated herself to silence. It was best to let Elle look around so they could get back to Kuwait City before dark.

Elle turned back to the village and walked further in. Cassandra followed close. She called out a formal greeting in Arabic. There was of course no answer. She "listened" for any pulse in the distance and found nothing.

Elle stopped and toed a piece of fabric in the sand. She bent and lifted it up, then squinted at the streams of sand flowing. It was a black head covering, probably what an older woman would wear.

"This would not be abandoned in the street," Elle said. "Even if these people were nomadic, this would not be left behind. And they left their shoes."

She watched Elle wander toward one of the buildings. She peered inside the narrow entryway and pointed her camera into the dimness.

Zahavi quickly stepped forward, gun drawn. He slid inside at an angle. Cassandra followed. She called out the same greeting. The interior of the structure was dark save for stray pinpoints and bands of light that seeped through cracks in the walls and ceiling. There was a small cot, neatly made, and several plastic crates topped with implements for a makeshift kitchen.

The light from Elle's camera further illuminated the space revealing a dusty swirl circulating through the air. She pointed the camera lens in a slow pan around the room.

"No signs of any struggle here," she said as if she were disappointed.

"We'll keep looking," Cassandra said.

Elle led the way out of the building. Zahavi was already checking a tent, partially collapsed from neglect.

"You might want to check this out," he said.

Elle picked her way across the dusty path and poked her head beneath the flap Zahavi provided. Cassandra watched as she leaned in filming the interior.

"Did you clear it?" she asked Zahavi.

The man gave her a smug glance. "Just because there is no one around here for you to translate doesn't mean you get to tell the rest of us how to do our jobs."

Elle extracted herself from the tent. "It's a wreck in there. Everything is tossed."

Alexander appeared behind them. "There is something you'll want to see."

He led them to a makeshift pen for goats piled with the bleached bones and horns of the abandoned animals, their skins and rotting fur buzzed with flies. The smell of their decay was exacerbated by the dry air, and hot sun rolled from the pen in what seemed to be a solid wave.

"The poor things," Elle said. "They were left behind with no one to tend to them. They starved to death."

"Maybe they left the sick ones behind," Cassandra said.

"No," Elle said. "They were all left behind."

Alexander surveyed the sight. "Why would someone kidnap everyone in a village? Why not kill them on the spot?"

"They knew something," Elle said. "Rob said they were all sick, and they were loaded up and taken away. I think someone hired Ziggurat Security to clean up their mess."

"Good," Alexander said in a no-nonsense tone. "We'll look around a little more and then we'll head back to Kuwait City."

Elle nodded slowly in agreement, and Cassandra nearly let out a sigh of genuine relief.

"Fine," she acquiesced. "We'll look around some more."

They filed back toward the center of the village. Elle stopped cold and changed direction. Cassandra looked back at Zahavi and Alexander. They were watchful, but their vigilance was lax. For them, this was a walk in the park. It should have been the same for Cassandra, but something in the village just didn't sit right with her.

Elle rounded a broken tent and stopped in front of a shack made up of discarded metal signs. They were old advertisements for Western products. The sun and sand-wielding wind had faded and polished clean the luster of the paint.

Cassandra followed Elle as she circled the building. She watched the hesitancy in her steps as she caught sight of something that disturbed her. Cassandra moved in step next to her and stopped when she did. On one side of the shack, someone had painted a five-foot lightning bolt in runny black paint.

"The fuck," Elle whispered. She walked up to the design and touched the center. She turned to reveal her blackened fingertips.

Alexander removed the gun holstered to his leg. He and Zahavi slowly walked to the mouth of the shack, each taking a side, and aimed their guns inside. Alexander went in, Zahavi behind him.

Suddenly, Cassandra heard a stray pulse. It was an unsteady buzz like a neon light warming up after someone had thrown the switch. His static came in a rush as he stumbled forward and grabbed Elle by the shoulders. She screamed and he let out a primal bray.

Cassandra stepped forward and pried him away. She pushed him hard to the ground. She slipped the metal baton from her sleeve and jerked her wrist to fully extend it. She stood ready to attack, to protect Elle.

The man wallowed in the dust, groaning. She turned to see that Zahavi and Alexander had joined them, guns drawn.

"Are you okay?" she asked Elle.

She nodded absentmindedly, her eyes glued on the man on the ground.

His eyes were wild. His loose hair was black and seemed to stand on end. His white shirt was torn and stained with sweat, sand, and blood. The tattered sleeves of the shirt were rolled up, and angry red scars in the shape of lightning bolts had been cut into the skin of his forearms.

Elle pointed. "His arms. Those look like Rob's tattoo. Just like on the side of this building. It's part of the Ziggurat logo."

She looked to Cassandra. "Ask him what happened here."

Cassandra put her baton away. She stepped forward cautiously, her hands stretched out in front of her. She spoke to the man in Arabic using a low voice. He sat up and scooted backward, leaving scuff marks on the dry, dusty ground.

"We are friends, sir. Please, calm down."

The man flipped over onto his hands and knees. He scrambled forward a few feet until he lost his purchase and fell onto his stomach. Elle hurried past Cassandra and stooped next to the man before she could warn her away.

Elle touched the man's shoulder and he rolled over.

"Hey, no one is going to hurt you," she said gently in English.

The man hugged his arms close and muttered incoherently as he eyed Elle. She offered a smile, her hand still on his shoulder.

"It's okay," she said. "No one here is going to hurt you."

The man looked past her at Cassandra and then at Zahavi and Alexander. He grimaced, grabbed his beard with both hands, and pulled hard.

Elle wrapped her hands around his. "Wait, don't do that."

His eyes rolled in her direction, and he grinned. Elle looked to Cassandra.

"Ask him his name."

She did.

The man stood slowly. "Tarek Ahmad Al-Nashi."

"The woman with me is an American reporter called Elle Pharell. She would like to ask you some questions about what happened here, if you would be so kind as to answer them."

He peered past her at Elle.

"And those men?" Tarek asked. "Are they soldiers?"

"They are here for the protection of the reporter," Cassandra assured him. "No one here means you harm."

The man took a moment. He stared at his palms for a moment before tucking his hands, filthy with sand, blood, and black paint close to his chest. He nodded his head slowly.

"Are you here alone?" Elle asked.

Cassandra repeated the question for Tarek.

"They were all taken," he said with a sneer.

She told Elle what he had said.

"By soldiers? Forcefully?" Elle asked.

She translated.

Tarek grabbed his beard again and tugged hard. A frown creased his face. The sand stirred around them on a sudden dry wind.

"The soldiers came after they were taken."

Cassandra repeated his words in English without turning.

"What happened before they were taken?" Elle asked.

"Their bodies were robbed of their souls," Tarek sobbed before Cassandra could pose the question. "They were inhabited by jinn. They could not speak, and they were unclean."

As he spoke, Cassandra repeated his every word. Elle stepped forward.

"What do you think that means, Cass?"

She shrugged. "In Islam, there is the belief that the human body can be possessed by spirits called jinn."

"Could a mental illness have been mistaken for possession?"

Zahavi spoke up. "I don't consider myself a religious man, but this just got…spooky."

Elle nodded. "He's obviously not in his right mind. Ask him if he too has been plagued."

She did and Tarek hid his face in his hands and nodded vigorously. "I hear the jinn. They whisper for me to relinquish my soul. They force me to be unclean."

He stretched out his arms to reveal the scars carved into his skin. "I seek refuge in the mighty Allah. Always."

Alexander spoke up. "Muslims don't tattoo themselves. It's a sin that can be weighed on judgment day."

Tarek grabbed his beard again and fell to his knees in the dirt. His tears fell freely, muddying the sand. Elle stepped forward to comfort him once again.

"Ask him about what happened when the soldiers came."

She did, anxious of what would come out of the mad man's mouth next.

"Americans," he said. "They came and took most of them away."

"Most of them?" Elle asked. A sudden breeze stirred her black hair. "What happened to everyone else?"

Cassandra posed the question to Tarek.

"They followed their master into the desert," he said.

"Who is their master?" Cassandra asked without translating the last answer to Elle.

"A sorcerer," Tarek whispered. "He cursed my people and poisoned the land. The Americans took everyone away, but they returned. I see them out in the desert. The sorcerer controls them."

"What?" Elle asked. "What is he saying? What did you ask him?"

"I asked him what happened to the people who weren't taken," she said. "He says that someone who practices black magic has them in the desert. He believes they are all under this sorcerer's control."

"Was this a person he knew from the village or an American?" Elle asked.

Cassandra asked and she translated as he spoke.

"He is the son of Shaytan. He took the soul of my sons and their wives, my grandchildren. He calls for me. I hide from them by making myself unclean. I don't pray in the mornings or at the setting of the sun. I call out to Allah for his mercy."

Cassandra sensed deception. He was withholding something. Tarek still had the scruples to keep some information to himself. With all of his talk of Shaytan and black magic, he realized that something else sinister had happened to the people in his village.

An anguish filled Elle's eyes as she listened to the man's words. She blinked her eyes rapidly as she turned and walked away. Cassandra followed. She caught up with Elle in a few strides.

"Before he died, it seems Rob had an obsession with religion," Elle said. "Tarek's delusions are different, but I can't ignore the parallel. Rob said that the people here were like zombies, and he didn't feel as if he were much better."

Alexander joined them. "What are we going to do with this guy?"

"That's a good question," Elle said. "We could take him back to the city. I can get him a full evaluation."

When Alexander and Zahavi exchanged dubious glances, Elle looked to Cassandra. "We can't leave him here alone. Who knows how long he can continue to survive out here."

She nodded as dread filled her. She remembered Thora's words from only days before telling her that Elle was expendable. The reporter's death was not her prime directive. She was there to muddy her investigation. There were many other ways the village could have met its fate other than the story Rob Loera told. The Kuwaiti desert could be a harsh place, and even the people who knew its dangers well could find themselves lost.

She could try to get rid of the man, Tarek. Make it look like natural causes. She just needed time. Elle was watching her, and it felt as if she could see her intentions. Reading pulses would be a parlor trick compared to one intuitive enough to read naked thoughts.

"Tarek said that the others wander the desert at night," Cassandra said. "Maybe we could catch a glimpse of them if we wait around."

"Would that be safe?" Elle asked.

"Out of the question," Alexander said. "How many people are we talking about? Are they all crazy like Tarek?"

"There can't be very many," she insisted. "If there are more people they will need aid."

Elle stepped close to Alexander. "I can come up with more money, for all three of you."

"What good is money if I'm not alive to spend it?" he asked.

"We're not talking about an army here," Cassandra spoke up. "You saw how easy it was to subdue Tarek."

"I suppose you'll beat them all back with your little stick," he said.

"I can handle myself if that's what you're getting at."

Alexander rolled his eyes.

"So far, no one has thought enough about these people to notice their disappearance," Elle said. "If we don't check this out no one will."

He shook his head. "You really need to think on this," he said to Elle. "You have the man Tarek. Simply take him back to the city and report this to the proper authorities."

"We'll stay the night and scope things out. If it gets rough, we'll leave," Elle said. "I'm sure you've been in tighter spots."

Alexander grinned. "Americans. The foolhardy who will walk off the edge of a cliff chasing their ideals."

Elle shrugged. "I can't argue with that sentiment."

Alexander looked to Cassandra. "I'm sure Zahavi will agree to stay. Let's go tell him about the change of plans."

He led the way. Elle touched Cassandra's shoulder.

"Thank you," she said simply.

Her heart fluttered, and at the same time guilt hardened in the pit of her stomach. There was no other option for her at this point. She would kill Tarek sometime during the night and convince Elle that they should leave. If that plan failed, she would have to kill them all and leave them in the desert.

Elle smiled. "It's nice to have someone on my side on this who understands."

"I want to help you find the answers you're looking for," she said.

She meant that and wished with all of her heart that it were true.

CHAPTER SEVEN

They made camp at the sturdiest building in the little village. It was made of stone and mud bricks. The inside was empty save for a few dusty rugs on the floor and pictures on the wall of the past succession of emirs. There were also framed black-and-white photos of people, families and children and elders. According to Tarek, his people used the building as a public gathering place to discuss matters of the village.

A door in the ceiling led to the roof where one of the men in the village would stand and sing the call to prayer. Cassandra stood with Elle and looked out at the desert that stretched on for miles beneath the endless blue sky.

"It's so harsh and beautiful at once," Elle whispered.

"As is the duality of many things," Cass said.

She followed Elle around as she filmed the village, sifting through the remains of the lives of the vanished people. Cass concluded that they must have lived for days in disarray before Ziggurat came in to collect them. She could see no sign of any past surveillance. Ziggurat would have picked the place clean. It all looked very sloppy.

She didn't understand how Olympus could allow such faulty work. It was irresponsible and inhumane. It angered her that Elle might have to die because some pet project had gotten out of hand.

As the day began to fade, they returned to their makeshift camp. Tarek had cleaned himself up a bit. He wore a clean shirt borrowed from one of the men. He stared toward the west and the setting sun. It was time for prayer, yet the man didn't pray. He seemed to believe his piety would attract evil to him.

They shared their food and water with Tarek. He seemed comforted to have people around, even if they were foreigners. Elle sat on the floor next to him. Cass sat close by ready to translate.

He talked a bit about the Gulf War and how, when the refineries burned, the skies turned black for miles. Elle asked Tarek more questions about his family and life in the village. When she asked about holidays, he spoke of Eid Al-Adha, the Feast of the Sacrifice, and how he saved all year for two sheep to sacrifice, butcher, and distribute throughout the village. His voice quavered with sadness and then anger. In frustration, he threw the bottle of water he held across the room. She and Cassandra exchanged worried looks.

"We were not sinful people," he said. "Yet we were still cursed."

"Do you remember anything out of the ordinary?" Cassandra asked. "Any vehicles or strange people?"

"The small planes flew over the village," he said. "Too small for a man to fit inside."

"Drones," Elle hissed.

"You don't know that for sure," she said, though she certainly did know. That meant that Ziggurat had purposely exposed this little village to a psychoactive substance.

"Planes too small for a man to fit in?" Elle asked. She studied Tarek who once again clutched at his beard. "Ask him if he is frightened."

She posed the question and repeated the answer.

"Yes, he is afraid of the sorcerer."

"Is he afraid that the soldiers will come back?"

Tarek said that he didn't fear the soldiers.

"Ask him about the day the soldiers came," Elle said.

"It was several weeks after everyone in the village became sick of the spirit," he said, a faraway look in his eyes. "The jinn poisoned them with insanity. They committed unclean acts, and one man ate the flesh of his young child. Then the white trucks came, and people in space suits, and the soldiers."

"Space suits," Elle said. "It sounds like he's talking about hazmat type suits. Perhaps the village was poisoned."

Cassandra didn't like the direction this line of questioning was taking. Elle had distracted them both with questions about the village life. Cassandra lost her grip on the exchange and missed the opportunity to guide it in a different direction.

"Don't you think you're stretching his words?" she asked though she knew Elle was intelligent enough not to do such a thing. "The guy is not in his right mind."

"Neither was Rob, but there were still facts in what he told me," Elle said.

"But how much of what this man is saying is the truth? How can you sort through it all?"

"We'll find out what exactly is wrong with him, if it was chemically induced." Elle paused. "Look, I know you're trying to look out for me, but I've been doing this for over a decade. I know I can't put Tarek on display and claim that Ziggurat used drones to poison the village with a chemical that made everyone insane."

She nodded, relieved. "Of course, I'm sorry."

"You're forgiven," Elle said as she watched Tarek stand.

He walked to the doorway and stared out at the darkening day beyond. The two of them watched him for a minute before turning to each other.

"So, do you think we could ever hang out after this?" Elle asked.

She smiled brightly. "I'd like that. Really."

"Good. Be warned. I can get pretty wild on a night out."

She laughed. "I've been known to do some damage."

"I kind of figured that," Elle said.

At the door, Tarek let out a short wail. He backed away, his hands up at his beard. He squatted and moaned. They immediately went to comfort him.

Cassandra heard footsteps above her and looked to the ceiling and the opening that led to the roof. Zahavi's face appeared, disfigured by the play of light from above and below.

"We've got company," he said.

"Who do you see?" Elle asked.

"They're moving pretty slow, but I'm sure they're your missing villagers."

She watched Elle run to the stairs and climb up to the roof. She closed her eyes and counted to five. She hadn't expected more people to show up. This was her time to act. There could never be anything between her and Elle. She was not Cassandra Hunt. She couldn't be Cass to one pretty reporter. She was the Gorgon. Her past was intangible. It came to her in fine silver streams like sand in an hourglass.

She would have to kill them all.

Her eyes on Tarek, she stooped and removed the small gun strapped to her ankle. She stepped close to Tarek, pressed the muzzle to his neck, and pulled the trigger. A small hiss escaped the gun as compressed air injected a dose of one of Thora's deadly concoctions.

Tarek shrieked and moved away. He slapped his hand over the injection site on his neck. It burned like hell. She suspected that she knew this from experience.

"Run," she said.

His eyes darted toward the ladder, then rolled up to the ceiling as the serum began to work its way through his bloodstream. Depending on how Tarek reacted to the poison, she would dose Elle later. Nothing violent. Elle would fall and sleep. She would watch and she would apologize. Elle deserved that much.

"Run," she said again. "Run while you can."

Tarek stumbled backward crashing into the doorframe. He quickly gathered himself and sprinted out into the quickening evening. She stepped out of the building and hugged the sides before running for cover to the side of a nearby tent. From her vantage, she could spot Tarek running for his ridiculous shed painted with lightning bolts.

She heard Elle shouting for her and paused. She clinched her fist. She would have to face her soon, and when she did, she would end her life. Whatever she thought they could have was a fantasy. She lived in the shadows, a specter with no life to call her own.

She balled her hand into a tight fist as if she could fight off the tears that suddenly came. She willed her legs to move away from Elle to the lightning bolt-covered shack. She slid inside and stared at the dark interior.

Empty.

She took a step forward and spotted the shard of red light on the floor. Another step and she saw a rug slightly wrinkled at the corner. She pulled the rug back and saw a metal door with a latch.

She pulled at the latch and a door sprang from the floor. She peered down past a ladder at what looked to be about seven feet to the bottom. A dull red glow emanated from the gap. She climbed down the metal rungs and landed on dusty concrete, her baton ready.

She spun around to see an endless stretch of tunnel in front of and behind her. She could see Tarek leaning against the wall tripping along as he continued to make his escape. She jogged after him, her footfalls echoing throughout the cement corridor.

As she approached, Tarek looked back at her with wild wide eyes and collapsed. She grabbed him by the collar and nearly lifted him to his feet.

"What is this place?"

"The Americans," he huffed, not able to catch his breath.

"What Americans?" she asked.

"Before the war," he groaned. "The tunnels were there before the war."

His eyes rolled back in his head. A trickle of blood escaped one nostril.

"You have to help me," he said, reaching for her and grabbing her jacket. His legs collapsed and he fell forward. She caught him and held him upright until his pulse faded to an echo, the wavering activity of a dying brain.

"I'm sorry, my friend," she said. "You know too much."

She lowered him to the floor and studied his face. Tarek was dead. She stood over the man for a minute or so, her breathing heavy, and a stinging in her eyes. Did killing always make her feel this way? She doubted she would be a very good assassin if she shed a tear for her victims. Perhaps she felt that way because she had just betrayed Elle. There was no turning back.

She looked away from Tarek's body and to the end of the tunnel in which he had run. It must have gone on for miles. She had an idea where it ended. Ziggurat did have a facility in Kuwait after all. It was literally underground. It had existed before the Gulf War, and it seemed a few locals knew about it.

She climbed back up the ladder and into Tarek's shack. When she slipped out, she heard shouts and a gunshot. She sprinted to the edge of the village and saw Alexander in the middle of a crowd of about forty ragged people. Sand rose from the ground in clouds as they shuffled forward. Alexander turned and shot one of them point-blank. The man crumpled to the ground. The others didn't react to their comrade's death. They sluggishly moved forward, reaching out, tearing at his clothes, and pulling at his arms. He fought at them, but they swarmed like ants over a fallen butterfly.

Behind her, an engine roared and the car piloted by Zahavi, Elle in the passenger seat, roared onto the scene taking out the edge of the swarm. The Suburban stopped and the driver's side door swung open. Zahavi stalked forward, his gun raised, and began to fire into the crowd.

Blood splattered from their limbs, and they didn't seem to care. A few of them left the swarm and stumbled toward Zahavi. He backed away firing. About a half-dozen more of the ragged people left their attack on Alexander for Zahavi. He kicked one of them in the stomach and tossed the man to the ground.

Cassandra watched a steady stream of people trickle from around tents and ramshackle buildings. The village had suddenly come to life, and not all of the people looked like typical natives. There were people of many nationalities in lab coats and skirts and ties. Even stranger was the fact that none of them emitted any primary brain activity; there was only a steady, identical hum like a chorus of crickets.

They crowded around the Suburban, reaching at the movement in the windows. She could see Elle inside, her face a blur of panic. She stepped back. She could walk away and leave them to their end. Thora could have a clean-up crew out to wipe the place of any evidence that a village had ever existed there. Likewise, Thora could return her to the pod and likewise wipe all traces of the night, and Elle away. Once again her mind would be barren of any memories. She could slip into the shadows.

A different pulse caught her attention. It was different from the identical hum, and was unrecognizable to her, which meant she truly had never come across one like it before. The stray pulse came to her in rapid bursts that faded as they bloomed, with an underlying current that lingered in between.

She turned and peered in the direction of a partially collapsed tent. Someone was in there watching her. She took a hesitant step in the direction of the tent and stopped. She heard tires on sand and looked over her shoulder to the Suburban. She saw Elle sat in the driver's seat and bumped over several members of the crowd to get to Zahavi and Alexander.

She turned back to the tent.

"Who's out there?"

She waited for her voice to cause a change in the stranger's pulse, but the pattern remained without faltering. It meant that the person inside the tent was focused enough to block the stimulus of her calling out to them.

Perhaps it was another wraith. She wondered if Thora would allow some other handler to send their charge into Kuwait to make sure things went smoothly. She thought then of Elle. Anyone else faced with saving two well-armed strangers or their own ass would not risk their life. Especially a civilian with no experience in combat or weapons. Anyone else would have been so frightened out of their minds, they would have driven away. Not Elle. She was trying to help.

Cass turned away from the tent and ran back to the Suburban.

CHAPTER EIGHT

Only minutes had passed since Elle sat with Cass and Tarek, listening to his speech through a woman whom she was beginning to develop a strong curiosity about. They even talked about hanging out. She felt well on her way to having proof of what Ziggurat did to those people and to Rob. She would get Tarek the help he needed. She would start a fund to properly care for him and other victims that would surely turn up.

Zahavi called her up to the roof. Everything after that was a complete blur of panic.

In the darkening dusk, Elle saw a group of people walking tightly together as if the desert were a bustling city street.

"They're moving pretty slow, but I'd say they're your missing villagers," Zahavi had said.

"Maybe they're looking for aid," Elle said.

"They don't look friendly," Alexander called. He offered her a pair of binoculars and she peered through them. There was something not right about the people in the distance. They didn't speak or otherwise interact with each other. When one of them stumbled and fell, the others didn't react at all. Their eyes were dead.

She looked to Alexander. "Let's get the fuck out of here."

"That's the best idea you've had all day," he said.

As they headed back down to the main building, Elle noticed that Cass and Tarek were gone. She ran to the doorway and looked out. She called for them. Zahavi and Alexander crowded past her and headed for the Suburban.

"Wait," Elle said. "Tarek and Cass."

Alexander turned on her in fury. "Where the hell are they?"

"I don't know," Elle said as her panic rose to high tide.

"I knew we shouldn't have trusted that bitch," Zahavi spat. "I doubt you will see her again. She has what she came here for."

Elle was drowning now. "That's not true."

Alexander grabbed her arm and pulled her toward the SUV. Zahavi followed. Elle went along a few steps, docile with shock. When she realized the men didn't plan to look for Tarek or Cass, she stopped in her tracks and snatched her arm away.

"I won't leave without either of them."

Alexander tried to reclaim his grasp. "You stay with Zahavi. I will go search."

"I'll go with you," she insisted.

"You're insane," Zahavi said and stepped close, stooping a bit and leaning close so they could be face-to-face. "The field trip is over. You'll do what we tell you or we'll all leave now without your pet habib and your little girlfriend."

She shoved him as best she could. Zahavi didn't even stumble at the impact. He grinned.

"Enough," Alexander shouted. "There is no time for arguments. Elle, please, allow me to go look for them."

"I don't trust you," Elle said. "I don't trust anyone at this point."

"I know," he said. "There are dangerous people about; you have to think of your life right now, and mine and Zahavi's."

Elle felt tears gather in her eyes. "What if she just went after him?"

Zahavi scoffed.

"Allow me to do this. Get in the truck with Zahavi, and I will return shortly."

He tried to smile to reassure her, but it was more of a grimace. He gave her a little push, and her feet began to move of their own volition toward the vehicle. She climbed into the front passenger seat and buckled her seat belt.

She watched Alexander trot away, his gun drawn. He disappeared behind a tent. She looked to Zahavi. The big man wore a nervous expression in the place of his usual smug one. Elle would have welcomed the change under different circumstances. She looked back at the last place she had seen Alexander. Nothing stirred.

Zahavi started the engine. Elle gasped, sure he was about to drive away, but he only left the Suburban idling, the headlights off.

Two gunshots sounded in the distance, one right after the other.

Zahavi swore in his mother tongue and threw the vehicle into drive. They sped through the village, skirting a makeshift building and knocking a tent loose. The headlights illuminated the dark shadows as the Suburban rolled through the uneven pathways between the structures. Elle heard two thumps and let out a short scream when she saw two bodies tumble into the darkness. The lights cut through the darkness of a clearing and fell on a throng of people.

Zahavi stopped the Suburban and jumped out, slamming the door behind him without a word to Elle. He fought off a few and one fell to the ground. He drew his gun and began to fire on the crowd. She expected the people to scatter, but they remained in a thick mob. Zahavi moved in close, firing. A few people fell to the ground but continued to move, crawling. One ragged woman took three slugs to the body before she collapsed to the dust.

Elle flinched at each shot, but she couldn't tear her eyes away from the scene. It was surreal to see the people unperturbed by the gunfire, the bullets that tore into their bodies, and the sprays of blood glittering in the headlights.

She groaned as the crowd parted enough to reveal Alexander prone on the ground. She reached out for the door handle but paused. Outside, the people drifted away from Alexander and crowded past Zahavi. They were headed in the direction of the Suburban.

Elle clicked the locks and ducked down on the floor between the front seats. She held her breath. Outside, she could hear more gunshots. She shivered. Perhaps if they didn't see movement inside the car the people would move on. She admonished herself for being frightened, and hiding like a child.

The first face floated by the window, passing across the driver's side window, and stopped in front of the window opposite her hiding place. More appeared, their faces slack and expressionless, their eyes staring and unblinking. Sores and scratches covered their skin beneath layers of dirt and grime. They crowded the windows and smeared the glass with their filthy fingers.

They climbed onto the hood, obscuring her view through the windshield. There were more shots. It meant that Zahavi and Alexander had not been torn apart, and that they were still alive. She had to do something or they would both be killed. Elle climbed into the driver's seat and switched on the engine. Her movement caught the attention of the ragged people outside the Suburban.

As she settled in, the horde continued to press against the window. They began shaking the glass with renewed vigor. Elle put the car in reverse and let it roll backward a foot. She looked over her shoulder and saw the back of the vehicle nudge the crowd. She saw a figure fall, and the Suburban rocked as the wheels rolled over the figure. She grimaced and stamped her foot on the brake. Beyond the windshield, the people milled forward. Elle took a deep breath and pressed her foot to the accelerator. She gritted her teeth at the impact of metal and fiberglass on human skin and bone. Their faces didn't change, and they remained soundless. They fell before the Suburban and beneath the tires. The vehicle rocked as it rolled over the obstacles. A thumping noise she would never forget echoed through the interior.

Her field of view cleared, and she could see Zahavi standing over Alexander, struggling with one of the horde with his bare hands. More of them weren't far away from joining the fray.

Elle began to honk the horn. The stumbling attackers didn't seem to be phased. Elle hit the accelerator and closed the short distance between the Suburban and Zahavi, bowling over more of them as she went.

A quick knock on the driver's door captured Elle's attention away from the horror of the scene. She let out a ragged gasp when she turned to see Cass there struggling with the mob.

Elle pulled the door handle and scooted over to the passenger seat. Cass fought off their reaching hands, and shoved one of them away from the Suburban. She slid into the driver's seat, swiftly kicked away a body, and slammed the door, catching several hands as she did.

Elle felt a short bleat of alarm escape her mouth to see fingers bent between metal. She saw blood flow as Cass struggled to close the door. On the other side of the door, the owners of the broken fingers showed no sign of pain. Their breath fogged the window as they continued their relentless reaching.

Cass shoved the door open, knocking them away. Once the Suburban was secure, she turned to Elle.

"Are you okay?" Elle nodded and pointed to the windshield. Zahavi still struggled with the group. Cass reached over her to open the glove compartment. She removed a gun. Elle gasped. She had no idea there had been a gun there the entire time.

"I need you to drive," Cass said.

They exchanged seats climbing over each other.

"We need to get in close," she said. "I'll clear the way first."

Cass rolled down the window and fired at the group that surrounded Zahavi. They dropped as bursts of blood sprayed above their heads like fireworks. Elle stared in horrified amazement as Cass picked off about eight of them. Zahavi recovered and gathered Alexander in his arms. Elle coasted forward. Cass opened the back door and helped Alexander and Zahavi into the Suburban.

"Drive," Zahavi ordered.

Elle revved the engine and peeled away from the village. In the rearview mirror, she watched Zahavi shake Alexander. There were ugly bruises around his collarbone and throat. The blood that stained his face wept from a gash on his forehead. Cass turned around in the seat and put her fingers to the unconscious man's neck. She slowly moved them away. Her eyes met Elle's.

"He's dead," she whispered. "His throat has been crushed."

The vehicle rocked as the tires bumped and rolled back onto the paved road.

Elle stomped the brakes. She put the Suburban in park and turned to look over the seat. Alexander lay still. Unbreathing. And the blood. It made her think of Rob.

"Don't say that," she groaned. "Please don't say that."

Zahavi gripped Alexander's shirt in both fists and began to tremble. He looked up at them, eyes shining with grief. He slid away and retreated to the second row seat. He removed his jacket and covered his friend's face.

"We have to go," Cass said, her voice hoarse. "We have to get out of here."

Elle sped away the night blurred by her tears.

❖

By dawn, they had arrived back at the hotel. Elle's throat and eyes ached from crying. Once she parked the Suburban, she buried her face in her hands. She felt Cass's hand on her shoulder and raised her head.

"What are we going to do?"

"I'm going to take Alexander back to France," Zahavi said.

Elle turned to see his face gaunt in the glow of a lit cigarette. His eyes were rimmed red and shaded by grief.

"He has an ex-wife and one kid in college now."

"Shouldn't we tell the authorities what happened?" Elle asked, looking from Zahavi to Cass.

"No," he said. "And if you try to fight me on it, I'll take you back to the desert."

"Hey," Cass said. "There's no reason to make threats."

"He went looking for you and the crazy man," Zahavi growled. "How convenient that he never found the two of you, that you returned alone."

"Those people were everywhere," Cass said, her voice low and even. "We barely escaped—"

"What happened to Tarek?" Elle asked.

"He took off when you guys went to the roof," Cass said. "I chased after him, but he ran into a crowd of those people."

"You're a good shot," Zahavi said coldly. "You went right for their heads. You didn't hesitate. I've never seen anything like it."

"I've had gun training," Cass said.

"Yet you don't carry a gun," Zahavi said, eyeing her with a look of disgust on his face. "I frankly don't want to know. I want to take my friend to France."

Cass gave a short nod. "We won't stop you."

"Hold on a second," Elle shouted. "This is crazy. Alexander was murdered in the desert by a crowd of mindless zombies. We should let someone know."

"Explain to her." Zahavi glowered at Cass. "She doesn't know the way things are done among people like us."

Elle looked to Cass. "What the hell does that mean?"

"It means we don't involve the authorities," Zahavi said.

"Alexander is wanted by several international agencies, as well as the locals," Cass said, her eyes darting between the two of them before settling on Elle.

"Not everyone agrees with his tactics, and there are people who feel wronged by him. The authorities would investigate, hold his body, or come after his family when they come to claim him. Let Zahavi handle this."

Elle let the information soak in. Who could so coolly plan to smuggle a body out of the Middle East? Killers. People who weren't squeamish about one of their travel mates being nearly torn apart.

"I'm going to tell someone about the people in that village."

"They are not my concern," Zahavi said, a feral hardness in his eyes.

"I'm sorry about your friend," Elle said. She truly was, and she didn't want to get in the way of Zahavi taking care of Alexander. He had died such a horrible death trying to help her.

"He should have told you to go home," Zahavi said bitterly. "Report the village, get those people help, and go home."

She and Cass climbed out of the Suburban wearily. As Cass gathered their gear, Elle watched Zahavi use a bottle of water to wash the blood from Alexander's face. He spoke quietly in Hebrew as he did. Elle came to the conclusion that he was praying. She tried to remember the last time she had prayed for anything. Her parents raised her to be religious, but of course, she was too stubborn to share in their beliefs after junior high when she decided she could think for herself.

She felt Cass's warm hand on her shoulder. "This is his journey now."

"Am I doing the right thing?" she asked.

Zahavi watched her as he climbed into the driver's seat of the Suburban. He gestured with his eyes to Cass.

"You're keeping the wrong company."

He peeled out of the parking garage leaving the two of them standing there, Elle looking to Cass whose face briefly contorted into a snarl of disgust. She glanced her way.

"We're better off without him," Cass said. "He would've just gotten in the way."

"Of what?" Elle asked.

"Finding out what happened to that village."

Elle glanced around them, suddenly paranoid of who could be watching or lurking between the parked cars. She felt as if those ragged cannibal people had followed them from the desert to squeeze their necks until they were bruised and broken. The entire night flashed before her eyes, the last vision, Alexander's death. She realized that more than what was considered in-between conversation silence had passed and she hadn't spoken a word.

Elle nodded numbly. "I should have stayed in Texas. Another man is dead."

Cass placed her hands on Elle's shoulders and lowered her head until they were eye-level.

"Don't say that," she said. "You were looking for the truth."

"I should've known not to try," Elle said. "The truth is hardly ever found. It gets lost and muddled, and after a few months no one cares."

"You'll still care," Cass said. "You won't stop looking. We won't stop looking."

Together, they walked inside the hotel. People were just beginning to rise for the day, and Elle could smell coffee brewing somewhere. Soon, the city would be business as usual, tourists, and workers, and suits darting from one air-conditioned cool building to another. She saw the dead faces of those people in the village. They could have been any of the people in the hotel.

In the elevator, she turned her attention to Cass. She thought of Zahavi's accusations that Cass seemed more than just a carefree translator. She thought of the words he had said in parting just minutes before.

"Where did you learn to shoot?" Elle asked.

"My parents," Cass said. "They were really serious about me becoming some kind of special ops."

"Zahavi said that you don't seem to be military trained."

Cass shrugged and turned her cool hazel gaze on Elle. "I wish it weren't the truth and that I had a more wholesome upbringing."

Elle leaned forward. "What do you mean?"

"Look," Cass said. "Zahavi is upset. It was my idea to stay in the village overnight, and if I hadn't run off after Tarek we could have gotten out of there safely."

Elle touched her shoulder. "You were trying to help me."

"It's impossible to earn the trust of a man like that," she said, her eyes steely, haunted.

"He knows you're not exactly who you say you are," Elle said cautiously.

"Who do you think I am?"

"I haven't decided yet," Elle said.

The elevator stopped on their floor and they parted ways.

Once in her room, Elle kicked off her shoes and checked her phone messages. Her mother had called her several times, as had Anne. Her next course of action was to shower. She took her time, soaping and rinsing several times. She thought of Tarek. And Alexander. Rob. She cried. It was all over. She had nothing to link Ziggurat with Rob's death. They could deny he even ever worked for them and no one would question them. She would be the crazy one. The slanderous reporter.

When she got out of the shower, a soft knock sounded at the door. She peeked out the spy hole and saw Cass with a room service tray of all things. She should have known her words would leave Cass unsettled.

"Let me dress," Elle said.

She pulled a button down flannel and jeans from her suitcase and put them on. When she opened the door, Cass was still there, as patient as ever. They sat at the nook and ate steak and some kind of rice with a flatbread.

When they were finished, Elle shamelessly stretched out on the bed. She didn't have the energy to banter or call Anne or figure out what to do next. Not only had she not gauged how hungry she was, but how tired. She hadn't slept since her nap during the drive out to the desert the day before. She had driven all night while Zahavi mourned and Cass kept vigil, a gun on her lap. Now Cass stood near the bed, unarmed but still watchful. She had done nothing but protect her fiercely throughout the whole ordeal in the desert.

Elle's eyelids drooped as sleep began to claim her.

"You should rest," Cass said. "I'll go and put my ear to the ground. Maybe I'll hear something about what happened to that village if I ask the right people."

"What do you mean by the right people?"

"The type of people who may be willing to trade information," she said. "It's not as exciting as it sounds."

"Then I want to come with you." Elle sat up.

"You're exhausted," she argued.

"So are you," Elle said and pulled back the covers as she made room for another body.

Without a word, Cass climbed into the bed and slid next to Elle. They turned on their sides and faced each other.

"I want to ask you something, Elle."

"Okay."

"What made you jump in the driver's seat last night?" she asked. "To try and save Alexander and Zahavi?"

"I don't know. They needed me," she said and tilted her head. "What made you rush through all of those people to join me?"

"I came back for you," Cass said. "But I've been in tough situations before."

"So have I," Elle said. "And I've met some courageous people. That's the way we should all be."

Cass nodded. "I take it there's no one who will have my head for being here with you." Elle chuckled. "No, though I doubt you would ever worry about someone coming for your head."

Cass looked away and then back at Elle. The way her eyes changed with her mood fascinated Elle, and she found herself wanting to know their full spectrum from hazel to gray.

"I'm glad you were there."

She turned over, suddenly overcome by emotion. She began to cry, softly at first, but then the sobs came, wracking her body. She felt Cass move close to her. Strong arms enveloped her, and when she shivered, they held her tighter. Cass rested her chin on the top of Elle's head.

"I have you," she said. "I have you."

Elle slipped into a vigilant sleep, conscious of the approach of nightmares. She re-saw the grisly happenings in the desert in the distorted trappings of bad dreams that rolled in and settled like a fog. She woke to the sound of Anne's ringtone. After a few confused seconds, she realized that she and Cass had gravitated closer during their sleep.

Elle stiffened and tried to move away, but Cass wrapped an arm around her waist and closed the gap of the inches between their bodies. They settled together easily, as if they were not total strangers. She felt good, her heartbeat strong and steady. Perhaps their bodies were too exhausted to make their physical closeness anything more than the need for comfort and reassurance.

"It's Anne," she said, smiling despite herself.

"Okay," Cass said sleepily and wrapped both arms around her. Elle chuckled.

"I'm going to answer the phone."

She slipped out of Cass's grip. She scooped up her cell to receive Anne's call.

"There you are," she said in greeting. She sounded worried and agitated. "Well, how did it go out there?"

Elle sighed. She thought of all that had happened, and her eyes began to water.

"What is it?" Anne asked urgently. "Have you been hurt?"

"No," Elle whimpered. "I'm fine."

"Tell me," Anne said.

"Alexander is dead."

"Who?" Anne asked.

"Tammy's contact," Elle explained. "He was killed in the desert."

"What happened?"

She took a deep breath and told of the previous day's events. Tarek and his story about the drones and the insanity that followed. She told about Alexander's death and Zahavi taking off with his body. She told of Cass springing into action and taking out all of those people. When Elle was finished, Anne sighed.

"These don't sound like the type of people you should stay in company with," she said. "You need to come home right away."

Elle nodded. "I agree with you, but I want to stick around for a few more days and see what I can dig up."

"I was afraid of that." Anne sighed.

"Something crazy is going on out in the desert," Elle said. "There are a bunch of people wandering around like zombies. I watched them kill a man with their bare hands. That is why Rob was out there. He was cleaning up someone's mess, and he was exposed to whatever harmed those people."

"That's a hairy theory," Anne said. "It'll be difficult to prove."

"Those people are out there somewhere," Elle insisted. "They should be easy to track."

Anne sighed her exasperated sigh. She was worried and anxious for Elle to return. Elle wished that she could forget what happened and just go home. She thought of Tarek, and Alexander, and mostly of the woman in the bed in the next room. She could see her in the mirror beyond the reflection of the bathroom's open door.

"How are you holding up?" Anne asked.

"I'm fine."

"And that translator? Where is she?"

"She stuck around," she answered as she watched Cass's sleeping form under the sheet.

"Seriously?" Anne asked.

"What?" Elle asked.

"I know that tone. Don't forget I've known you over twelve years. I know how you sound when you're smitten."

Elle moved away from the door and further into the bathroom. "What if I am?" she whispered. "She saved my ass out there, and she stayed here with me instead of running for the hills."

"Well," Anne said. "It seems I owe her my gratitude."

"I'll let her know," Elle said. Anne had always made it a point to be snarky and jealous toward her paramours. She especially enjoyed poking fun of their professions and affectations. It was as if she could sense Elle's lack of devotion to her lovers. They always took second place to her work at the *Green Patriot*.

"We all miss you here very much," Anne said.

Elle smiled. "I miss you too."

"Congresswoman Pharell calls me every day to tell me how inept I am."

Elle laughed. "I'll call her today, I promise."

"You'd better," Anne said. "Let me know when you're on your way home."

She called her mother next. She answered after a half dozen rings, out of breath.

"Thank God," she said. "Do you know how worried your father and I have been?"

Elle smiled wanly. It was a phrase she had heard many times since she was sixteen and sneaked out to a concert.

"I'm sorry, Mom. I kind of left in a hurry."

"I would say so," her mother said. "When are you coming back?"

"In a few days," she said automatically, though she didn't know what would happen once she reported what happened in the village to the proper authorities.

"Sounds vague," her mother answered. "Are you running out of excuses for freaking your parents out or do you just not care anymore?"

"Mom, that's not fair," Elle argued. "I'm thirty-four years old. I didn't know I still need my parents' permission to leave the country."

"Of course not, only Anne Humphries."

Elle rolled her eyes. Her mother had always been jealous of her relationship with Anne and saw her as some sort of replacement parent. There was no point in arguing with her when she was angry. Regina Pharell had a famous temper, and her words could sting. Elle had long ago learned to steel her own emotions when her mother was involved.

"I would have called, but I knew you'd have one of your famous freak-outs," Elle said. "Where is Dad?"

"We're out at the clubhouse for a few rounds with the Williamses," she said.

"Can I talk to him?" Elle asked.

There was silence, and she could hear her mother pass the phone. "It's your daughter, and she's being the worst right now," she said loud enough for Elle to hear.

"Well, there's my little globetrotter," Matthew Pharell said in greeting.

She smiled at the sound of his voice. "Hey, Dad. How's everything?"

"Good," he said. "Going to put the hurt on the Williamses this morning, and your mother says I can have a scotch at lunchtime."

Elle laughed. Her father was so good-natured and mild she wondered how he managed to put up with her mother for nearly forty years of marriage.

"I'm sure you can finagle two scotches," she said.

He laughed. "We'll have to see about that."

"Is she super pissed?" Elle asked of her mother.

"We both are," he said.

"Come on, Dad—"

"You're our only one, Elle," he said calmly. "You've always been independent. When you were a baby, you cried to spoon feed yourself. What a mess that was. And then you started walking. You would toddle off and not even look back for us."

"I get it," she said.

"What I've never told you was how worried your mother was all the time," he said. "Your feminist, well-heeled mother was distraught that her baby was so independent. She wanted you to remain a baby, and I believe you were ready for college at four."

Elle laughed, but it made her sad. "I was lucky to have intelligent, well-adjusted parents."

"Just take care of yourself out there," he said. "Your mother has good news."

"What is it?" Elle asked.

There was a rush of air as the phone switched hands. "We're going to be in a magazine spread," she announced, explaining how she received a call from the editor of a magazine. "Black mother and daughter teams. We're going to be in the politics section."

"It sounds nice," Elle said, though being on some over glossed fluff-fest in between some reality star mother-daughter duo and an ad for shampoo didn't particularly excite her.

"You could pretend to be a little more excited," her mother said.

"I am," she said. "I'm just tired. Jet lag."

A least it was partially true, and her mother seemed to buy it. They discussed what they would wear and what candid shot they would use from their everyday life. Her mother had in mind a photo the three of them had taken at a formal dinner in DC. Elle agreed but teased her mother and suggested they use a picture from last year's ugly Christmas sweater party. She was glad to end the conversation on a positive note.

When she left the bathroom, Cass was sitting up in bed stretching languidly. She wanted to join her, but inhibition made her hesitate. She needed to get focused. They had already wasted time snoozing together in a lover's embrace instead of searching for answers. What the hell was she doing?

Yet Elle could have cursed when Cass swung her legs to the floor and announced that she wanted to go for a walk to stretch her legs.

"I'll just get my shoes on," Elle said and looked around the bed for her sneakers. "We need to talk about getting in touch with someone of the highest rank we can get."

She looked up to see Cass regarding her with a wavering glance. "How did you sleep?"

"Pretty good," Elle said. "Thanks for staying with me."

Cass smiled. "Thank you for asking," she said. "It's been a long time since I've been close to someone without, you know."

Elle found her shoes and slipped them on. "The same here."

Cass moved close searching Elle's face. It made her want to shut down or laugh and say something flirty, anything to avoid the want she saw in Cass's eyes.

"Can you please explain it?"

Elle stammered. "It's probably nothing. We like each other. I don't know about you, but you could search Google on how gay I am. We're two red-blooded women, and we were nearly killed not too long ago. We drove for hours with a dead man in the backseat."

Cass sighed. She touched Elle's face.

"It was fucking traumatizing. I think we're in shock," Elle said. "That's it. We're probably suffering from PTSD."

Cass gave a small smile at her babbling. She leaned in and softly touched her lips to Elle's with her own. They shared several short kisses. She straightened again as if she were measuring something. "When I came back for you I was so scared that something happened. I don't think I've ever been so frightened for someone other than myself."

Elle took one of her hands in her own and cradled it close to her chest. "Maybe it's two people finding comfort in each other after going through something horrible together."

"But there is something else," Cass said.

"I feel the same. I thought I was trying to preoccupy myself."

"I'll be that if you need me to," Cass said, slipping around her, and Elle had to close her eyes, heady from her proximity. She quickly regained herself.

"That wouldn't be fair to you, Cass. It wouldn't be fair to either of us."

Cass leaned in closer, and Elle tilted her head up. When their lips made contact, Elle felt a shiver work its way from the base of her spine to her core. The kiss was deep in an instant. They fell into each other, and for a few moments, were lost. She was vaguely aware of the feel of Cass all around her and inside her. She heard herself groan brazenly.

Elle broke the kiss with a giggle. She stepped backward.

Cass pursued, but Elle stopped her.

"How about that walk?"

Cass sighed. "Lead the way."

They walked down through the lobby and out to a courtyard lined with trees. They admired a massive fountain spraying jets of water high in the air. Elle couldn't help but think of that night in the desert, Alexander dying in her arms as Cass disappeared into the night. She never wanted to know fear like that again.

She felt Cass's arm around her shoulders and felt comforted.

A scream pierced the air. They turned in the direction of the glass-paneled lobby and saw several dozen ragged people flooding the finely appointed space. Recognition allowed her to take in more details of the crowd. Perhaps it was the space and the fading light, but upon seeing them again, Elle really saw them, as individual people, not a faceless mob. They were not all brown-skinned and dressed in rural desert garb. Many of them wore casual clothes, and a few of them wore lab coats that were tattered and grubby. Underneath the layers of grime on their faces, their skin was pale and ashen.

Hotel patrons and workers began running for cover, running out into the courtyard.

Cass caught Elle's hand and pulled her toward the back of the courtyard and an exit gate that led out to the street. Before they could reach the exit, it flew open and a horde began to pour in by twos and threes.

Stunned at the sight, Elle was hardly aware of Cass pulling her along in an opposite direction. They moved through a panicked crowd to a side door that led to a stairwell crowded with people. She felt Cass's arm around her waist as they fought their way through.

An alarm sounded, a blaring electronic shriek that brought a new surge of panic in the stairwell. They ran up the stairs and through a door promising in several languages to lead them to the lobby and the exit.

People poured toward the door. Elle saw a woman in a business suit fall and scream, reaching her hand for a fleeing man. She disappeared from Elle's view beneath a blur of scurrying feet.

Cass stopped then stepped back quickly as a ragged man staggered in. The hotel patrons spread out, crushing themselves against the walls in order to give the man a wide berth. His wooly hair stood on end, and blisters covered his face. He stumbled in a circle on one leg, the other dragging behind at the ankle, bare, filthy, and festering from a blackened wound.

He turned and began to slide their way. Cass stepped forward, extending the baton she apparently always kept hidden in her sleeve. She struck the man across this face. The blow didn't seem to deter him. Cass stepped behind him and brought the baton across his neck. Elle heard a hollow, wet crack.

The man dropped heavily, gasping for air. Cass reached for Elle's hand. Together they headed into the lobby and a panic of screaming, fleeing people. A female hotel worker dropped what looked to be a pry bar with a wooden handle as she attempted to fight off a shirtless man in tattered pants. He grabbed her throat, and his bony arms rippled as he squeezed.

Cass let go of Elle to bowl into the man. He fell to the floor and flailed clumsily for a few seconds before he slowly began to pick himself up. Cass retrieved the pry bar and punched the handle between his eyes. He fell to the floor and stayed there.

Cass motioned for her to follow her to the exit. She looked beyond the glass doors at the crowd. No hotel staff or patrons remained on the inside of the glass. Only Elle, Cass, and the horde remained.

Cass stepped forward swinging the bar at a trio of filthy sleepwalkers. The blunt crook of the metal impacted with the face of one of their attackers. One of them staggered and fell. Before he could hit the floor, Cass moved on to the second. She used the end of the handle to dislocate one of the horde's legs at the knee. He teetered over, clawing at Elle, his fingers tangled in her shirt.

Elle screamed and pushed at the man. He smelled foul and his eyes were wild. Through his tangled hair, she could see Cass brain the third, a female in filthy casual clothes. She crumpled, and Cass turned to see Elle fighting with the second.

She sprang forward and shouldered Elle's attacker to the floor. She grabbed Elle's hand and half-dragged her to the check-in desk.

"Get over," Cass shouted. The gray color dominated her eyes. They were hard and cold, darting around for any sign of danger.

Elle looked behind her and saw a surge of them trudging their way, climbing over furniture and each other in a blind charge. Elle scrambled over the desk and turned expectantly to see Cass join her. She jumped on the counter and stood facing the dozens of ragged people, the pry bar still in her grasp.

Cass fought off twenty of the stumbling, scrambling horde. Since meeting Cass, Elle wondered if she was some sort of athlete. Cass incapacitated the attacking people as if it were a sport. Her movements seemed choreographed. Elle could hardly believe her eyes as Cass moved with an unnatural quickness, an otherworldly grace.

She turned and leapt to the floor next to Elle.

"We're moving," she said and rushed Elle along through a door and into an office space. A few people cowered with makeshift weapons. They watched as Cass and Elle hurried past.

They ran, hand in hand, along a corridor past a laundry room and heard the screams.

"They're behind us," Cass said.

"How did they find us?" Elle asked, out of breath. "How did they get out of the desert?"

A worried expression passed over Cass's face. She still clutched the pry bar just below the handle. Blood stained the head and dripped onto her shirt.

"It's like they're after us," Elle said.

Cass didn't say a word. At the end of the hallway, an exit sign glowed like a beacon. Cass stopped and cautiously cracked the metal door. Elle could see a dark alley. It appeared to be empty and still. Cass slipped through the exit and she followed. Outside, sirens, screams, and shouts echoed through the night. There was complete chaos out on the street.

Cass rushed to one end guiding Elle along. The two of them moved calmly through the melee past a strip of shops.

"Which way is the embassy?" Elle asked.

"We're not going to the embassy," Cass said.

Elle stopped, ready to argue.

"They can't help you," Cass said. "And those things will just show up there."

"We'll be safer there," Elle said.

"No, we won't," Cass said. "Someone is sending them after us."

"But how? And who?"

Cass shook her head. "I'm not sure."

"That's just crazy," Elle said.

"No, it's not. It's mind control, Elle, a very low level, but that's what it is." She grabbed Elle's hand and pulled her along. "I'll explain when we're somewhere safe."

A black van sped down the street and came screeching to a halt. The sliding door bulged before ripping open. The same dazed looking mob began to spill out onto the sidewalk, scrambling over each other in the rush.

Elle didn't need any urging to run. She sprinted away from the scene, keeping pace with Cass. There were a few people strolling along, window gazing and going in and out of shops, who watched them pass with curiosity. Elle saw their faces change as they heard the screams in the distance as other pedestrians came face-to-face with the small mob of what—according to popular culture—looked to be zombies.

Cass ducked into a parking garage, and Elle followed close on her heels. She heard more screeching tires and the scrape of metal on cement. They turned to see another black van dart into the structure, followed by the mob.

Cass pulled Elle among the parked vehicles. They ducked behind a white Mercedes to catch their breath.

"We need to find a vehicle," Cass said.

Elle nodded and followed her lead as they hunkered and ran, Cass testing the doors of cars at she went. It occurred to Elle that she meant to steal a vehicle. She wished the police would show up. She didn't understand Cass's reasoning, and she kept seeing images of her on top of the check-in desk swinging the pry bar.

Cass stopped suddenly. Elle paused and heard the shuffle of feet close by. Under the car, she could see the play of the overhead lights as their pursuers passed on the other side.

"Stay down," Cass hissed.

She straightened and ran around to the back of the car. With a grunt, she raised the bar. Sparks flew as the crook of the bar crashed into the blade of what looked to be a machete. The wielder of the big knife climbed over the trunk of the car, followed by a flock of his cohorts. Elle scrambled backward only to find herself snagged by a dozen hands.

She screamed and fought at them. The mob surged on her, blocking all light. She kicked her legs and they grabbed her ankles. They smelled of excrement and disease. She could feel their breath as they loomed in.

The light returned and there was Cass, shoving her way through them. Elle glimpsed a spray of blood, and for a second, she saw Rob's face behind that burst of red. The machete clattered to the floor. Elle's attackers fell one by one and there was Cass, her shirt and neck and chin splattered with blood. Less than an hour ago, Elle had kissed her lips. Now she wanted to be sick.

Cass reached for her hand.

Elle didn't take it.

"There's a bike. I can wire it," she said. "Come on, Elle."

She stood numbly and scanned the carnage around her. A pile of twitching, mangled bodies still reached for her.

"We have to go," Cass said. "This way."

Elle followed her to a gaudily painted orange and red sports bike. She watched as Cass laid the bike on its side. She used the thin edge of the pry bar to remove the seat. She looked up at Elle and reminded her to keep watch.

Elle glanced around the garage nervously. "You're a regular Girl Scout, aren't you?"

Cass smiled wryly as she straightened the bike and straddled it. She turned to Elle.

"I'm not getting on that thing with you," she said.

"I know how to handle a bike," Cass said. "I won't let anything happen to you."

Elle shook her head and took a step backward. The hotel, the desert, and now the parking garage. It was all too much.

"Who are you?"

"Please, I have to get you out of here," Cass said. "I'll do whatever it takes. I promised I would stay with you."

Elle took a hesitant step forward and then another when she saw the van cruise past. Cass started the motorcycle's engine, and Elle slid onto the seat behind her.

She held on to Cass's waist as the bike surged forward. The world around them blurred as they sped out of the garage and into the night with the black van catching up steadily.

"Fuck," Elle groaned into Cass's shoulder as the bigger vehicle's headlights blinded her. She could feel the heat coming from the grill of the van as it neared. She looked over her shoulder and saw the shadowy figures behind the dash with those same dead, expressionless faces.

Cass cut a corner, crossing over a sidewalk as she went. Elle felt her teeth click as they hopped the opposite curve. She heard the tires of the van squeal as it turned then sped forward in an attempt to recover the lost distance. She felt the motorcycle pick up speed as they encountered other traffic. She felt Cass's body steer through the cars. Behind them, the van slowed to a stop.

Elle felt the bike slow. Cass guided them into a parking lot.

"Are you okay?" she asked.

Elle nodded. "What the fuck is going on?"

"I don't know," Cass said. "We're going to find out."

She turned and started the bike again.

"Where are we going?" Elle asked.

"Someplace safe," Cass said.

Chapter Nine

The night darkened as she pulled the bike into a silent, suburban neighborhood. Not a thing stirred as they passed houses like squatting monoliths with glowing eyes. She was very conscious of Elle behind her, trembling, emitting that hum so unique to her. While Cassandra was hyper vigilant, Elle was exhausted. Someone was after them and they were sending a mind-controlled horde to do their dirty work. She thought of the stranger from the desert. He or she had a unique pulse as well.

She turned the bike down a dark road and stopped at a tall, narrow house. She punched a code at the front gates and they slowly swung opened. She coasted the bike up the drive and directly to the front door.

"Whose house is this?" Elle asked.

Instead of answering, Cassandra simply turned the knob, the code at the gate having activated the rest of the house from its slumber. She and Elle entered the well-lit foyer with white marble floor that looked to have veins of gold. A spiral staircase led to the second floor. She went to what looked to be a home security keypad and pressed her face against it. Elle moved close to see the white band of light scan her eyes.

She straightened, blinking rapidly. "This is a safe house. We can get cleaned up and eat, then rest without worrying about those things finding us."

"Why are we here?" Elle asked.

"Because we don't know who we can trust right now," Cassandra said. "We don't know how big this is."

"You're talking about the Zombie people," Elle said.

She nodded in reply and motioned to her blood splattered clothing.

"I'd like to get cleaned up."

"It seems to me like you're stalling. You know something about what's going on and you're not telling me. Instead of going to the authorities, we're hiding. Have we done something illegal?"

Cassandra reached across the distance between them and touched her shoulder. Elle moved as if she were going to step away from the contact but seemed to think better of it.

"I will answer everything I can."

"What the fuck does that mean?" she asked.

"It means I don't have all the answers," Cassandra said.

Elle eyed her shrewdly. She was angry, and she had every right to feel that way. She had every right to walk right out of the safe house. If she became insistent, Cassandra wasn't sure what she would do.

Cassandra sighed. "Please give me a moment."

"Fine," Elle said. "Twenty minutes."

Cassandra led her up the spiral staircase to the second floor. She showed Elle to a bedroom and opened one door to reveal a closet full of clothes of various sizes. She then showed her a bathroom stocked with towels and toothbrushes in plastic wrap.

"What is this place?" Elle asked.

"A safe house."

"I get that part," Elle said. "Who keeps up with the place? You?"

"No," Cass said. "People I know."

"What sort of people?"

"The sort who shelter people in a fix."

She turned and quickly walked away before Elle could ask more questions. She knew that she couldn't run from her for the rest of the night. Asking questions was Elle's specialty. It made Cassandra feel inept and vulnerable, as if Elle could ask enough questions to strip away all her secrets and leave her exposed.

She went to the opposite side of the house. Behind a Kalmakov print was a secret panel that led to a communication room the size of a closet. A firewall shielded the entire house from sending or receiving signals from cell phones or any other form of civilian communication.

She stood before a panel screen and recited the code that would contact Thora, pausing when the device clicked and relayed her voice through a system of security checks.

Thora's face appeared on the top half of the screen. Her eyes scrolled up and down Cassandra's image. "You look worse for wear."

"I'm still standing," she said.

"What is going on there?" Thora asked.

Cass filled her in about the journey into the desert, finding the man Tarek, and his subsequent disappearance down an underground tunnel. She told her about Alexander's death.

"And the reporter?" Thora asked before she could continue.

"She's here with me. At the safe house."

Thora let out an audible breath. Cassandra knew it well as the sound she made to thinly veil her annoyance. She hardly showed any emotion beyond that. Cassandra knew for sure though she couldn't recall any occasions.

"I couldn't leave her out there," she said.

Thora snorted. "You could have indeed left her and her other companions dead in the Kuwaiti desert for some kite's supper."

Cassandra had to keep herself from wincing at her words. She took a breath. "Then we would have had Anne Humphries to contend with."

"Anne Humphries," Thora scoffed. "Your concern is not thinking about the outcomes of your actions."

"I wasn't thinking. I just acted."

Thora peered at her through the screen. "Why don't you admit that you didn't have the grit to kill the reporter?"

"That is not true," she insisted.

Thora raised her palm, a signal that she didn't want to hear any more argument.

"I take it you have gained her trust."

"I have."

The next words Thora spoke she said slowly, enunciating each syllable. "Then kill her and leave her body for the housekeepers."

Cass winced again. She thought of Elle's question of who kept up the safe house. Housekeepers stocked food, tidied, brought fresh linens, and disposed of any trash; sometimes their clean up involved the removal of bodies.

In that moment, she hated Thora and wondered how many other times she hated her only to have her memories of the occasions washed away.

"If that is your directive," she said simply.

"It is," Thora said. "She has outlived her usefulness and tainted my life's work."

Her mind spun with scenarios. She could tell Thora about Elle's strange pulse. Thora would want to examine her. She might want to wash her. Cassandra quickly killed the thought.

She could tell Elle about Thora and Olympicorp. She could tell the truth about who she actually was and they could run away together, drop off the grid.

She could kill Elle. Pull her into an embrace like the one they had shared earlier and smother the life out of her.

"It seems you have disturbed a hornet's nest of sorts." Thora changed the subject. "Ziggurat has been having troubles in the past few weeks. The soldiers they released back into the civilian population have met the same end as your reporter's friend. In the last few days there have been disturbances at the Ziggurat training facilities in North Africa and Eastern Europe."

"Disturbances?" Cassandra asked.

"Shootings, mass suicides, rioting," Thora explained. "This Kuwait thing could get out of hand if we don't get to the source of it."

"Are the underground tunnels part of Ziggurat?"

"They had a facility there years ago," Thora said. "As far as I know, it is defunct."

"What if that isn't the case?"

Thora paused. "If it were I would be aware."

Cassandra saw her chance and took it. "I connected with someone out in the desert. Their pulse was strange."

"Strange?" Thora asked. "How?"

"I couldn't read it," she said. "It was very strong, overbearing. When I called out to whoever it was, the pulse didn't falter. It frightened me. I wanted to get away from there."

On the screen, Thora rose a bit in her seat. "Impossible."

"It seemed like he was perfectly synced with all the people in the desert."

"All of them?"

"I figured it out at the hotel. They were on the same wavelength. Like a hive mind."

"An anomaly, I'm sure," Thora said.

"It sounds like a sleepwalker operation," she said. "The alteration of a mass population's pulse, and introducing poison into the air to induce a walking catatonic state."

"That was way before your time," Thora said. "And not many are privy to that knowledge."

"Yet I am," she said. "I have to know the past in order to predict future happenings. Isn't that what you've programmed me for?"

Thora looked taken aback, but recovered quickly to her stoniest countenance. "Do you know what happens when a sleepwalker operation goes awry?"

She thought of Tarek's description of a drone flying over his village just before things began to go bad. Chances were that she and Elle had already been exposed to whatever catalyst poison Ziggurat was testing.

"Still, they came after me and Elle at that hotel at great risk," Cass said. "Either someone from Ziggurat has gone rogue or someone at Olympus thought I could be done in by an army of brain dead civilians."

On the other end of the call, Thora fell silent. "You raise a valid concern," she said. "Don't believe this changes anything. The reporter will meet her end soon. I have made my decision on the matter."

"Yes," Cassandra said. "I will search out more information on this end."

"We have a man who knows of the goings on in the area. His name is Amir."

She felt a chill at the mention of the name. Not the chill of fear, but of something much different. The way Thora said the name, she was unlocking the part of Cassandra's brain that held her memories of the man. The chill was the short flood of information that came. She saw him in her mind's eye, a squat bearded man who dealt in the sale of women and girls.

Along with the flood came a vision. Bright white behind her eyes as if a camera's flash went off in her brain. Then she saw Elle dead on the marble tile in the foyer.

Cassandra blinked rapidly. The screen went blank. She stepped out of the small room and slid the panel back in position. She replaced the painting.

She went to the nearest bathroom and began to methodically strip away her bloody clothes. She stepped into the shower and ran the water a little hotter than she could stand. She stood under the stinging blast hating herself for what she was. For failing Elle.

The ever-intrepid Elle found her that way. Cassandra heard her attempt to silently enter the bathroom. She peered at her through the shower curtain and steam. Cassandra stared back at the woman she would have to kill.

"Your twenty minutes are up," she said and waved her hands at her face. "How can you stand the water so hot?"

Cassandra didn't answer.

Elle's brow creased and she threw back the curtain and turned off the faucet.

"What's wrong?"

"Nothing." Cassandra folded her arms across her breasts.

"It doesn't look like nothing," Elle said. "It looks like you're in here cooking yourself."

"If you must know, I'm having a moment."

Elle's eyes softened. She turned away and retrieved two towels from the corner.

"I'm sorry," she said as she handed one to Cassandra. "I'm being a super bitch. You must have saved my life a dozen times between this place and the desert."

She dried herself a bit and wrapped the towel around her chest. Elle handed her the other for her hair. She could do it. Lunge at Elle and snap her neck. It would be quick. Her pulse would fade to nothing.

"You were right not to trust me," Cassandra said slowly. Elle stepped back as Cassandra stepped out of the tub. "I'm not who you think."

"I figured as much," she said. "The way you got us away from those zombie people."

Cassandra studied her for a moment. "I work for them. I work for Ziggurat."

Elle stepped back again. "What do you mean?"

"They've been watching you since Rob Loera died," Cassandra said. "They knew you were coming here, and they sent me to keep tabs on you."

Elle didn't say anything for a moment. She blinked and knitted her brows together; her lips parted to let out an indignant breath.

"You lied," she whispered.

"I was doing my job."

"And you climbed right into bed with me," she said, her voice hardening into a harsh timbre. "And Tarek. Did those people kill him or did you?"

Elle's hand crept up to her trembling lip. Tears magnified her eyes. Cassandra regretted telling her that version of the altered truth. It had been foolish of her to think she could be remotely honest.

"I'm not a killer," she said. Another lie. She wished she could take it all back, just so Elle wouldn't be standing there looking at her that way, as if she were seeing her for exactly what she was, a monster.

"How am I supposed to know what you are?" she asked. "Zahavi didn't trust you—"

She reached out for Elle's hand, but she backed away. Cassandra followed her until Elle backed into the counter and sink. She caught her arm and pressed against her. It took little effort to trap Elle's trembling body with her own.

Her face wet with tears, Elle turned away. "No," she said. "No."

"I've risked much to be with you right now," she said and raised her hands to the ceiling. "Of all places, here."

"What?" Elle shouted. "Your life? What about Tarek, and Alexander, or Rob?"

"Elle. Listen to me please. I'm here to help."

She looked up, her eyes fierce. "You work for Ziggurat."

"Not after this. I want to help you."

"Why? So you can continue to keep tabs on me?"

Cassandra snaked her arm around Elle's waist and felt her stiffen. "Bringing you here was the point of no return. Once they figure out what's going on—"

"Then we should part ways now."

Elle moved to get away, but she held her. Elle's pulse sang but not from alarm or fear. When Cassandra tightened the grip on her waist, resulting in a new wave of trembling. Her fury faded, giving way to something else.

"Why?" she asked breathlessly. "Why would you turn against them for me?"

"Because you're kind and brave," Cassandra whispered. "And beautiful."

"Bullshit," Elle said. Their faces were inches away.

"You don't believe me?"

"Of course I believe you," Elle said. "That's not why you're crossing a murderous billion dollar corporation though."

Her intuitiveness amazed Cassandra. "Elle…"

"You're like Rob aren't you?" she asked. "You're just more in control. They trained you, but they didn't ruin you."

Cassandra let go of her and backed away, but Elle quickly closed the gap between them. Suddenly, she was on the defense. Elle reached up and touched either side of her face.

"It's okay," she said. "Let me help you."

Cassandra nodded, and Elle pulled her closer until their lips met. She seemed softer than she did in the hotel, her body even more lush and welcoming. Wanting to feel Elle's hands on her skin, she let the towel drop to the floor.

Elle groaned in response to the gesture and cupped Cassandra's breasts. Another groan resonated, and she was partially aware that it came from her mouth. At the moment, her entire being was centered around Elle Pharell's hands and fingers as she gently massaged her breasts.

When Elle stepped away, Cassandra followed. She led her to the adjoining bedroom and the bed with a black wrought iron frame. She quickly moved past Elle and sat. When she moved in close, Cassandra pulled her on top of her lap.

Elle peeled off her tank top and bra revealing her full red brown breasts tipped with ebony nipples. She straddled Cassandra's legs, knees on either side of her hips. She writhed as Cassandra's hands traveled the curves of her waist and back beneath the yoga pants. She straightened, encouraging Cassandra to taste her breasts. They quivered as her breathing quickened, the nipples hardening. She kissed and nuzzled them gently.

She continued her exploration of Elle's ass. Her hands moved low to the two mounds of flesh and then up to the identical dimples at her lower back. Elle brought their lips together as her hands played at her throat, sliding up the sides of her neck to the spots behind her ears and up to her scalp where fingers tangled in her hair.

After a time, Elle broke the kiss. She cradled Cassandra's head and rocked her hips as a heat grew between their bodies. Elle let out a cute little mewl. Her pulse hummed high and crackled like electric sparks. She was ready. To Cassandra, her beauty was transcendent, some divine secret humans were not supposed to know, and played at when making love.

Cassandra lay back on the bed taking her prize with her. She helped Elle slide the yoga pants over her hips and down her legs. Elle glided over her for a kiss. They moved together, and she relished the feel of skin on skin. Their hips met and bonded as if magnetized, linking them as their legs, arms, hands, and lips roamed and explored in kisses and caresses.

Cassandra rolled them over. She broke away from Elle and kneeled on the bed to better see all of her. Elle watched her with heavy lidded eyes, her breasts sitting high like ripened fruit, the curves of her waist extending to the flare of her hips clad in nothing but a pair of bikini cut black panties.

Elle hooked her thumbs under the sides of those panties and raised her hips off the bed to remove them. Cassandra moved to offer aid but found herself turning Elle over to see with her eyes what her hands had touched. She kissed Elle's neck at the base of her skull and heard her suck in air as her flesh goose pimpled.

She hovered over her, kissing her way down her spine to those delightful dimples just above the swell of her buttocks. She kissed those dimples and placed her hands on either side of Elle's ass, lightly caressing her there.

Elle gasped and wiggled her hips.

Cassandra slid her hand along the mattress between Elle's thighs. She lifted her hips, and Cassandra turned her wrist and palmed Elle's mons, giving it a gentle squeeze. Elle groaned and lowered her hips, sandwiching Cassandra's hand between her body and the bed.

She used the heel of her hand to grind against the moist folds of Elle's sex. She dipped her fingers inside. Elle began to rock her hips, rubbing her wet clit against Cassandra's hand. She literally had her in the palm of her hand.

The sight and the feel made her aware of the heaviness growing at her abdomen and the twinge in the muscles of her back and stomach as if her body envied Elle's abandon.

She removed her hand from between Elle's legs. She used it to hold her down while she kneeled between her parted legs. She straddled one of her thighs and pressed against her ass until her own clit rubbed against velvet skin in a sweet friction.

The pleasure was so intense she felt her mind slip away, her heart stopped, sound ceased to carry, time stopped. There was only that wonderful hum of Elle, and the heat between them. She thrust against Elle's ass, a tension building in her body. She slowed herself and moved away, out of breath and giddy.

Elle turned over and propped her torso up with her elbows. She grinned. Her eyes lidded with desire. Cassandra dropped on her side next to her. Elle copied her pose. She searched her face with those sparkling eyes.

"What is it about you, Cass?" she asked.

CHAPTER TEN

Cass shook her head and gave one of her half smiles. "It's you," she said. "You bring out something in me...I can't explain."

Elle moved close and wrapped her arms around Cass's slender body. She rolled them over and kissed a trail from her breasts to the dark blond thatch damp from her arousal. After a quick gaze into her eyes, she parted Cass's legs and tasted of her.

Her response was explosive. She arched her back, bucked her hips, and cried out. Elle couldn't help but smile around the hot sliver of Cass that she held in the cradle of her tongue.

Elle licked and sucked until Cass sobbed with delight and stiffened so much she seemed to rise off the bed. Elle kissed that same trail back up to Cass's lips. She covered her with her body as they kissed and situated herself over her parted legs. She moved her hips until their clits met.

They rejoiced in shivers and paused to gaze at each other. Elle started first. She rocked her hips in a silky rhythm. Cass joined her. She moved more erratically, steadily changing her pace and direction. Each move they made brought a number of sensations, skin chasing skin, breath on skin. Their wetness spread, and through the haze of it all, Elle imagined they would drown in it. As she neared the crescendo of their labor, Elle found herself so weakened by desire she had to rest her entire body on Cass. They shared a kiss as cool and refreshing as ocean spray. They murmured beatitudes into each other's mouths.

When Elle moved to straighten, Cass constricted an arm around her.

"I've got you," she whispered.

She began to match the movement of Elle's hips. They rocked and shuddered together, and gave a singular cry as they paused at the pinnacle and sank into the bed in a sweet decline.

They caught their breath and calmed each other with absent-minded petting. Elle drifted into a sticky-sweet sleep to Cass's fingers playing up and down her spine.

She woke in the dark room alone. She sat up in bed and called for Cass. She waited a moment and switched on the bedside lamp. There was a note on the stand, cream-colored paper with blocky handwritten letters.

I went back to the Al Mansar.

Stay Put.

Elle frowned at the note. "Are you fucking kidding?"

She slid out of bed and roamed around the house calling for Cass. No voice called back to her. Cass had actually fucked her, lulled her into sleep, and taken off like a thief in the night. Had that been her plan all along? She had fallen for the seduction, once again distracted from the terrors in the desert.

"What the fuck are you doing, Pharell?" Elle asked herself.

A mantle clock in one of the safe house's room read three a.m. She went upstairs for a second shower. She locked the door and took her time bathing, reliving the events of the past few hours. She thought of making love with Cass, and before that, Cass's confession of working with Ziggurat.

She had found Cass in the bathroom standing under a shower of steaming hot water. Elle recognized the look in her eyes as the same tortured expression Rob wore the day he killed himself. Of course, the two could not be any more different physically, but that look was identical—eyes vacant, not unlike the mass of people that had attacked them. It was a wide-eyed, wild look. A tic at the corner of the eyes. She felt as if she knew it well.

Elle's stomach growled audibly. She finished up her shower, dressed, and went in search of food. She wandered until she came upon a kitchen. The countertops were black marble, and the cabinets had clear glass fronts trimmed with chrome.

Elle inspected each one and found the spaces fully stocked with dishes, glasses, silverware, and foodstuffs. She helped herself to some crackers from one of the cabinets. She munched as she continued her search. In one of the kitchen drawers was an actual register till, each compartment stacked with currency from all over the world. She picked up the pile of yen and flipped through it.

She wondered what other treasures the house guarded. She went back to looking for wine. She found what she was looking for behind a narrow door. She smiled when she spotted a wine rack stocked with a variety of flavors. The labels were all in different languages.

Elle rolled her eyes. "Where is the genius linguist when you need her?"

She chose what she could translate from the gold Italian script on the black label that the wine inside would be sweet and red. She searched around for a wine opener until she found one in a drawer. She uncorked the bottle and didn't bother to wait for it to breathe. She took a long pull from her full glass. The wine was full-bodied and sweet but not cloying. She sat at the counter and ate an assortment of cheese, crackers, and cured meats. Once she had eaten her fill, she wandered the house with her wine glass, wondering what secrets she might find. She was surprised at the absence of books or music, or anyone's personal touch or taste.

Elle's thoughts strayed toward home. It was late morning in Austin. Anne was more than likely at the *Green Patriot* office/studio giving everyone hell, and just below the surface, she fretted about Elle's absence.

Elle returned to the bedroom and lay among the sheets that seemed to still hold the warmth of her coupling with Cass. She smiled and was sure it was her imagination. After a moment reveling in the fresh memories, she went to the bathroom.

She paused in front of the mirror to check her hair. A movement to her right caught her eye and she let out a startled scream when a woman appeared behind her. Elle turned, nearly hopping onto the counter.

No one was there.

When she turned back to the reflection, she saw the woman there. She looked to be about Anne's age. Her silver hair was cut into a stylish bob. She was dressed in a black suit with a white blouse and pearls.

"Ms. Pharell," the woman said.

Elle stepped close to the mirror, then dashed out of the bathroom and traced the length of the wall with her hand as she stepped into the hall. She knocked on the wallpaper thinking it would sound hollow. She realized she wouldn't be able to tell either way and returned to the bathroom.

"Well?" the woman asked expectantly. "Is this not what you wanted? To speak with someone from Ziggurat?"

Elle frowned. "Yes, but I didn't expect you to contact me through a mirror."

The woman gave her a stony look. "I suppose I should have expected you to behave in such a juvenile fashion."

"Excuse me?" Elle asked in disbelief. "I don't believe I caught your name."

"And you won't," she said. "I am contacting you on the behalf of Ziggurat."

"Are you a lawyer or something?"

"No," she said. "I have come to formally warn you."

"Of what, or should I ask who?"

The woman's lips pulled flat into a straight line "Cassandra Hunt, who you so affectionately and boisterously call Cass, seems to be playing us both for fools."

"And we're supposed to bond over our betrayal?"

"Ms. Pharell, I was once young myself. You're in a strange land with a beautiful stranger, and danger at every turn. I can understand how you would end up in bed with her."

Elle took a pause as her mind connected all of the dots. "Have you been watching us?"

The woman didn't answer. She only waited in smug silence.

"You fucking perverted old bat," Elle said.

"The house is under constant surveillance. I'm sure Cassandra knew this," she purred.

Elle folded her arms as if she could physically ward off this new bit of information. Not only had Cass slept with her and left her, but she had left her with the enemy. She was the enemy.

"Oh, don't blame yourself. She's a pro. I should know. I trained her. She has a knack for figuring out what a woman wants and giving just enough of herself to gain their trust."

"Who are you people?"

"We are ghosts. We play by a different set of rules."

"And Rob? How did he fit into all of this?"

"Sergeant Loera couldn't take the strain of the new world he was shown," she answered with that same smug look. "That was very unfortunate."

"And the people from the desert?" Elle asked. "What did you show them?"

"You ask for dangerous knowledge," she said. "You would broadcast it to the world, and that would bring strife of an even larger scale."

Elle shook her head. "Cass is frightened of you and your people."

"Yet she navigates the terrain so well. She is a survivor. I take it you have been witness to her feats. She is an exacting killer. A masterful liar. In certain circles, she is the Gorgon. Anyone who gets too close to her meets their end."

She regarded Elle silently, letting her words settle and seek out her uncertainty. The old woman was playing her; there was no doubt of that. There was some truth in her story. She wanted to shock Elle and test her out.

"Did you think you could take her back to Austin and your menial life?

"Do you want to take down Ziggurat?" she asked before Elle could reply. "You could avenge your friend."

"I have a feeling any satisfaction you offered me for Rob would be manufactured."

The woman gave a dark chuckle. "You'll regret not listening to me. I'll leave you with another challenge. Call her by that name I mentioned and you will see what she is."

That said, the woman faded from view, leaving Elle alone once again. She stared at the mirror for a minute.

"Fuck this," she announced.

She left the bathroom and went in search of some decent clothes. She didn't have a phone or her passport. Everything had been left behind at the Al Mansar.

In the bedroom where she had left her dirty clothes, she found clean jeans, a white T-shirt, and a black leather jacket. Her sneakers were still in good condition. She returned to the kitchen drawer and helped herself to a wad of money: a mix of Kuwaiti dinars and American dollars. She suspected that whoever kept up with the house wouldn't miss it and would replenish the kitchen drawer stash.

She stuffed the money in her jacket and opened the door to the garage. A black Audi, a BMW, and another blasted motorcycle. She chose the Beemer and tried to convince herself that it was not at all stealing. She thought of Cass and wondered if she could get into trouble over this. The keys to the BMW hung on a pegboard. She scooped them up and used the remote to unlock the car. She looked around for a garage opener and found only a keypad.

"Shit," she muttered. "Of course it would be hard to commit grand theft auto."

She would walk to the nearest phone and call a cab.

"I'll go straight to the embassy," she said aloud. "I'll tell them what happened in the desert. I'll tell them about this house. I'll tell them about Ziggurat."

She marched to the front door and turned the knob, almost expecting an alarm to go off. Nothing happened. She stepped out into the early morning darkness and took one glance inside the house.

"What about Cass?" she whispered to herself. Was it true that she had risked her life by forsaking Ziggurat and bringing Elle to the safe house? She couldn't worry about that, and she couldn't let the fact that they had slept together influence her decision. It had all been a mistake.

"I'm sorry," she said, and left the safe house.

CHAPTER ELEVEN

There was complete chaos back at the hotel. A crowd had gathered before police could properly contain the site. Locals, tourists, hotel workers, guests, and police roamed the scene. As Cass arrived on the scene, medical personnel wheeled eleven body bags from beneath the grand entrance of the Al Mansar and into a coroner's van. The police made an attempt to contain the onlookers, but they were under-staffed and inexperienced. She slipped past the cops and back into the hotel.

Most of the carnage had taken place on the ground floor. Several officers and hotel workers guided guests up to their rooms if they chose to stay on.

She wandered the areas not cordoned off by the police and behaved like a pesky American, asking questions, and exclaiming that there was so much blood. An irritated investigator finally chased her off with a uniformed escort to show her to her room.

"Were any of the terrorists captured?" she asked wide-eyed as they rode the elevator.

"No, miss. None of them were terrorists," the officer said. His English tumbled slowly as he carefully enunciated each word.

"Are you certain?" she asked. "A mob of crazy people, attacking everyone with their bare hands."

"I assure you, there are no terrorists in Kuwait City."

They arrived at the rooms Elle had rented. She used the key to slip inside. She knew something was off before she could get both feet into the room. She looked over her shoulder at the officer who waited dutifully in the hallway. She gave a slight smile and closed the door behind her. She scanned the dim room. The place was tossed. The mattress had been flipped, and the drawers of the bureau hung open.

She was not alone. She felt another pulse in the room, very faint as if the person were dying. She thought of the black case she had stashed in the small closet. The gun inside.

"Where is the reporter?" a male voice asked.

Cass blinked and saw him in the corner next to the curtained window. His pulse grew stronger as she became fully aware of his presence. Another wraith? Sent by whom?

"She is someplace safe," she said carefully.

The man stepped forward. He was Anglo. Sandy-red hair. Blue eyes glowed beneath his heavily tanned brow. He was tall, lanky, and gaunt. When he spoke, his words were dressed in a Texas drawl.

"Are you her protector then?"

"Yes," she answered.

"But you come from Ziggurat?"

"Sort of," she answered.

He edged closer. "And the reporter?"

"No. She is a civilian. Just like you."

A smile twitched at the corners of his thin lips. "I was once a civilian."

"And now?" she asked.

"I command the great legion," he said and spread his arms. "I only have to think it and they will descend like a cleansing plague."

He had been there in the desert watching her and Elle fight off his great legion. They were pawns to him, not people with homes and families waiting for them to return.

"What happened out there?" she asked him.

"We were underground. There is a facility run by Ziggurat with tunnels that lead all through the desert. It was all top secret. Project Sandman. They hired ex-soldiers that the war had nearly used up. You know, the type with just a little fight left. We signed contracts with clauses that forbid us from ever speaking to anyone about what we saw."

"And then?"

"Cepilon," he said. "It was some gas they were testing out on the locals. I heard there was a leak, but I found an empty canister in one of the ventilation ducts later."

"Who would do such a thing?" she asked.

"We used to have a joke," he said. "Ziggurat doesn't hire anyone who isn't just a little bit crazy already."

She nodded. A large group of people working and living sequestered from the rest of the world and seeing horrific things, it was enough to drive anyone mad. Thora said things were falling apart at Ziggurat facilities around the world. There had to be some kind of connection.

"They locked us down there. Called it a quarantine. Then they never came for us. They meant for us all to die down there. But I looked after everyone. I fed them and clothed them. Even the poor people from the village."

"That was very kind of you," she said.

He smiled. Back home in the States, people would have avoided him in the street. His clothes were torn and dirty, his face extremely sunburned. He had that wild-eyed look of a crazed vagrant.

"I went to Kuwait City once for supplies. I saw my old friend Rob and the reporter on TV. He didn't remember me or Ziggurat." Suddenly, he looked pained. "I called him and Rob said, 'I'm sorry, man, but you got the wrong dude.' And that's when I realized what Ziggurat was doing to us."

"Rob is dead," she said.

"I know," he sobbed. "I got in touch with all the guys. None of them remembered. I felt it when he died. Just like I was able to hear the reporter. I heard her mental noise."

"Mental noise?"

"The sound of thoughts," he said. "Like the hum of a neon light. It took me a while to figure it all out. I had plenty of time down in quarantine when they forgot about us. It would keep me awake at night, all of this humming and buzzing. I had to learn how to turn it down."

She took a step back, as he had drifted closer during their conversation. She had hardly noticed. What he described was the ability to read pulses, and suppress his own, the latter of which she had never heard about.

"Is that how you knew to come to this hotel?"

"Yes. For the reporter. She will help me like she helped Rob," he said. "She can document my work. She can explain it to the world."

Cass took another step back. She felt strange, unsure of how much time had passed. She blinked, and in her mind saw the lamp on the bedside table on, the shade off, and the man very close, touching her face lovingly with hands. She blinked rapidly and the room was dim again. She gasped and brought a hand to her cheek. She should not have come here.

"I can hear yours. It's quiet. Like a secret," he said methodically. "Like the grass at night with a little wind. Rush-rush-rush. Rush-rush-rush."

She found it hard to focus on his words, but at the same time was lulled by them. She felt the same way she did when she spoke to Thora.

"You should go back to the desert," she said. "It wasn't smart of you to bring your people here to the city. The authorities will want to put a lid on this."

He gave her a puzzled look. "There are many of us."

"They will hurt you and your people."

His eyes turned cold. "Did the reporter send you here to tell me that?" he asked.

"Yes," she said. Why not? If he had some sicko fixation on Elle, it wouldn't hurt to play on it if he would cooperate. She should have known things would not go so smoothly. She felt his pulse spike.

"Well, she's wrong," he thundered. "Once she sees me face-to-face she will know. I heard that song that comes from her head."

He perceived Elle's pulse just as she did, as a glorious song. He would want to be close to her too. It all fed into the delusion that she would accurately document his struggle.

"Tell me where she is," he said. "I would never hurt her, you know. And you could even join us in righting the world."

His words made her think of Thora and her talk of rebuilding the world with the two of them among the new pantheon of powers that would rule.

"I can't do that..." she said calmly. "What is your name?"

"Thomas Lyles," he said.

"Thomas," she said. "You're making things very dangerous for us all."

"I'm a danger to the unrighteous," he said. "Are you unrighteous? You never told me your name."

"I'm the Gorgon," she said.

He seemed to ponder her introduction. "You're fighting me," he said. "Giving me some bullshit code name. You're a warrior. I can see that."

"That is what I have been trained to be," she said. "That is what I have been molded to be. I can't be wrangled by a fucking bum."

His anger crackled forth in his pulse. "The reporter, you've clouded her mind. You've made her think you're her protector, but you'll turn her over to them."

"No," she said. "I would never—"

"Life means nothing to them," he said. "You know what they do to the little people who get caught up in their machine."

She knew. Yet she couldn't let this lunatic unnerve her. She felt her breath catch in her lungs, her hands ball into fists of their own volition.

"I'd never let that happen. Not to Elle"

He chuckled. "I'll find her. I have scouts all over this city. They will get close enough to become caught in the tether of her song."

For a second, a shaft of light filled the room. The door opened revealing the dark forms gathered in the hallway. They poured into the room bringing darkness with them. They brought with them the foulest stench.

She fought one off only to have another of Lyle's legion clamp clammy hands on her arms. They crowded in, filling the room. They piled their weight on her until her knees buckled. She struggled and managed to free her arms. She threw her elbows, striking at the grappling silhouettes. She could hear and feel their ragged breath on her face as they forced her toward the floor. She used her arms to prop herself up and braced her body against the onslaught of grabbing hands tugging at her clothes, her hair. A rubber soled shoe settled on her hand, along with the weight of its wearer. She felt an arm snake around her neck and squeeze.

All the while, they continued to pile into the room. She could feel them all around her until their mindless static became a deafening roar. Even if the arm around her neck loosened so she could breathe, she doubted there would be any air.

It was not long before a blackness even darker than the crush of bodies in the lightless room began to claim her mind. She was losing consciousness. Thomas Lyles's horde would tear her apart. Elle would be a sitting duck at the safe house. He would find her.

Cassandra used the last of her remaining strength to push against the horde, though she knew her efforts would be fruitless. There were just too many. An anguished groan escaped her. She felt so weak, as if she were merely the translator she pretended to be, that she was not the Gorgon. The realization hit her harder than a ton of bodies.

The tangled net of limbs shifted suddenly and lifted away from her as one.

She rose, gasping for breath, and saw them flying in every direction. They hit the walls, crashed into the furniture and each other. The light from the hallway took on a strobe effect as it was covered and uncovered with a confetti of falling bodies.

She ran toward the light, tripping over the limbs of those that had fallen. She reached the doorframe. A pile of squirming people nearly blocked her exit. She stumbled and scaled over them. Before she leapt over the crest of writhing bodies, she peered over her shoulder one last time into the room.

There were literally wall-to-wall people struggling to get to their feet as they scrambled over each other. Whatever phenomenon had freed her seemed to be over. If Thomas Lyles was in there among the rubble of flesh, she couldn't tell. In the hall, there was a mound of people against the wall. The strange force had ejected them from the room.

She jogged up the hallway away from the scene. She almost expected to see more of the legion on her way out, but there were only the police and investigators trying to piece together the night's events.

She hurried back to the sport bike borrowed from the safe house garage. She wanted to get back to Elle, and hoped she wouldn't be too angry that Cass had left in the night. Elle's anger was the least of her worries. There was Lyles and his legion to think of, and of course Thora, and Olympus. As she neared the house, a familiar pulse rang out at her through the night. She stopped the bike and as it idled, she "listened." It was Elle, only blocks away, and she was frightened.

Cassandra turned the bike down a side street. After traveling a few yards, she realized that Elle was on the move. She scolded herself for dragging Elle into this. She should have never brought her to the safe house. She had compounded her mistake by sleeping with Elle. It broke her heart to regret such a pleasurable experience. Elle clinging to her as they strived together for the moment of climax. Cassandra had no memories of anything as exquisite. Thora would never allow her to keep the memories of Elle. She would see them as bane and steal them away.

She found herself in front of a small café, closed for the night, as it was four thirty a.m. A figure stood in the shadow of the front entrance. Hiding.

Cassandra cut the engine and kicked down the stand. When she dismounted, she noticed that Elle had crouched down a bit. Her pulse shifted. Elle was frightened of her, and it broke her heart.

"Hey," she said. "What's wrong?"

"You lied to me," Elle blurted. She straightened. "You left me. You fucked me and then you left me."

Cassandra flinched at the bite in her tone. "I'm trying to protect you."

"From who?" Elle asked. "You?"

Something was wrong. She reached out for her, but Elle moved away. Her dark eyes shone with anger.

"Please don't touch me," she said.

"What happened while I was away?"

"How astute," Elle said in a cultured purr that sounded like a spot-on impression of Thora. "Strange you should ask what happened in what is supposedly a safe house."

"What did she say to you?" Cassandra asked.

"She said you're playing us. She said you're a killer and a manipulator."

She felt a sigh escape her. "Do you believe that?"

Elle tossed her hands in the air and let them fall. "What the fuck am I supposed to believe, Cass? She knows that we were together earlier."

"Goddamnit, Thora," she groaned. "She told you that?"

"Yes," Elle said. "Through the bathroom mirror of all places. Did you know? Did you know there could possibly be someone watching us?"

"I wasn't thinking," she said. "I'm so used to being monitored. It never occurred to me."

"What?" Elle asked. "Monitored? Oh my God, what the hell are you?"

"Just calm down. We need to focus on getting out of here."

"I am not going anywhere with you," Elle said. "You should have taken me to the goddamned embassy if you truly fucking cared about my well-being."

"So those things could show up there too?"

"They're people, Cass, or should I say the Gorgon?"

She felt her entire being sink out of her. To hear that name coming from Elle's lips. Thora was trying to trigger her again. Having failed at her earlier attempt, she was attempting to shock her into killing Elle.

"What is that? Your code name?" she asked bitterly. She looked up at Cassandra, a glint of sadness on her face when she saw her panicked expression. She could hold the truth from her no longer.

"It's the other me," Cassandra said.

"The other you?"

"The one Thora controls. The one who does horrible things."

"And Thora doesn't control you?"

"She does, but I can still think for myself. I can be afraid. I can have pity, and I can care for someone," she said.

Elle looked doubtful. "So if Thora told you to hurt me…"

She moved close, no longer able to stay so far from Elle.

"I would never hurt you."

"I know." Elle's resolve visibly crumbled and she began to cry. She allowed Cassandra to put her arms around her.

"I'm going to get you back home, Elle. When you get back to Austin. You have to forget about me, the village, Tarek, the hotel, this house. Everything."

"Wait. What?" Elle asked.

"This is bigger than the two of us. I need time to figure this out."

"You said you would help me," Elle said in a small voice.

"They would never let us get close enough to find anything concrete," she said. "They operate on secrets, things that would be dangerous for you to know."

"Thora told me that," Elle said. "She also told me not to trust you."

She looked around them. They needed to get back to the safe house and out of the country before Lyles's eyes honed in on them.

"I need to get some things and then we can move on," she said. "We need to do this quickly, Elle."

She folded her arms. "I'll go, but we have to discuss this me-going-back-to-Austin thing."

She returned to the bike and felt comforted when Elle slipped on behind her and placed a hand at her hip. She started the bike and guided them back to the house. Elle sighed as they walked through the garage door and into the kitchen.

She stopped for a bottle of water from the fridge and spied the opened wine bottle on the counter.

"I see you made yourself at home," Cassandra said. "You picked a good vintage."

"It was the only label I could read," she said as she rinsed out the glass and placed it in the sink. She was nervous to be back there. She wished she could comfort Elle, but the hardest was yet to come.

"Where's my phone?" Elle asked. "Didn't you go back to our rooms?"

"There was trouble at the hotel," she said. "That's why we've got to move."

"What do you mean? What kind of trouble?"

"They were still there," she said. "Waiting for me to return to the room. I almost didn't make it out."

"You fought them off at the Mansar without a problem."

"I'm not Superman," Cassandra snapped. Her mind flashed back to the clutter of people flying through the dark hotel room. Some force had projected from her body, and it was strong enough to move bodies. She turned away from Elle and went back to the communication room.

"When were you going to show me this?" Elle asked.

"Never," Cass said.

In a three-layered trunk, she found a few decent handguns. She took a compact automatic Uzi as well. Elle watched in amazement as she perused the weapons. "There is stuff stashed all over the house," she said and reached into her jacket pocket and removed a wad of bills.

Cassandra couldn't help but to smile. "How far were you going to go on that?"

Elle tightened her lips to suppress a grin. "I was going to the embassy. Fuck you."

"Please?" she asked.

Elle followed her out of the house and into the garage. Cassandra entered the code to open the garage. She glanced at Elle who jerked her thumb at the BMW. Cassandra smiled. How could she refuse her?

"Wait," she said once they were settled in the car. "I'm not going home. Not yet."

"Don't fight me on this," Cassandra pleaded.

Elle didn't answer. She folded her arms.

She sighed in response. "There was a man in the room. He said his name was Thomas Lyles. He said that he knew Rob Loera. He worked for Ziggurat at a secret facility here in Kuwait. Things went south and everyone went zombie except him."

Elle frowned. "Things went south? What does that mean?"

She drove out of the garage. Out of the corner of her eye, she watched Elle turn in her seat to see the house in the growing distance.

"I think they were testing a biochemical for war," she said "Something that doesn't kill people but turns them into—well, you saw them for yourself."

"You should have taken me with you," Elle said.

"I'm glad I didn't. He's fixated on you," she said. "He saw that you helped Rob, and he wants to use you to document his restoration of the Middle East. He's crazy, and he has several hundred people under his control."

"How can he have those people under his control?"

She thought of Thora's attempt to trigger her to hurt Elle. She wondered if she had always felt the pull of resistance. She supposed she had never cared.

"It's possible."

"That's insane." Elle shook her head. "I don't believe you."

"There are things out there that not everyone is privy to," Cassandra said, not able to look at Elle while spilling secrets. She focused on the road ahead. "There are things that are just whispered about in the darkest circles. Mind control has been around for centuries, but the Nazis and the Japanese fined-tuned some processes during and after World War II."

"Is that how Thora controls you?"

She took a moment before she answered. She wanted to tell Elle the truth, but she knew that would be welcoming danger into Elle's life.

"Normally, yes, she does, but something has changed, Elle. The things she sent me here to do, I've been able to resist doing. I have to get you home before she pushes me to do something awful."

"What do you mean, push?"

She looked to Elle. She thought of waking up in the pod full of gel. "However she controls me. I'm not certain of the process."

"So, what, you hear her voice in your ear?"

Cass looked down at her hands. "No. It's a biological pro-gramming, something they change on a physiological level. I don't hear voices. It's more like an urge, something I just know I have to do or a person I need to meet. A way I need to be."

"Have you ever not done what you've been programmed to do?"

"If I ever have, I don't remember," Cass said. "They erase my memories."

Elle's eyes widened. "You're talking the stuff of conspiracy theories."

"It's the truth," Cass said.

"My friend Tammy would kill to meet you."

She glanced at her. "I've already said too much, Elle. Let's get out of here. I need to get you to safety."

To her relief, she agreed. She slipped her hand into Cassandra's. The warmth of the contact made her feel more than alive.

"We'll figure things out as we go."

CHAPTER TWELVE

In the end, she trusted Cass with a confidence she couldn't explain to herself. Together, they packed up some supplies and left the safe house in one of the cars from the garage. They went to another hotel where Cass somehow secured a passport. They had lunch and were on the road again toward the Saudi border.

"Where are we going?" Elle asked.

"I'm going to drive you to a small airfield," Cass said.

Elle felt restless as if it weren't time for her to leave. All the answers behind Rob's death were at her fingertips. "What we should be doing is going back to the desert to check out those tunnels. Since they're all in the city, we could slip in."

"You should forget those tunnels. You should forget everything you've seen."

"I can't do that," Elle said. "There is no one to erase my memories."

"Elle," Cass said. "Thora will be watching."

"Fuck Thora," Elle said. "Rob is dead. Tarek is dead. Alexander is dead. All of those people are mindless zombies, and God knows what they've done to you. Ziggurat needs to be exposed for the monsters they are."

"Ziggurat is only part of a bigger machine. These are people who know how to deal with secrets. They can pave things over and ruin your credibility."

"You could help me," Elle said. "We could help each other."

"It's too dangerous," Cass said. "I wouldn't be able to keep you safe."

"You have so far."

"Our luck would run out eventually," she said, a haunted look on her face, as if it pained her to think of the consequences.

"You're the Gorgon. It sounds like some kind of superhero."

Cass cringed visibly. "Don't say that."

"Say what 'the Gorgon'?"

Cass stamped on the brakes, and several cars swerved around them.

"This isn't a game, Elle. Thora wants me to kill you, and Lyles thinks you're part of his insane prophecy."

Elle could only stare at her. Cass stared back, the golden warmth drained from her eyes, leaving only cold gray. She turned her head away slowly toward the road. Cass pressed her foot to the gas and drove forward. Her hands shook as they gripped the wheel. Elle noticed that she breathed in short puffs.

"So why haven't you killed me?" she said, though she knew her words were adding fuel to the fire.

"I don't know," Cass said. "Maybe I have a death wish."

"You know it would be wrong," Elle said. "You know whatever truth I find and expose could help you get away from them."

"No," she said. "I can't do that ever."

"What they are doing to you is slavery," Elle said. "You're brave enough to see that for yourself. Let me help you."

"Like you helped Rob Loera and Tarek?" Cass shouted.

Elle felt her body shrink away as anger flared up her spine. "How dare you? Don't use them to push me away so you can live in denial about who you are."

"I just can't walk away," Cass growled. "Somewhere along the way, I'm sure I would have done that. I can't be saved, but I can keep you safe."

"You could do more than that," Elle said. "If I'm willing to take the risk—"

"Because you seem to have a strange delusion that I am some kind of superhero."

Elle chuckled bleakly. "I've never gone that far."

They were silent for a few moments. Elle felt terrible for Cass; she seemed so conflicted. Perhaps Elle had sensed her turmoil upon their first meeting. The whole incident with Rob had made Elle sensitive to someone sharing his struggle.

"My mother is a US Representative," Elle said. "She has connections."

"The American government?" Cass asked. "I feel safer already."

"So I'm just supposed to go home and forget all about you?" Elle asked. "Allow Ziggurat to get away with murder?"

"Things would only get worse for the both of us," Cass said. "You have to understand."

"I don't want to."

Cass rolled her eyes, and Elle reminded herself that she was angry with the woman she felt such a loyalty for in such a short time. She wanted so much to save her from a fate like Rob's. That name the Gorgon was the gun to Cass's head.

Elle followed her gaze out the windshield and to the highway where a chain of people filed side by side across the road. The taillights of the car in front of them flashed, but not in enough time. Several of the people on the road collapsed, broken in a heap. More quickly filled the gap.

Cass brought the car to a stop. She slammed the shift into reverse and peeled backward; the interior of the car muffled the squeal of tires against the pavement.

"Oh shit," Elle gasped. "How did they find us?"

Cass didn't answer, her brow bent as she studied the rearview mirror. She swerved the wheel to the left and they passed a blue sedan that honked angrily.

"It's Thora," Elle said.

"It's not Thora," Cass said. "It's Lyles. He's tracking your pulse."

"Like my heartbeat?" Elle asked, puzzled.

Once again, Cass didn't answer. The car slowed as she reached a dusty median. She crossed it, leaving a cloud of sand behind them and took the opposite route.

"He must have some of his horde around the main exits to the city," Cass said, glancing in the rearview mirror. I can't risk trying to plow through."

Elle studied her closely as they sped away from the scene. Cass wasn't telling the truth, not entirely. She was holding back.

"What is this pulse thing?" Elle asked.

"It's the ability to read brain patterns. I can tell what someone is feeling and predict how they will behave in any given situation. I can also tell when someone is lying or has bad intentions. Everyone's has a different feel, especially yours, Elle."

"Mine?"

"It's unlike any I've ever come across, I think."

"So Lyles has this ability?"

Cass nodded. "I think he's developed it into some sort of empathy. He must have been exposed to whatever chemical Ziggurat sprayed on the village."

"So he's psychic?" Elle asked.

"All the spooky phenomena that is the paranormal is a science in some powerful circles," Cass said. "Everyone has that ability to see what is not in front of them, and everyone experiences it, some more than others. Part of my training was not only physical and mental, but psychic. Only the best master all three."

"And that's you," Elle said, still not able to get over the feats Cass had performed at the Mansar. "I knew it. You are superhuman."

"I'm not," Cass said.

"Okay, so back to Lyles," Elle said. "He's some kind of empath, and that makes him able to control all those people."

"The poison broke down their brain function giving them all the same pulse. Lyles was able to link them all together into one consciousness. He may be able to see through their eyes."

Elle stared off into the distance. What Cass spoke of was unheard even in the most established conspiracy circles.

"What's so special about my brain that makes him want me?"

"I don't know," she said almost sheepishly and grinned. "Your pulse is different. It's like a tingle down my spine and the back of my skull, and sometimes it gets into my cheeks."

Elle smiled. "You felt all of that when you first met me?"

Cass grinned. "Yeah."

"It feels pleasant?"

"Very."

"And when we…"

She laughed. "It definitely enhanced things significantly."

"I'm jealous," Elle said, putting on a mock pout. "You weren't even going to tell me. I feel used for my…vibes."

"Vibes," Cass repeated and laughed. She straightened in her seat and studied Elle with a puzzled look.

"What?" she asked.

"I'm thinking your pulse may be what drew Rob Loera to you and why you were able to calm Tarek down. They were all part of some kind of programming or, they were exposed to Cepilon."

Cass looked at her. "We need to change destinations," she said. "There's someone with a private airfield in Kuwait, but he's not a good guy."

"How do you know him?"

"I don't remember, but seeing him will trigger all the memories," Cass said.

"How does that work?"

"Whenever Thora sends me on a mission, she equips me with the memories I need."

"So they aren't all erased?"

"No, I suppose they aren't, just blocked. She sets up triggers when I'm briefed. I don't know what will happen when I see him, Elle. I may act differently. Just go along with it."

Elle agreed. They drove back into the city, past the suburban neighborhoods and swanky shopping centers to a forgotten area of town. Before they reached their destination, Cass stopped the car and went to the trunk. She returned with a full, black burka.

She made a disappointed face. "Really?"

"I don't want anyone to recognize you," Cass said. "Just keep your eyes low and don't speak. Stay close to me and don't touch me."

"This is bullshit, you know."

"Safety first," Cass said with a wink and helped her don the burka.

Her eyes now framed with black cloth and lace, Elle watched out the window as they drove a few more blocks to a gated warehouse guarded by burly men. As they pulled up to the gate, more men appeared. They were dressed in linen chinos and loose shirts that contrasted with the automatic rifles they pointed. Elle gasped and looked to Cass.

"It's okay," she whispered without looking at her. "Look down at the floor. Let me do the talking."

That said, she rolled down the windows and spoke in Arabic.

One of the men spoke back gruffly and some boys appeared. Elle watched from the side mirror as the boys lay down on their stomachs to check beneath the car. Cass left the driver's seat, her movements slow and deliberate. There was some argument over the weapons they found there, but Cass remained cool. Elle tried to remain outwardly apathetic, but she couldn't help but spy through the mirrors to see what was going on.

Once the men were satisfied with the search, the gates opened. One of the men gestured with his gun that they could pass through. Cass rolled the window back up before she spoke again.

"So far, so good."

The men directed them to a lot lined with dozens of luxury and exotic cars. Elle spotted a brown-skinned man with a black beard. He wore an impeccable suit and was trailed by several busty white women in skintight dresses.

Before she could complain, Cass explained. "They're not famous American journalists," she said. "To be honest, they have it just as bad as women who have to dress like you are now."

"How is that?" Elle asked.

"You'll see," Cass said. The car stopped and two men opened the doors. Elle hesitated before she stepped out. She looked up into the hard, dark eyes of the man who towered over her.

Cass said something in Arabic, and to Elle's surprise, the man's eyes softened a bit. She stepped out of the car, and he passed a metal detecting wand over her. When nothing beeped, he motioned for her to go stand next to Cass who had her hands raised as a young man vigorously frisked her.

A short, stocky, bearded man appeared. He was handsome despite the extra girth, with small pouty lips.

"Agent Hastings," he announced. "You've picked a good day to come."

She grinned wryly and spoke in what Elle could only describe as a smoky, sexy British accent. "Amir. I see you have made your way in Kuwait City."

Elle fought the urge to do a double take at Cass's change.

"The Disneyland of the Middle East," Amir groaned. "It will do."

His eyes roamed to Elle.

"You've brought a gift?"

"I'm afraid not," she said. "I need to get her to America."

"Of course, of course," he said. "Follow me."

The inside of the warehouse was tricked out into a casino. There were craps and card game tables as well as roulette wheels. What got Elle's attention was the gated ring surrounded by well-dressed, shouting, cheering people. Inside the ring, two men were beating each other senseless.

Cass/Agent Hastings didn't seem at all alarmed. As they walked, she chatted with Amir about his business. They climbed a set of metal stairs to what had probably once been some supervisor's office. The cement floor inside was decorated with various animal skins, the walls with trophy heads in between monitors. Elle spotted a rhino and cringed.

"I take it your yearly safari was fruitful," Cass said.

Amir rolled his eyes. "Africa is not what it used to be, my friend."

"Some people will say it's for the best," Cass said smoothly as Amir directed them to sit in an area around a long, low table. Elle sat at Cass's left, and Amir took the chair across from them.

"Christianity is to blame," he said excitedly. "It's a filthy stain on the world, and everyone is too busy debating about it being a stain in the first place to clean up the mess."

Cass smiled good-naturedly. She didn't look to Elle at all, virtually ignored her. Amir glanced at her occasionally as if trying to see through the transparent fabric mesh over her eyes.

He offered Cass a scotch and she accepted. Elle wanted a scotch, but no one bothered to offer her a drop.

Elle's eyes wandered to the flat screen monitors. Most of them showed the action below. There were cameras on the card games and craps. A few monitors showed still pictures of young women in bikinis or skimpy dresses. The women wore stylish makeup, and a few of them smiled, but most of them stood expressionless. Numbers, followed by three letters, flashed on the bottom of the screen. Five-digit numbers that changed in increments of a thousand.

Her body heat rose under the veil as she realized with anger and sadness what exactly was going on. She was witnessing an open bid war on the women on the screen. She thought of Cass's words earlier.

"Tell me more about your friend," Amir said. "Is she from Africa?"

Elle switched her attention back to the man as he began to rattle off what she guessed were pleasantries and greeting in various languages. Elle didn't look at him, only down at her lap.

"Enough," Cass said coolly. "If you're quite finished harassing my charge."

"You must be in a tight spot to have to bring her here," he said, and his face pulled down in a mock sadness. "And America. Not an easy country to get into."

"You have Caribbean connections," Cass said.

"Is that where the lovely flower is from?"

"You know I cannot tell you," Cass said.

"Yes, I know," he said. "It's been a very busy few days for me. First, I had some guests from the desert. They needed a mass amount of transportation in a quick hurry, and so I provided them some vehicles that could not be traced." He raised one finger. "He also asked me to be on the lookout for a white woman traveling with a black woman, a reporter he wants to get his hands on."

Elle felt her heart leap into her throat. She looked to Cass who didn't look her way.

"Your new friend is not like us," Cass said coolly. "He's a freak."

"Religion is for the weak-minded, but that man is shaitan himself," Amir said as he worried with the collar of his shirt. He leaned forward. "Most men want to carve a place out for themselves in the world. He wishes to eat the entire thing."

There was a tense moment of silence.

"Still, I am a businessman," Amir said. "If you can offer me a better deal than the American, Lyles. Perhaps we can solve this civilly."

"I am not in the position to make a deal right now," she said.

"Of course," he said. "We are friends. You know, Mr. Lyles turned over one of his charges to me. It watches me day and night. It also fights for me in the ring downstairs." He laughed. "A real bruiser. Bashed a man's skull in with his bare hands. No one wants to go near him. Some of my friends downstairs are anxious to see it in action, but no one who is serious would dare."

He produced a remote from his pocket and turned in his seat as he pointed to one of the monitors. The "it" Amir spoke of was a human behemoth who towered over his bulky opponent. His disheveled hair fell in waves over his face and down his shoulders. He stood barefoot in ragged pants, and his great chest heaved with every breath he took.

The other fighter danced around him. He moved and quickly executed a combo to the giant's midsection. The attack didn't seem to faze him. The lumbering giant took a swipe at the man, but missed. The fighter moved in again. This time he could not escape a massive fist. The blow knocked the man off his feet and sent him crashing into the gate.

"Kill it," Amir said. "Free me of that mad man."

"Is that all?" Cass asked.

"I like you, Agent Hastings," he said. "If anyone can put the dog out of its misery…"

"Why not kill it yourself?"

"He sees through them," Amir said. "He's taken their souls. I want him to know you killed it and leave me in peace."

Cass leaned forward resting her elbows on her thighs. "He'll see me."

"Dispatch the monster, and I'll make sure you are far away from here before he can make one move."

Cass took the time to mull over the idea. Elle sat on the edge of her seat about to spontaneously combust, she wanted so badly to tell Cass what a horrible idea Amir's offer was. They exchanged looks, and her eyes softened when they fell on Elle, as if she were trying to tell her that everything was okay. Her eyes darted away quickly, and Elle felt loneliness at not being the object of her gaze.

"Deal," Cass said. "Give me ten minutes to prepare."

No longer caring who saw her face, Elle pulled the veil halfway over her head where it rested like a nun's habit.

Cass and Amir turned her way.

"Hello, Ms. Pharell," he said with a satisfied smile.

"Hello," she answered. "I think I'll have a scotch as well. A double."

CHAPTER THIRTEEN

Elle, scotch in hand, paced the small, doorless room as Cass taped her hands for the fight. She still wore the burka around her shoulders.

"Can't this guy be bought off or something?" Elle asked. "You should have let me talk to him. No, I should have just talked to him. This fighting thing can't happen."

"It will," Cass said. "Don't worry. I've seen specimens of his caliber. He's the product of the many super soldier recipes out there. They need maintenance. Care. That video we saw was more than likely taken when Amir first acquired him. By now, he won't be so swift or strong."

"How would you know that?" Elle asked.

"I've seen one, or fought one. I don't know." She couldn't recall because she didn't know the occasion. They were the very first group of genetically altered humans meant to brutalize the world. They were called Titans because they were outdated, primeval, like in the myths.

She busied herself with the tape, keeping her wrist straight and getting just the right tension for support, then she wrapped through each finger and thumb. She found herself entranced by the ritual and barely felt Elle come behind and touch her shoulder.

"So Agent Hastings is a cover?"

"To Amir, I am a British SIS agent fallen from grace and gone rogue." She shook her head at his naiveté. "He's an intercontinental stool pigeon. Everyone's lookout man and errand boy."

"He was selling women," Elle said. "Like they were cattle."

"There are women who have it far worse than burkas," Cass said.

"I'm going after him next," Elle said. "As soon as all of this is over. I'm going for Amir." Her eyes widened as she gestured with her hands. "That's what we could do."

"And what would that be?"

"You and I could travel around the world putting shit right. You could kick ass, and I could report on it."

Cass chuckled despite herself. "That sounds like the stuff of prime time TV."

Elle placed her hands on her hips. "What do you know about prime time?"

"Enough to know that real life is a lot messier," Cass said. "The endings are not tied up in a tidy package. They're left frayed, if there is anything left at all."

At those words, Elle's eyes took on a sad cast. "What happens if you don't make it?"

"I will," she said. "I'm getting you home. I promised."

Elle pulled her into a soft embrace. She leaned her head on Cass's chest and muttered her worries. "I'm supposed to forget you after that. Forget everything. I don't know if I can."

"We can only solve one problem at a time," Cass said. "We go back to our normal lives and wait for the right time."

"What if you forget me?" Elle asked.

"I'll try not to," Cass said. "Please trust me."

One of Amir's men stuck his head through the curtain. "Everything is ready."

Cass gave a nod and turned to Elle. There was such a tender look of concern on her face it nearly broke Cass's heart. She was certain that no one had ever looked at her that way. She took Elle's hand in her own and leaned down to kiss it.

She stood and let go of her hand softly. She turned and walked through the curtain, Elle on her heels. A quiet anticipation had taken over the warehouse. The well-dressed onlookers had abandoned their games to turn their attention to the ring. She heard their whispers and felt their individual pulses and static. Some of them touched her as she passed as if her bravery could heal them of their apathetic existences.

One of Amir's goons opened the gate. She turned and looked to Elle one last time. There were tears in her eyes. She gave her a smile before walking into the ring.

The giant waited patiently. In person, he was even more monstrous. On the street, he would have been an abnormally tall man, his height earning curious stares. His arms reached past his knees and bulged with muscles and ropey veins. More than likely, he had been born a normal human, just as she had been. Some child neglected and abandoned. Easy pickings for Olympus.

Like her, they would have taken him to a facility for testing. Their paths diverged there. He had been found not to show any special talents, an average or below average intelligence. They would have started to train him the way one would train an animal. More than likely, he had been the guinea pig for many experiments. He had survived them all.

Just as she predicted, the giant didn't seem as sharp as he had in the video. He had probably been the subject of some long-going trial. He stood placid, expectantly, like one of those bears trained to dance. For a second, she wondered if he would fight at all.

When he saw her enter the ring, a kind of scowl crept over his face. His nose was a massive lump; a scar across his forehead pulled his brow low over his eyes.

He let out a bellow and took a lumbering step forward. In the next stride, his pace quickened and one of those massive arms arced up at his side. His fist came in a blur with what seemed to be the force of a wrecking ball.

She leaned backward and felt the wind of the intended blow. She ducked and rolled, not stopping lest he trample her. She scrambled to her feet just as the giant made a mad grab at her. She dodged the scissor-swipe of his arms and sidestepped, managing a well-placed kick to the side of his knee. She felt satisfaction at the pop and the giant's subsequent collapse onto the injured knee. Once he was at her level, she rounded with an overhand punch that connected with his craggy jaw. She heard another snap as his neck bent at an odd angle. The giant was stunned.

Another kick put him on his ass. She struck again, aiming for the bridge of his nose. He turned his head and the blow bounced off his cheek. Her hand began to sting immediately. Before she could move away, an arm snaked around her waist. She hit him with a few short punches to the face but couldn't get enough momentum to inflict any pain. A large hand locked around the back of her neck. She felt his arm extend in a whipping motion, taking her along with it. She flew backward and crashed into the fence. She landed on her hands and knees. Pain blossomed in her injured hand.

She looked up to see the giant lumbering toward her. It made her grin to see him favoring his leg. She got to her feet and met him head on. She dodged the mighty fist and stooped, punching him in the groin. She rolled forward between his buckling knees. He grabbed the end of her ponytail and yanked her back in front of him. She crossed her hands in front of her face as the shadow of his fist came down. The blow pushed her arms into her face, barely cushioning the impact. She turned her head and kept her arms up as the giant rained down a savage attack. He gave up on her face and began to hit her stomach and ribs. She resisted the urge to drop her hands and brought up her knees.

She felt herself being lifted from the ground and dropped back to the cement. She landed on her back, determined to remain in her protective position. The battering stopped. She felt the giant lumbering around her. Hot, heavy breathing mixed in with the cool air of the warehouse like the beginnings of a storm.

She unfolded herself and got to her feet. She had to use both hands to deflect an attack from one of his monstrous fists. Though instinct said to tuck the arm of her injured hand, she knew she could not.

He lunged and she dodged his grasp.

The titan was tiring. She doubled her pace. It was all about endurance now and being fast enough to avoid those arms. Her entire body ached. Her hand and wrist throbbed. She circled the titan, matching his movements.

He lunged again. She moved but wasn't fast enough. He caught hold of her ankle, dragged her close, and climbed on top of her, using his weight to pin her to the floor. He seemed to take a moment to catch his breath and sagged against her, his arms at her side, head on her chest. She tried to roll and trap one of his arms. She raised her legs around his torso and waited.

The giant rose, using his arms to get off the ground. She tried to lock an arm around his neck in a chokehold, but she couldn't get good purchase. He dropped his arms, flattening her beneath him. She felt the air rush out of her.

He rolled over and wrapped one of his meaty arms around her head, covering her eyes and ears. She struck and kicked, but her blows didn't affect the giant. She kept her chin tucked to avoid being choked. He folded her head into his armpit. She sucked in a breath and the rancid smell of his sweat. He squeezed between his tricep and the rock solid muscle of his chest. His grip tightened.

CHAPTER FOURTEEN

Cass's head disappeared in the bend of the big arm. The bulging veins on the giant's arms swelled with the intensity of his hold. Cass continued to land punches, but they were weak and ill-aimed.

"No," Elle said. She freed herself of the burka and ran around the gated fence with Amir's guards hot on her heels. She reached the gate and quickly unlatched it. Another guard was so transfixed by the fight that he didn't hear the surprised shouts from his comrades.

She scrambled through and bolted across the ring, Cass hung limply from the large, lumpy flesh. She shrieked and halted as the giant turned, dropping Cass to the cement floor. She landed on her side and didn't move.

The giant staggered forward, his malformed features turned up into a mockery of a smile. He toddled forward, his arms stretched out like a baby who wanted to be picked up. Elle scrambled away, her knees nearly giving out as the smell of the man reached her before he did. She turned and ran for the gate, but the goons had closed it. She looked up at the office to see the silhouette of Amir as he stared down at the ring.

The giant came at her and stopped. He fell to his knees and reached out. He touched her face with rough, dirty fingers. He smiled. His eyes looked surprisingly calm.

A second later, they widened and the giant screamed. Startled, Elle screamed as she watched him fly backward. He spun and she saw Cass clinging to the giant's back. He spun around to the opposite side of the ring, his long arms reaching around to snatch at her. He rammed backward causing the whole fence to shake.

Elle felt a hand on her shoulder. She turned to see a man with a sandy colored beard. He smiled serenely.

"Ms. Pharell," he said. "How nice to finally meet you in person."

"Lyles," she said. "Please call that thing off. It will kill her."

"Come peacefully and hear what I have to say," he said.

She stared at him in disbelief but tore her eyes away from Cass to listen to whatever madness he wanted to spout.

"Document my plan, upload it to your site, and I will return you to the embassy," he said and offered his hand.

"Call it off first."

He touched the side of his head with his hand. He bent his head.

The giant grabbed Cass's legs and cast her into the fencing. She fell hard to the concrete floor, curled up in a ball, and was still. The giant stalked toward her prone body.

"Call it off!" Elle screamed in Lyles's face.

The giant stopped and shook his massive head. His shoulders drooped, and he trundled off to the side. Elle moved to go to Cass, but Lyles caught her hand and pulled her toward the open gate. She tried to plant her feet, but he dragged her forward through the crowd.

As they guided her away, she caught sight of Amir who watched passively. The silver-haired woman stood to his left. She was speaking to him. He gave a slight nod at whatever she was saying.

"Thora," Elle called out. "You cold-hearted bitch. You stay away from her."

A brief smile touched Thora's lips as Lyles pulled Elle through a bay door and into the glaring sunlight where a van waited. Elle recognized a few of the guards from before. They didn't look at her. It was as if she still wore the burka and veil over her eyes. A man in black tactical pants and a shirt with a badge with a lightning bolt in the middle waited in the van. His eyes had the same dead look as the members of the horde.

Lyles pushed her forward as the man in the van reached out. She could smell him before he snatched the front of her clothes. He pulled her into the van and placed her on the seat. He held her by the wrist until Lyles got into the driver's seat.

"Where are we going?" Elle asked.

Lyles didn't answer. He started the van and sped away. She watched the warehouse disappear as they peeled around a corner and back through the rundown neighborhood. She tried to remember the twists and turns, but everything was happening so fast. She eyed the man next to her. He didn't seem to be aware of her or the world around him. He only stared forward, his breathing a bit heavy for someone at rest. She had never seen one of Lyle's horde when they weren't trying to kill her or Cass. A nametag clung to his filthy tattered shirt by a few threads. It read Maines. Both of them had black lightning bolts inked on their forearms. Rob had the same tattoo, as did Tarek.

"Relax, Ms. Pharell," Lyles said. "Or may I call you Elle?"

"You just took me away against my will," she said. "I think we've crossed the line of formality."

"We had a deal," he said. "Don't be sore."

"Are you fucking kidding me?" Elle asked. "You didn't even let me see if she was okay."

He drove in silence for a moment as if mulling her words. "She's a big girl," he said. "She's high-level, but you know that."

Elle didn't doubt that. Cass had survived the monster's massive grip. Could she survive Thora's clutches? Elle felt her fingers curl into a fist. She couldn't do a thing to save Cass now. She was trapped in a speeding van with a crazy man.

"She's inhuman," Lyles said. "She doesn't think like you or me. She has been trained to disregard things that would hinder us. Pain, for instance. Fear. Love."

Elle narrowed her eyes. "Fuck you."

The side of his mouth turned down. "I'm sorry to upset you, but you must know."

"I know about the pulse. I know for some reason mine is different and it attracts people like you, Cass, and Rob. Even that monster."

"He's something else isn't he?" Lyles said. "A killer, just like Cass. Except he doesn't come wrapped in a pretty package."

He looked away from the road to stare at her.

"It's their game. Hiding the truth," he said. "Concealing it. I'm only telling you for your own good. It's impossible for Cass to tell you. They filled her with too many falsehoods."

She had to escape. She had to get back to Cass. Elle leaned across the man in the security uniform for the door handle. Maines flipped her back upright in her seat and returned to his vacant stare.

She raised her butt from the seat and slid over the back.

"Hey," Lyles shouted.

There were no handles for the back door, and she managed to give it one solid kick before Maines dragged her back to the passenger seat. She screamed in frustration and banged on the windows. She doubted anyone could see her through the heavily tinted glass. She punched at the glass. She wished she was strong like Cass.

"That's enough of that," Lyles said. He pointed a gun at her. She thought of Rob and felt a shiver up her spine.

"You won't shoot me."

"They're cartridges in this gun instead of bullets. A powerful sedative that would set us back at least a day. Don't you want to go home, Ms. Pharell? As soon as possible?"

She settled down in her seat.

"I miss the States, you know. I grew up in a little place in Kentucky. I miss the winter. Coming home to a warm, modest dinner and a not too cold can of beer."

"Sounds nice," she said. "But you've come a long way from that."

"Some people have to do that," he said and grinned. "We are those people. We leave the world we know and we end up seeing what's behind the curtain and under the trap door."

Elle thought of Cass's words warning her about knowing too much.

"I agree with you, but the way you're going about it, using those people. You control them, like you're doing to poor Maines here."

He grinned. "Nothing gets past you does it, Elle?"

"I would hope not," she said.

"Maines is a Tennessee man. We're practically neighbors," he said. "We worked together for Ziggurat for about eight years in the underground facility. It was top-secret stuff. It was a chance for good old country boys like me and old Maines to move up in the world."

Lyles chewed his bottom lip and blinked his eyes rapidly to hide his tears. They surprised and shocked Elle.

"Maines went a long time before the gas got to him. We had orders to keep things in line. We took care of everyone for some time."

"Gas?" Elle asked.

"They called it Cepilon," he said. "They were testing it on the nomads of the area, flying over with drones and spraying them."

There had been some truth to Tarek's ranting. Those villagers were guinea pigs for Ziggurat, which meant there was something more to their outfit than security. They used men like Maines and Lyles to keep their secrets.

"So how did the Cepilon end up affecting everyone else?" Elle asked.

He shrugged. "An accident I suppose. Something leaked or someone was careless."

"And everyone just started to…turn?"

"The first case was this pretty little red-headed technician." He smiled a bit. "One morning, she woke up and she had forgotten how to speak. By the end of the day, she was like one of those folks with Alzheimer's, and by morning she was gone."

"What happened next?" Elle asked.

"It all went to shit," he said. "It was thought to be an isolated incident for a few hours. Then other people became confused and crazy. We were put under lockdown. Everyone was scrambling, but we knew it was all over."

"So, everyone turned but not you."

"We're all tested before we get signed on to work for Ziggurat. It's all word of mouth hush-hush and all that. They were very interested in me. Wouldn't say why. They put me in this pod thing, pitch-black, filled with this jelly that was supposed to suppress sound and any other stimuli. After about ten minutes, I took a nap. I dreamed these wild, vivid dreams. I saw my momma and daddy at home arguing about his drinking. I dreamed about my sister singing her baby to sleep. I dreamed about the room around the pod, and I saw that pretty redheaded scientist checking my vitals. I saw her go back to her room and take a nice shower and wash her hair."

He laughed. "When they woke me up, it was three days later. They wanted to know about what I'd dreamed. I told them. It seems I wasn't dreaming at all. I had left my body and visited those places."

Elle narrowed her eyes. "You're fucking with me."

He grinned. "No bullshit. Momma always said I had a gift for the sight. I could find lost things. Once, her wedding ring slipped off in the yard. I dreamed of the exact spot where it had fallen and went out for it the next day."

"And after that?"

"I could hear what people felt," he said. "Their sadness. Their anxiety. So much anxiety. Like a tension wire, singing. Different feelings have different sounds. When people genuinely laugh, I hear bells."

"So what am I feeling now?"

He shook a finger at her. "Now you're a strange case. You just sing. It's way different from that tension wire anxiety. You sound like an exotic instrument. Like a theremin or someone who can play a saw."

"I sound like a saw?"

He laughed. "Yeah. It's pleasant. I bet Rob liked it."

"Rob had the same ability?"

"Yeah, he went into the pod too," Lyles said and then looked sorrowful. "It was too much for him so they cut him loose."

"He didn't remember working for Ziggurat."

"They have to do that."

"How could you work for someone like that?"

"It was money, and it was a promise," he said. "I discovered a lot after things went to hell at the facility. I had to report to the higher-ups. They trusted me with the whole operation."

"And they betrayed you."

"I just looked around one day and saw all these people that needed to be cared for. I was the only sane one at the nuthatch. Those poor people. I decided to save them all. Save this world from itself."

"You'll get them all killed," Elle said. "If you try to make these people into some kind of army you won't be doing any good."

"Listen, I don't think I'm some sort of prophet. I just know that I'm supposed to take charge of those people and use them to make the world a better place."

"Exploiting them," Elle said. "I think you were affected by the Cepilon, just in a different way. You're not thinking rationally about this."

His cheerful, excited exterior faded for a second, an affectation, just as she had suspected. He gave a cold, disgusted look as he tossed a phone on the seat. It was hers.

"You got three minutes to call someone to let them know you're okay and that you'll be sending a video. Don't try anything funny. By the time anyone can get to you we'll be done and gone."

With shaky hands, she picked up the cell and dialed Anne's number. Anne picked up right away.

"Where the hell are you?" she asked in greeting.

Elle felt her face collapse from emotion, and for a second she couldn't answer.

"I'm sorry," Anne said. "I didn't mean to yell at you. What's happened, Elle? Please talk to me. Tell me you're okay."

She nodded and finally found her words. "I'm fine. Fine."

"Where are you? What's happening?"

"I...we had to run," Elle said. "The hotel was attacked."

"I saw that," Anne said. "I've got people on the ground there looking for you."

"I was at a warehouse," Elle said. "Cass is there. I don't know if she's hurt—"

"Warehouse?" Anne asked. "Elle, tell me where you are right now."

"I don't know," Elle said. "I was taken."

Anne cursed under her breath. "What is going on over there?"

Lyles reached for the phone. She clutched it for a second and then handed it over.

"Hello?" he asked. "Who do I have the pleasure of speaking with?"

He smiled when Anne spoke and then gave a mock wince. "Well, Ms. Humphries, it sure is good to hear a fellow Southerner. You were reared in Mississippi I take it. A fine, unassuming place. Listen, I have Ms. Pharell here safe and sound. She is going to report a story for me and when you have it loaded on your site, I'm going to set her free."

He smiled as he listened to her. Elle could hear her shouting through the phone.

"Now it seems Ms. Pharell has gotten herself mixed up with some pretty tough characters, my former employers. It seems I have done you both a favor by getting her away from them."

He paused.

"To hear her tell it of course it's different, but let me tell you from someone who has slept and ate amongst the evil, that these people are snakes. I'm the knight in shining armor here."

He paused again.

"I'm glad you see it my way. I'm going to hang up now and you won't hear from me until tomorrow. No harm will come to her. You have my promise."

He hung up and smiled. "Now that was pleasant. You don't know how long it's been since I've talked to actual Americans. A good old Mississippi drawl."

Elle settled back in her seat and waited. She kept her eye on Maines. The city gave way to suburbs and then desert. Lyles turned off the road. The ride got bumpy as the van navigated the unpaved terrain. It was obviously not equipped for off-road, and she swore she heard the exact moment when the shocks gave. They stopped at a ridge and Lyles climbed out. Maines followed, his face expressionless. Elle went too.

"This isn't the village," she said.

He jerked his thumb west. "The village is that way. This is the entrance to the facility."

Elle threw up her arms. "Where?"

He walked a few feet and jumped down into the narrow valley. He reached up a hand. She took it and climbed down with him. A dark metallic door built into the wall of the ridge hid the entrance. Camouflage netting further concealed the door beneath the ridge.

There was a sign in English, Arabic, and several other languages warning of radiation along with the yellow trefoil symbol.

"Just a precaution," he said and gave the door a push. It slid sideways on a track revealing a small chamber and another door and a glowing keypad.

He walked inside and motioned for her to follow. Maines came up from behind and gave her a little push. She followed Lyles. The door slid closed leaving them in complete darkness. Elle gave a small gasp, her brain haunted by the story about pods and sleeping for days.

She heard a beep, and the inner door swung opened revealing a tunnel lit by long fluorescent bulbs that gave off a red light. She followed Lyles, truly curious of the place. Sand dusted the floor for a few feet. After that, the floor was smooth and pristine. She felt the draft of air conditioning.

Lyles whistled as they made their way. They passed places where the corridor branched off, and there were heavy metal doors with codes on them. They turned down one of the branches.

"How the hell do you find your way down here?" she asked.

"You've got to know your way," he said distractedly.

He stopped at a double door and pushed the handle. It opened to a cafeteria of all things, dimly lit and not as pristine. Elle crinkled her nose at the stink of unwashed bodies and stale food. People sat on the floor silent and staring. They were dressed in casual business clothes and some of them wore lab coats. They were disheveled and dirty, their complexions darkened with days of grime.

"My God," she said under her breath. "How many are there?"

"Your little friend took out a few dozen, so I don't know," he said. "There were eighty-one people in this facility alone. I picked up a few strays on the way."

"You're exposing people to Cepilon?"

He ignored her. He passed through the people. They all sat cross-legged with their hands in their laps.

"They're in repose right now," he said. "Resting."

"They're dirty and miserable," Elle said. "Who feeds them?"

He laughed bitterly. "You sound like the U.N. now. There's more to life than bread alone, Elle Pharell. Your daddy the minister should have taught you that."

She felt a streak of anger rise through her. "My father, or any other sane person, would never go for what you're doing here."

The people stood. As one, they raised a hand in salute and remained in that pose, statue still. Elle glanced at Lyles. There was a pride on his face that she found sickening.

"I'm sorry to upset your sensibilities. Let's go."

She went with him, glad to leave the horror show in the cafeteria. They walked down another corridor just off the cafeteria. It was a sort of dormitory littered with the remainders of people's lives. She noticed more of the legion standing in the rooms, not moving. It occurred to her that Lyles had them posed in place so he wouldn't have to feel so lonely when he passed through.

He led her to a smaller room with monitors and a few computers. He motioned for her to sit, and she gave no argument. He opened a refrigerator under a counter and produced several bottles of water. He handed her one.

"How often do your friends get water?" Elle asked.

"Twice a day."

"When you're around," Elle said.

"I've made plenty of sacrifices for them," he said.

She shook her head. "You've never sacrificed your freedom."

Lyles slammed his hand on the metal table between them, startling Elle. "What do you think is going to happen to them?"

"They can get treatment—"

"And who would treat them? Who would be in charge of that? The government? Whose government?"

"I don't know," Elle stammered.

"I'll tell you what's going to happen," Lyles said. "Those people's families will never see them again. It'll all be about the

Cepilon. They'll want to know how it works and how it affects the brain."

"I wouldn't let that happen," Elle said.

"Of course," he said. "Media. The great equalizer. The savior of us all."

"It's a better plan than letting those people be killed," Elle said. "It's better than letting them suffer."

He stood and walked around the table. "It's too late. Things are already in motion."

She watched as he produced a camera.

"You want to help?" he asked. "Let's prepare what you're going to tell the good, ignorant people of the world."

Chapter Fifteen

When Cass opened her eyes, she saw the titan. He obediently lowered his head as one of Amir's men fixed a large yoke around his thick neck. The bystanders were gone. She sat up and looked around the ring for Elle. She spotted Amir.

"Where is Elle?"

He shrugged. "Gone with Lyles."

"You bastard," she said, quickening her step as she moved toward him.

She stopped when she saw Thora, dressed in black linen. She too held a yoke. Cass's eyes fell on the blinking blue light on the apparatus. Instead of bringing comfort, she felt fear.

She took a step back.

A small frown creased Thora's well kempt brow for a second and then disappeared. She smiled.

"It's time to go home, Cassandra."

She shook her head in reply.

"You've had your fun," Thora said. "But now it's over."

"Where is Elle?"

She rolled her eyes. "With Lyles. Your friend Amir is smart. He gave me what I wanted, and Lyles what he wanted. The fight with the giant was meant to stall you."

"I'll be sure to repay him."

"Don't worry about that," she said. "Once I get you home, I will wipe every trace of this mission from your memory. And if you continue to be stubborn, I will go a little deeper. You won't be the same, but that is something I will have to deal with."

"I'm not going with you. I have to find Elle."

Thora's mouth tightened into a straight line. "The wisest thing you can do now is forget about her. Let me wash your mind of her. Save her life and spare yourself."

Cass blinked back tears. "Would you protect her?"

"What's done is done," Thora said.

The tears flowed freely over the lids of her eyes. She let out a sob. "It's not fair that I have to let her go."

"You're not thinking clearly," Thora said. "Everything you claim to be is a lie. You killed Tarek, the man she was trying to save. What would she say if she knew what you really are? She would never understand."

Cass thought about it for a moment. "Something happened at the hotel. It was like a power burst right out of me."

"Impossible," Thora said.

"It did," Cass said. "What have you done to me?"

Thora grinned and stepped forward. "Do you know what this means? I haven't even activated it yet."

"Activated what?"

"The Aegis," she said. "A device that turns the very air around you into a weapon."

"It's in my head isn't it?"

"Amazing," Thora said. "Your brain has activated the Aegis on its own. Let me show you how to control it. Come with me and we can start."

"No," Cass said and moved past her, toward the gate.

"Do you think they would allow Lyles to continue to bring attention to himself?" Thora asked. "The Pantheon has known what happened at the Ziggurat facility for some time, and they have known about Lyles. It became an impromptu experiment." She smiled, amused by the idea. "Things got out of hand, as they do sometimes."

"Why send me?" Cass asked.

"A training exercise," Thora said. "I wanted to see if you would be affected by Lyles's newly gained ability."

"More games," Cass said. "No one's life has worth to you."

"You're wrong. Your life is of value and so is mine," she said. "We have something they want. We can't turn away from that. They won't let us."

"And Elle?"

"She is a tragic casualty," Thora said. "She won't be the first or the last."

There was something about the way she spoke those words that gave Cass pause. The second spike in her pulse was also a clue.

"What do you mean by tragic casualty?"

Thora sighed. "A clean-up crew will follow Lyles and your reporter to the desert and kill everything that's crawling around out there. The tunnels will be collapsed."

Cass opened the gate and walked out of the ring. She heard Thora's heels on the concrete as she pursued.

"You betray me," her voice thundered as she flung the yoke to the ground. "You would throw my life's work away. I've given you the world."

Cass turned to see Thora with a gun raised.

"You'd kill me?"

"I would incapacitate you," she said. "I would heal you."

"Yes, you could, and you could wipe my mind and turn me into a drooling idiot, an emotionless robot ready to do your bidding and crawl between your legs."

Thora made a face of disgust. "How dramatically ridiculous."

Cass turned and walked away.

She expected Thora to shoot. To cut her down, but she rounded into the shaft of a shipping dock flooded with sunlight, and no gunshots followed. She came across a beefy man in front of a black Maserati. She bowled into him, knocking him to the ground. She placed her foot on his neck.

"How long has it been since the woman I came with left?"

"A little over an hour," he answered.

"Give me the keys to this piece of shit," she said.

He dug into his pocket and removed a set of keys. He tossed them to her.

She climbed into the car and peeled out of the lot. She had to get to Elle. It wouldn't take Thora long to come up with a backup plan.

CHAPTER SIXTEEN

L yles insisted that they sit side by side for their "interview." She cooperated with the mockery with the hopes that he would fulfill his promise to release her. Together, they planned a statement and questions. He set up a video camera on a small tripod opposite them. As he directed, she was to begin with an opening statement that he edited.

"Hello, this is Elle Pharell reporting for the *Green Patriot* from Kuwait, just a few hours out of the city. I'm here with Thomas Lyles, ex American military and former employee of Ziggurat International Security."

She glanced at him and saw him nod his head thoughtfully. He crossed one leg over his knee and leaned forward intently. Sometimes when he looked at her, she got the feeling he was trying to hone in to her pulse and take over her mind. The man was insane, and she wanted to get away from him as soon as possible.

"For those of you not following what appear to be terrorist attacks in Kuwait City, yesterday afternoon, a minimally armed group of people stormed the Al Mansar hotel. Using only their hands and weapons such as sticks and primitive farm tools, the group attacked and injured hotel patrons and clashed with police before disappearing into the city without a trace, leaving behind a wake of destruction."

She paused again and thought of Cass creating a wake of her own as she fought off the mindless legion. She had to have escaped the warehouse. She would come for Elle. But would she know where to look?

"Mr. Lyles claims that the attackers are not conscious of what they're doing, that they were a part of an experiment carried out by Ziggurat on the unsuspecting people of Kuwait. Technicians for the company released a toxic gas over several locations they knew to be inhabited by rural nomads who live in the desert. The people affected were psychologically and cognitively damaged. Turned into zombies, you might say. I have encountered them firsthand, and I can tell you that they are clearly not aware of themselves. They have no emotional expression. They seem to have lost their ability to speak."

Lyles spoke up, impatient with her introduction. She let him interrupt. She wanted to show whoever watched the video, before Anne yanked it down, that she was not in charge of the interview.

"They are the products of old-fashioned greed," he said. "America, Great Britain, Russia, every country and corporation that has contributed to the degradation of the Middle East. They want oil. They want the Holy Lands. It has been a thousand years of systematic destruction."

She didn't know why she expected him to stay on the script he had written.

"What is your role in all of this?" she asked.

He didn't answer. He stared into the distance for moment.

"Thomas?"

He waved her away and stood up.

"We've got company," he said and reached for her hand. "Shit. We've got to go."

"Who's out there?" Elle asked.

"I don't know," he said. "An army."

"An army?" Elle asked. She stood.

"Take the camera. Leave it on," he said.

She did as he said and followed him out of the room. They hurried down a red-lit corridor, the camera bouncing in her hand. She hoped Lyles knew the place better than their pursuers.

They rounded a corner and both of them stopped when they heard gunshots.

Lyles punched the wall and let out a cry.

"They're killing them," he said. "Everyone in the cafeteria. They're fucking killing them."

Elle faced him. "What did you think was going to happen?"

"It wasn't supposed to go down like this," he said. "It wasn't."

"But it is," Elle said. "You need to get them to surrender. Stop making them fight."

"I didn't." Lyles's voice creaked and his eyes pooled with tears. "I swear."

"Oh shit," Elle said.

"They're exterminating us," he said. "All of us."

He backed into the opposite wall and sank to the floor.

"We've got to get out of here," Elle said. "This was never going to turn out for the best. You knew there would be casualties."

He looked up at her, his tears falling freely.

"Let me help you," she said. "Get me out of here."

He nodded and stood slowly. He began to walk down the corridor, using his sleeves to wipe at his face. Her heart broke for him and the people in the cafeteria, just as it did for Rob.

She followed him, keeping pace when his slow walk turned into a jog. They came to a metal door that stood partially open. He slipped in and motioned for her to enter. What she saw when she stepped into the room made her blood run cold. In a neat row were several metallic tubular containers with flat bottoms. Each had a gauge and wires connected to a keypad. Lyles grabbed a dolly from the opposite end of the room and rolled it to the tanks.

"What is that?" she asked.

"Cepilon," he said.

"What are you going to do with it?"

He grunted as he lifted the tube onto the dolly and secured it with straps.

"What are you doing?" Elle asked again.

"I'm replacing them," he said. "The ones they killed. I'll make more."

She touched his shoulder. "We need to get out of here."

He shrugged her hand away. "I'm not going to let them get away with what they've done. They don't get to decide who lives and who dies."

"Neither do you," Elle said and set the camera down.

Lyles picked it up and checked to make sure that it was still set to record. He shoved it at her.

"Hold on to this. No matter what."

He returned to his grim labor, glancing over his shoulder. "Trust me. These people aren't worth your sympathy. They're monsters."

Lyles rolled the dolly back into the corridor. He punched some numbers on the keypad. There was a beep and a series of clicks. He hurried away from the canister like a kid who had just lit a firework. Elle followed his lead as they left the scene.

"That shit isn't going to poison me is it?" she asked.

"No, we'll be well away from it when the time-release valve opens," he said. "They'll walk right into it. Even if they have masks…"

His voice trailed off as they hurried around another bend.

"You're immune to it," Elle said. "I wonder why."

"I'm betting that you would be immune to it too."

"What makes you think that?" she asked.

He didn't answer her. They came upon a ladder that led to the ceiling. Elle looked up to see the outline of a circular hatch.

"We're not going to stick around to find out, are we?"

She shook her head and climbed up the ladder behind him. She paused in her ascent and watched him pull back a metal latch and fling back the door, flooding the red light of the corridor with sunlight and swirling sand.

Elle had never been so elated to see the sun. She climbed up after him. On the surface, he pulled a sand-colored covering from a motorcycle. Elle thought of her escape from the hotel with Cass and her fear of the bike. Without hesitation, she hopped on behind Lyles. He kick-started the engine and the motorcycle started up.

Gritty, warm air stung her eyes as they sped away. Her heart hammered in her chest so hard and fast she was sure Lyles could feel it over the thrum of the engine. He skirted the scant desert vegetation as they sped across the ground.

Through her narrowed eyes, she saw several black SUVs up ahead, wavering through the heat like a vision. Lyles turned sharply and gunned the engine. Elle held tight and squeezed her eyes closed.

CHAPTER SEVENTEEN

Cass pushed the sedan past the 150 mark on the speedometer. She gripped the wheel until her knuckles whitened. She turned off the road and toward the village, braving the bumpy ride over unpaved ground.

A black shape in the rearview caught her attention. She took her eyes from the road and saw the reflection of a black helicopter flying low behind her. She muttered a curse and gunned the engine. She hit an indention in the desert floor. The undercarriage of the car scraped the ground with a shriek. The car bounced and she banged her head on the ceiling.

She gritted her teeth. There was no way she was about to let up on the accelerator. Just then, a hail of gunshots peppered the back of the car. In the rearview, she saw someone leaning out of the helicopter with a semi-automatic rifle. The mirror exploded in a sparkling spray of glass, fiberglass, and plastic.

The helicopter sailed over the car, and the shooter took out the back windshield and plugged away at the roof, making a manic tune of thunks, whizzes, and pings. She swerved. A bullet hit the dash and left a smoking hole.

She swerved again. More holes appeared in the hood. The village was up ahead. It would provide some cover. She guided the car toward the meager scattering of buildings. Steam rose from the damaged radiator. The car wouldn't last much longer. She maneuvered the car into a half spin and flew out of the driver's seat once the car stopped in a cloud of dust. She ran for the little stone building where just the day before she had suggested they camp out in.

Gunfire chased her as she dived across the threshold. She bowled into a crowd of standing bodies. Lyles's zombies. They packed the room, lined up in the stifling heat created by their bodies, waiting for Lyles to move them. A wave of disgust passed through her. She grabbed one of them by a tattered shirt.

"Lyles, you asshole," she shouted into the filthy face. "I know you can hear me. Where is Elle?"

The man only stood there, his face limp and expressionless. Outside, the helicopter thundered close by stirring sand through the entryway.

"They're coming for you, " she said, continuing to speak to Lyles through the mindless man. "Hope that they get to you before I do."

Just when she was about to give up the bizarre version of video-chat, the man's face suddenly became animated. "I've got trouble," he said in a gravelly voice. "Elle. Just south of the village."

She threw the zombie to the ground and watched as the man calmly picked himself up. The others began to silently file out of the building. She watched them, puzzled, and situated herself in the crowd.

She stepped out into the dusty air so clouded with sand that it choked her lungs. She moved cautiously, willing herself not to look up so that she would blend into the crowd. More of them milled out of the tents and ramshackle buildings.

When the gunfire started, Cass pushed forward. All around her, people fell into the dirt. She took shelter near the goat pen. She watched the helicopter maneuver around the crowd while the shooter mowed down unarmed civilians.

She thought of Thora's words, how casually she mentioned the execution of dozens of people, all to save what she called her life's work.

Cass removed the pistol from the waistband of her pants. She straightened and stalked forward, through the sand that blurred the air and the blood that stained the ground. She took aim and fired. Her first shot hit the base of the rotor, the bullet creating a small burst of sparks. The shooter spotted her and swung his rifle, but it was too late. Her second shot pierced the shooter's helmet in a burst of blood. He fell backward.

The helicopter wavered, and the pilot ascended, fleeing the scene.

Cass ran to the other side of the village. Looking in the direction of the horizon, she saw a motorcycle with two riders pursued by two black SUVs. She ran forward and was able to make out Elle's form on the back of the bike. Lyles steered the motorcycle haphazardly toward the village.

One of the SUVs pulled up alongside them and swerved. Lyles gunned the engine and the bike shot forward just inches from the front bumper of the SUV. Cass sprinted toward them as fast as her legs could carry her.

The SUV caught up to the bike and swerved again as Lyles struggled to keep it upright.

"No," Cass shouted. She felt that freezing sensation in her head and stopped in her tracks. Just like in the hotel room with Lyles, she felt the air press against her. In front of her, a horizontal column of dust rose from the ground, lengthening and disappearing.

The SUV that pursed Elle and Lyles came to a sudden stop, the grill caved in on itself, and the hood crumpled backward as if it were nothing more than glossy black paper. The windshield clouded as it cracked into thousands of pieces.

Lyles slowed the bike as they neared. She waved them forward. She looked up to see the terrified look on Elle's face as they passed. She reached for Cass, and she reached back. Their fingers barely brushed, but it felt as if they were as close as they were in bed together back at the safe house.

Cass turned back to see the second SUV barreling her way. A hand appeared out of the passenger window and fired at her. She raised the desert eagle and fired back, sending the shooter back into the vehicle.

She focused on that cold feeling that lingered. It intensified, blurring the edges of her vision white. Once again, the air seemed to solidify around her in a pressing mold around her body. The column appeared, marking itself in the sand. The pressure subsided, the column vanished, the SUV stopped and flipped forward. It fell in an arc on its back and skidded several feet before it was still.

The cold feeling in her head morphed to a piercing pain as if someone were prodding her brain with a frozen piece of steel from the inside out. She fell to her knees, her palms at the side of her head.

She looked over her shoulder and saw Lyles and his legion. Elle led the way. She ran to Cass and kneeled. She used her hands to search her for injuries.

"Oh my God, are you hurt?"

"No," she said. "My head."

Elle replaced Cass's hands with her own. "What is it?"

When their eyes met, the pain abated. Cass sighed and was able to catch her breath. She gave a small smile.

"I guess I'm okay now that you're safe."

Elle smiled back.

"Ya'll get out of here," Lyles said. "Take the bike. Get Elle to safety."

Cass nodded and handed him the gun. "There are a few rounds left in it."

"That's all I need," he said and looked to Elle. "Please don't think I'm a bad guy. I'm just somebody who got pushed too hard."

"I don't agree with using those people," she said.

"You don't have to," he said and handed over her cell. "Remember, I'm like Rob. My story deserves telling. So do those people's story."

"I'll try," she said.

He nodded and walked toward the wrecked SUVs followed by his legion.

Cass pulled Elle close, and they quickly made their way to the bike. As they sped away, she felt Elle press her face into her back as she wrapped her arms around her waist. She couldn't stop the tears that stung her eyes.

CHAPTER EIGHTEEN

Night had settled once they reached the tiny airstrip. Cass coasted alongside a hangar and stopped the engine. They both dismounted and turned, collapsing in each other's arms. Elle buried her face in Cass's chest. She didn't let go, even when she heard footsteps and the voice of a man speaking in Arabic.

Cass answered him, and Elle heard the man leave.

They parted and shared a short kiss.

"Come with me," Elle said.

"It would be safer for the both of us if I go back with Thora."

"What will happen to you?"

"I don't know," Cass said. "You shouldn't worry about me, and you shouldn't go after Ziggurat either."

Elle's thoughts strayed to the video camera under her jacket. It wasn't the proof she needed to nail the company responsible for Rob's death and the ruin of so many people, including Lyles. The same company that kept Cass in bondage.

"Let me handle them," she said as if reading Elle's thoughts. "I'll come find you. I promise."

Elle nodded. "Okay. I trust you."

"Good," Cass said.

Elle hugged her again. "I don't want to let you go."

"Me either," Cass said somberly.

The man returned. He began to talk. Behind them, a young man brought a gas can and poured some into the tank on the bike. Cass noticed Elle watching.

"Call home and tell them you'll be in Tel Aviv. This is Kadir. He'll take you there."

Elle nodded. She dialed Anne who answered right away.

"Oh my God, where are you?" she asked.

"I'm going to Tel Aviv," she said.

"We're on our way," Anne said.

"We?" Elle asked.

"Me and my contacts," she said. "I'm here in Kuwait."

Her heart soared, and in an instant broke when she saw Cass walking away, back to the bike. She called out to her, but she mounted the bike and kicked it to life. She coasted away and picked up speed once she cleared the hangar. She watched her until she was a speck of light on the dark road. And then she was gone.

Anne's voice shouted through the phone.

"I think we broke up," she said when Elle spoke again.

"Yeah," Elle said absentmindedly.

"Where are you landing?" Anne asked.

Elle found Kadir and let him speak to her. Once the arrangements were made, he showed her to the plane. It was a small jet with a plush interior. She wondered what Kadir did to pilot around such a jet. He introduced his son and copilot.

Elle was able to use the restroom to wash the grit of the desert from her face. It was only then that she longed for her suitcase and her things. She picked a seat and settled in. Kadir's son brought her a cup of red lentil soup and left her.

She heard the plane engine start and strapped herself in. It wasn't long before the takeoff started. As the plane climbed through turbulence, she thought of Cass, alone on that bike as she had been most of her life.

She drifted off to sleep and dreamed of black SUVs flying across the desert sky. She woke as the plane landed. It was morning, and she felt a sort of relief to see that they were safe on the ground. Her heart ached though, and she didn't want to give a conscious thought as to why.

Kadir stretched as he left the cockpit. "Are you ready, Ms. Pharell?"

She stood on legs numbed by the seven-hour flight. Kadir had his copilot open the hatch to the door. She walked down the ladder that led to the tarmac. She heard someone call her name and spotted Anne waiting next to a car.

Elle quickened her step. They met each other halfway between the car and the plane and embraced. She felt her world come back together in that instant. Though she still felt that ache, she felt safe and secure.

"I'm so glad you're okay," Anne said.

Elle nodded numbly.

Anne smiled and kissed her cheek. "Let's get you to the hotel," she said.

Elle followed her, but she couldn't help casting one glance over her shoulder at the plane and Kadir. She gave a small wave and climbed into the backseat.

"I need to call my parents," Elle said.

"They're waiting to hear from you," Anne said.

They were silent for a moment. Elle looked out the window watching the city of Tel Aviv unfold before her. She felt Anne studying her and waited for the inevitable question. Anne was never delicate about such things.

"So where's your little friend?"

"It's a long story," Elle said.

Anne patted her leg. "We have plenty of time to get down to that. You have that look in your eyes like Rob before he went off the deep end. Haunted."

"This isn't over yet," Elle said. "Rob isn't the only victim of Ziggurat. They do horrible things to people, experiments, mind control…"

The tears overcame her, and she began to sob. "Cass is going against them on her own. They'll kill her."

Anne hung an arm around her shoulder. "She brought you safely to me. I'm sure that wasn't an easy feat."

"She's very special," Elle said.

"I'm sure she is. I'm thankful to her."

They reached the hotel and Elle was grateful for a hot meal and an even longer hot shower. She called her parents. Her mother was more than annoyed that she had taken off to Kuwait without telling her. Her father was a little more forgiving, as usual. They had heard about what was being called in the media the Bedouin attacks. Elle assured them she had never been in any danger.

"I hope you've got this out of your system," her mother said and changed the subject to her niece's wedding in the summer. "Make plans to be there."

Her dad cracked a joke about the rehearsal dinner being a baby shower as well, and the three of them laughed. Elle didn't realize how much she missed them until that moment. When she hung up Anne was waiting with a bottle of red Israeli wine.

"You have a story to tell me," she said.

Elle sat down and accepted a glass. "Where should I start?"

Anne smiled wryly. "Try the beginning."

CHAPTER NINETEEN

S he went home. Thora kept her lab in a house on the southern coast of Greenland and stayed there for months at a stretch while she worked on projects and research. Cass had no immediate memories of the place. As she hiked down the snowy slope that led to the secluded property, she tried to recall any specific memories of the place and found she could not. Still, she had known where to come looking for Thora.

She knew the access code to the massive gates. She stood shivering in the sleet waiting for them to swing open. She jogged to the front door and entered the house. She heard a burst of static and then Thora's voice.

"I'm in the dining room."

Cass walked the polished beech wood floor carefully, not sure what to expect when she entered the white-walled dining room decorated with art. As she glanced around the room, she realized that she knew the works all by name and artists. She also knew Thora changed out the art regularly.

She sat at the black table topped with glass, her place setting in front of her, a plate with a slab of rare meat and something green along with yam puree. Thora loved yam puree.

Thora looked up from her meal. She picked up her wineglass and swirled the contents around.

"Well, you've returned."

"I've come to make a deal," she said, her voice raspy.

"A deal?" Thora shouted. "You walked out on me. You insulted me. You left me to fend for myself. They know what you did, and now we'll have to pay."

Cass felt her knees grow weak at the thought. She knew there would be a price to pay for crossing Ziggurat. She couldn't lose sight of her goal to keep Elle safe.

"I'll do whatever it takes to get us back in their good graces."

"And keep your lady love safe in the process. I suppose that is why you came here? To make sure that they don't go after her."

"I used the Aegis in the desert. It's a very powerful weapon."

Thora scoffed. "That won't save us."

Cass called upon that chilly sensation in her brain and it came. She heard Thora gasp as the air pressure changed in the room. Her empty place setting flew off the table and crashed into one of Thora's pieces of art. The canvas itself caved in.

When she looked back at Thora, she had resumed her usual calm repose.

"Sit down," she said. "Have some dinner."

Cass didn't move. She didn't want to fall for any of Thora's tricks.

"You're being rude," she continued and called for the maid/cook who appeared in a gray uniform. She was an older local woman who had worked for Thora for years. She eyed the mess and the broken painting.

"Another place setting," she said. "Sit," Thora said to Cass. "You've proved yourself. You're here of your own volition. You're your own person."

Cass sat. "I just want to make sure that Elle is safe."

"Of course," Thora said simply.

The maid returned with a covered plate, silverware, and a glass.

"Good to have you back, miss," she said quietly.

Cass cut a hearty slice from her steak. She hadn't eaten a proper meal for a few days. She chewed her bite of meat and watched Thora eye the painting.

"It took strength for you to return," she said. "It seems you will go through great lengths to ensure her safety. The question is: how far are you willing to go?"

Cass didn't answer. She tried the puree.

"Would you put the yoke back on?"

Cass pushed her plate away. "No."

"How do I know you won't murder me in my sleep?" she asked. "You're a very dangerous weapon now." Thora stood and walked around the table. "I will not only have to convince the Pantheon that you're back under my full control, I will have to convince them not to harm your Elle."

Cass regarded her with the coldest gaze she could summon. "How can I trust you?"

"You'll trust me because I have your best interests at heart," Thora said. She moved close and touched Cass's face. A smile pulled at her lips when Cass flinched.

"Do you?" she asked.

"I'm willing to help you, a gift for your return."

"And I would have to put on the yoke."

Thora paused thoughtfully. "You come to me and offer to sacrifice yourself for the reporter, so do it or walk away again."

Cass stood. "Please. Please make sure she's safe."

Thora turned and walked away, motioning for Cass to follow. They adjourned to the library. A fire roared in the fireplace painting the dim room with dancing shadows. Thora produced a black case. She opened it to reveal a yoke. That infernal blue light was winking. She lifted the device.

Cass stepped close and squeezed her eyes shut. She felt the cool metal and plastic as Thora locked the yoke around her neck. She thought of the sight of Elle smiling. She tried to hold that memory close in the hopes she wouldn't lose it.

She felt the prongs pierce her skin and the place between her vertebrae at the base of her neck. That familiar calm feeling claimed her. She thought of Elle beneath her, the feel of her body as they strained together in the most perfect labor.

The yoke began to take effect, and that calm feeling flooded through her body. Her heartbeat slowed; her eyelids dropped. She realized then that the feeling was not calm, but no feeling, a numbness that saddened her.

"There," Thora said as if she had supplied some sort of remedy. "Sit."

Cass felt her body react. She thought of Elle's words about slavery and found that she could not summon up the proper outrage.

Thora touched her face. "You gave me a fright," she said. "I have not been so worried in a long time. As you have noticed, we live a certain lifestyle."

She watched, detached, as Thora crossed over to the fireplace and used a metal poker to prod at the burning log that crumpled in a flurry of sparks.

"When one reaches the highest ranks of Olympicorp, the concept of fear becomes foreign. Power. Prestige. Privilege. You come to look down on the rest of the world. We are the master elite. We are above celebrity and politics. We have no boundaries."

She returned the poker to its place and crossed the room, back to where Cass sat. She touched her face, and the expression of tenderness she wore would have sickened Cass if she were able to feel anything at the moment.

"My dear," she said. "My darling Gorgon. You have had the blinders removed. It is my fault for shielding you from the world and its trappings. I thought if I kept your mind clean of too many memories you would only need and want me. But there is more to the human experience."

She leaned down and kissed Cass on the lips.

"I will take better care in the future. You will be clean again, and lucky never to have known love. Ms. Pharell will not be so lucky. She will look for you out of the corner of her eye for the rest of her days."

Thora produced an inoculation gun. Cass sat docile as Thora rolled up her sleeve and delivered the injection. She felt nothing, but she saw the blackness cloud her vision. She struggled to call on those memories of Elle, the sound of her laugh, the feel of her hands, but none of that would come.

Through the thickening black, she could only see Thora's face watching her. As even she faded from Cass's vision, she managed one word.

"Elle."

CHAPTER TWENTY

Elle sat poised behind the *Green Patriot* news desk. Her hair was perfectly coifed, and she was dressed in a plum colored suit with a black blouse beneath. It was her first broadcast since her return from Kuwait.

"Are you sure about this?" Anne asked. For days, they discussed exactly what story she would tell their viewers. As she promised Cass, she wouldn't talk about Ziggurat or the Bedouin revolt. As far as anyone was concerned, she took a short reprieve to mourn the loss of her friend.

"I'm ready as I'll ever be," she said.

"You look like you could use a martini."

Elle grinned. "I'll take you up on that offer at lunchtime."

"I bet you will," she answered. She turned to the production staff. "All right, everyone, we're filming."

At the door of the studio, the red light flashed indicating that recording had commenced.

"Hello, everyone. I've been away for a while, and I thank you all for your support during this difficult time. A few weeks ago, Robert Loera, a veteran of the wars in Iraq and Afghanistan, visited me at the *Green Patriot* studios. He was confused, frightened, in hysterics. I couldn't talk him down. He was armed. He put a gun to his head and pulled the trigger. Rob was a friend of mine. We worked together to bring awareness to the treatment, or lack thereof, to veterans with mental health issues. He had come a long way in the short time I knew him. He went from being unemployed and homeless to working a full-time job and owning his own property. He was doing well it seemed, and it just shows that the scars our veterans return home with are not always visible and that there is no quick path to healing."

She paused, her mind on Rob and his last seconds on earth. She had gone to his grave just the day before and promised the cold stone engraved with his name that she hadn't given up on exposing Ziggurat.

Anne gestured with her hands, waving her notes in her hand, and it occurred to Elle that her lapse into silence had gone on too long.

"Rob's story is similar to many veterans' stories all over the world, as well as the residents of occupied areas, anyone who has found themselves in the center of war. The psychological effects of war on the human psyche. There is only one clear answer to this."

She turned to the second camera for a different shot, a wider view of the desk and a bearded gentleman in a white shirt and a blue checkered bow tie.

"Today, we are joined by Dr. Daniel Rift, professor of politics and international relations at Hendrix College in Conway, Arkansas. Welcome, Doctor."

"It's my pleasure." He smiled. "I was so sorry to hear about Rob Loera's death. He was a true patriot."

"Thank you," she said. "You've been teaching a unique perspective on the history of post-traumatic stress, there at Hendrix. Can you explain how far back your subject matter goes?"

"My initial travels took me to fourteenth century France," he explained. She looked to Anne to see her nodding and giving a thumbs-up. Elle did her best to remain present in the interview. Since leaving Tel Aviv, she found it hard to concentrate and keep focus. Her sleep was decent, but it took hours and two to three martinis to put her under.

Dr. Rift talked about texts of knights extolling the horrors of battle as well as poor living conditions, lack of sleep, and malnourishment. She thought of Cass living such a harsh, unforgiving life, looking to Elle for salvation.

After the broadcast, Anne took her to lunch at their favorite Mexican restaurant. They talked about work and her mother announcing her run for Senate. Anne went on one of her tangents about elections. Usually, the subject would have inspired a spirited debate between them, but Elle bantered half-heartedly. Her thoughts turned to Cass, as they often did. Elle could see her so clearly in her mind, and remember every conversation, touch, and glance.

"It's gotten so that I can tell when you're thinking about her," Anne said. "I'm glad we're not on the air."

"I think about her every minute, Anne," she said apologetically. "Is she okay? Where is she? Has she gone back to those horrible people because she feels like she needs to protect me?"

"I think that was the point," Anne said. "She knew there was the chance that you two might never see each other again. How long are you going to wait, Elle?"

"However long it takes," she said, though she knew that was an unrealistic goal. "Or I could tell everyone what really happened in Kuwait."

"With no proof?"

"They know what I know," Elle said and took a sip of her margarita on the rocks. "They probably have an action plan ready."

Anne peered at her over her glasses. "So we just forget about it. We let it all go. Including your lady-Bond."

"I could never forget her."

"I didn't mean that," Anne said. "I meant moving on with your life from this whole Rob Loera thing. Stop pining for a woman you're never going to see again."

"It's very unfair of you to say that," Elle said.

"You're not being fair to the people in your life," Anne said. "People who haven't dragged you through hell before vanishing over the horizon."

Elle's anger swelled and flashed through her body. "Is that why you asked me to lunch? To fucking attack me?"

Anne frowned. "I wanted to take you to lunch because I want my best friend and my colleague back. It hurts to see you chase ghosts when I'm right here."

She opened her mouth to argue but held back. She took another sip of her margarita. What did everyone want from her? Her parents. *Green Patriot*s viewers. The sponsors. Anne. They all wanted something different. It was suddenly hard to manage all of their wants. What about what she wanted? She thought of Cass, and tears gathered in her eyes. She blinked them away. Anne was watching her.

"I'm sorry," she said. "I don't want to upset you, Elle."

"You didn't," she said sullenly.

Anne tilted her head. "I guess this is going to take some time."

Elle nodded and managed to muster up the strength to change the subject.

❖

Elle's home life was not much different. She spent most of her time in her apartment with a good stiff drink. It numbed the pain. She thought of Cass. She made other plans. Elle knew that Ziggurat would keep her under scrutiny. They might even come for her. The thought frightened her to no end.

She called a locksmith to add an extra bolt on the door. The manager of her apartment was pissed when he found out, and she received a letter from the leasing company a few days later. After re-thinking the lock situation, she decided that there was little she could do if Olympicorp came knocking.

She kept her blinds closed completely shut and the curtains at her patio drawn. She would often wake in the middle of the night and just before dawn looking for signs of Cass.

One late evening, exactly two months after the events in Kuwait, Tammy Crockett interrupted her vigil, researching gun safety classes. Elle had been avoiding her, and they had vague conversations where Tammy was sternly polite about Alexander's death and the story of what happened in Kuwait. She obviously saw through Elle's lies and trusted her to drop the bullshit soon.

"What's up?" Elle asked.

"This security footage at the hotel during those Bedouin attacks," she said. The tone in her voice told Elle that the story had crumbled.

"How the hell did you get that?"

"Oh, it wasn't at all easy," she said slyly. "It seems the Kuwaiti government swept up the surveillance footage, and won't let anyone take a peek. But they were foolish enough to e-mail it around. How silly is that in this world of hackers?"

Elle felt her stomach churn. "Tammy, whatever you've gotten a hold of, it can put us all in serious danger—"

"There is a very familiar face running around in that hotel with a very feisty blonde. I can't believe you kept this shit from me," Tammy said. "After I helped you."

"I didn't tell you for a reason," Elle said. "Fuck. I shouldn't even be talking to you about this at all. This is serious."

Silence. She owed Tammy the truth, at least some part of it. She sighed.

"Meet me at the Playbill in thirty minutes and don't tell me you're sleeping, heifer."

Tammy ended the connection. Elle rolled her eyes and groaned when she remembered exactly what the Playbill was. She got dressed and drove to the designated meeting place.

Tammy sat at a velvet booth. Elle maneuvered past a woman in a top hat, tails, and not much else. On the stage, a drag queen dressed as Liza Minnelli in *Cabaret* sang the title song.

Elle sat down and poured herself a shot.

"So what exactly did you get yourself into out there in the desert?" Tammy asked.

On stage, the fake Liza was working the crowd with a few jokes. Elle took the shot, sighed, and began to tell the whole story. She told Tammy about meeting Alexander, Zahavi and Cass. She spoke of the abandoned village and what happened that night. She told her how Alexander died. Elle left out the part about Thora, and the safe house.

"Shit," Tammy said when she had finished. Elle wanted to explain herself, but something on Tammy's face said that she didn't have to. Elle grinned. It was a comfort for someone else to see just what was at stake. She showed Elle the video of the Al Mansar lobby on her tablet. It was surreal to see herself running with Cass as she fought off the horde with that pry bar.

"I wasn't able to dig up anymore on Ziggurat, but your blonde I found," Tammy said as she scrolled her smartphone's video menu to reveal another clip. The still showed Cass on what appeared to be some sort of concept bike. Tammy tapped the picture and it came to life. Cass guided the bike through a crowd of people. A cop stood in her way. He touched the bike and she punched his lights out.

Elle looked to Tammy. "That's definitely her."

"It was from a few weeks before you met her. That was from a bank robbery in Prague. She iced a couple of dudes who happened to rob the same safe deposit box that very day. They tried to start a fire to escape."

"So what was in that package?"

"No one knows," Tammy said. "But the guy it belonged to was a German scientist who killed himself the year before the robbery. Guess who he did contract work for?"

"Ziggurat?" Elle asked.

"Bingo." Tammy turned up her bottle again and grinned.

"Oh my God. Why didn't I come to you sooner? You're a freaking genius."

Tammy shrugged. "I can't believe you fed me that bullshit story."

"I promised Cass I wouldn't report anything."

"You're not. I will. Don't try to talk me out of this."

"You don't know what they are capable of," Elle whispered.

Tammy lit a skinny brown cigarette. She took a deep drag of it and reached for the ashtray. "This could be big."

"What about Cass? She's innocent in all this."

"What if that's what she wanted you to think?" Tammy asked. "Just maybe you're being manipulated by this broad. She knows about Rob. Maybe she's giving you a sad fairy tale about being a mind control slave to play on your sympathies."

On the stage, the music slowed and "Liza" began to sing "Maybe This Time."

Elle shook her head. "She wouldn't do that. She protected me."

"Maybe she's not done with her game."

"You are way paranoid," Elle gently reminded her. "I've thought of breaking the story. I thought of having you break the story, but this is someone's life. This is our life. What I saw in Kuwait was frightening. I have nightmares of that fucking gas getting to me."

Tammy narrowed her large eyes. "You didn't trust me. That hurts."

"I'm sorry?" Elle asked.

"I bet Anne knows the whole freaking story."

Elle sighed. "Who do you think came to Tel Aviv to get me?"

Tammy resignedly pressed her cigarette among the ashes in the tray, killing the burning ember of tobacco on the end. "You know, all of this got me to thinking about how the shit that goes on in the world is all connected," she said. "I'm going to come up with a program that links all six degrees."

"Clever," Elle said.

"And I'll hold off on that story. I hope your girlfriend shows up. I have a ton of questions for her ass to answer."

"Who said she was my girlfriend?" Elle asked.

"You don't have to tell me," Tammy said. "I too have succumbed to the swirl."

Elle laughed. "I'm going home, Tammy. We're not all self-employed and can make up our own hours."

"You're not going to stay for the nightly *Dreamgirls* tribute?"

Elle sat back down and helped herself to one of Tammy's skinny brown cigarettes. "Okay, maybe I can stay for one more show."

CHAPTER TWENTY-ONE

Music. Something by Bach. Dominated by lively strings. A warm feeling passed through her abdomen. She tightened her eyes and smiled. The music opened her eyes, and through the bluish gel, she could see Thora's form moving busily over her. There was always much involved with her revival.

She felt another stirring inside her and raised her hand outside of the gel to grip the side of the pod. The open air made her gasp, and she sputtered as the gel filled her mouth and throat and nostrils.

"Steady now," Thora said and floated down close to her.

She frowned because the gel muffled Thora's voice. She wanted to be out of the pod and with her. She wanted to stand on her own two feet and just go. She gripped the other side of the pod. She felt Thora reach into the pod and plant her palm in her chest to push her back. She was saying something, but the Gorgon couldn't hear the words clearly.

Finally, she felt Thora's hands on her shoulders lifting her out of the pod. She sat up, choking the gel from her lungs and wiping furiously at her eyes. Thora quickly came to her aid. She helped her out of the pod to a metal chair.

"Do you know who I am?" she asked.

"Thora," she said.

"Do you know who you are?"

"I am the Gorgon."

"Do you know what day it is?"

She rubbed her arms. The room was freezing. She didn't know what day it was. She just wanted to be next to a warm fire. She wanted to soak its heat right into her bones. Her body tingled with want.

"Can't we go to the library now?" she asked Thora.

Her eyes widened at the suggestion. "No. Not just yet."

She stood. She wanted to walk the cold out of her body. She paced around still smeared with the gel. Each step that she took seemed to bring a new wave of energy. "I don't know what time it is right now. Is it day or night?" she asked.

Thora looked puzzled. "It's night right now."

She trudged a few steps around the sterile lab, working the numbness out of her legs. There was only one way out of the room. A seamless door that only opened when Thora came near it. She felt as if she had somewhere to be, that she needed to leave right then.

"It's winter time isn't it?"

"What a question to ask," Thora said carefully. "Do you remember the cold?"

She stood and brought a thin white blanket to drape over the Gorgon's shoulders. She used it to wipe away the gel and further dry her skin.

She nodded. "Yes, I remember being outside the house and coming in to dinner."

Thora leaned in to study her face. "Is that all? What do you remember before that?"

She tried to remember something, but couldn't. "Nothing," she answered.

"Very well," Thora said.

She went to the door. It opened. The Gorgon followed her into the library. The room smelled of books and Thora's fragrance. It was her favorite place to unwind, and it was there she often had the Gorgon touch and kiss her.

There were folded clothes on a chair. Black flannel pajamas and slippers. She dressed and stood before the fire. Beyond a window, she could see a frosty landscape. She remembered daylight and running across that field while filled with such an anxiety. Had she been late to dinner?

She watched from the fireplace as Thora set up a cold dinner. She beckoned the Gorgon to a chair. She did as she instructed and they sat together eating in silence. She could hardly focus on anything but the food in front of her. Once her hunger was somewhat tamed, she found that her mind drifted back out the window and to the field beyond.

"Why don't I remember anything?"

"Finish your sandwich," Thora said.

She did, but she burned to remember something more than that day. She decided to focus on what she was doing rather than feeling. It had been a particularly brisk day, and she didn't wear a proper coat in her memory. She had just come from someplace fairly warm where the sun shone. In her mind, the scenery changed. She was suddenly running on rocky, sandy soil. She felt that same anxiety. That she should hurry. A black car flew over her head and landed. The memory of the sound of the crash made her put down her sandwich.

She stared at her empty white plate. Then she saw her. She was reaching for the Gorgon through a cloud of dust. A heartbreaking fear shone in her eyes. The scenery of her memory changed again, and there was the woman again, unclothed, beneath her, eyes burning with a different sort of intensity. They moved together beyond physical closeness. She could feel the other woman. Her skin and her heat and even deeper, the blood as it rushed through her veins.

Elle. She had to get to Elle. She looked at Thora who was speaking, but once again, she couldn't make out her words. She looked to the fire, and she saw Elle in her mind once more, angry, and then sad, her eyes shining with tears.

"I will never forget you."

"I'm sorry," Thora said. "What did you just say?"

The sandwich turned bitter in her mouth, and her lip began to tremble as her eyes began to tear. Elle. Where was Elle? Was she safe?

She stood and looked toward the window. She would run. She had to get back to the States. She felt Thora's presence behind her. She didn't recall seeing her move.

"This will not do," Thora said softly.

The Gorgon felt something cool and metallic pressed into her neck. Then came the hiss of compressed air and the sting of a needle. She suddenly felt very heavy, and all the light went away. She slipped away thinking of Elle's smiling face. She smiled back, certain that no matter how many times Thora put her in the pod, she would never forget Elle.

CHAPTER TWENTY-TWO

She stayed close to Thora as they moved through the streets of Manhattan. The sun shone high and the sky was blue and cloudy. A pleasant day. It was summer, and most of the people they passed were dressed for the weather. Thora had picked out her suit. It was a lightweight material that kept her cool despite the weather.

The Gorgon's gaze followed a police officer on a motorcycle. She was to be vigilant of law enforcement when out in the world. Her objective was to protect Thora should anything arise. She carried her black case. They were going to a meeting of the Pantheon, and many of the members would not be pleased to see the Gorgon.

She was a breathing, conscious weapon. They were smart to fear her.

A doorman allowed them in and they rode an elevator to the top floor. She followed Thora to a conference room where several members of the Pantheon waited for their arrival.

Thora made her rounds while she waited at the door. As she made her way around the table, she placed gray foam shapes on the polished wood, a couple of cubes, a sphere, a pyramid, and a cone. She placed a pocket-sized projector on the table, and it beamed a perfect live picture of Cass's brain.

"I know you're all anticipating the results of my latest endeavor. Ladies and gentleman, allow me to present the Gorgon."

At those words, the Gorgon removed her jacket just as Thora had said to do that morning. The rigorous training exercises she did daily had built the muscles in her arms. She looked to the objects on the table. A chill traveled from the base of her neck and into her skull. As the cold claimed her brain, the objects floated from the table.

As the objects levitated in the air, there were gasps from the Pantheon. Just as Thora had said, she ratcheted up the power. The objects flew in all directions, and one of the windows cracked along its length. Once the air cleared, the members of the Pantheon returned cautiously to their seats.

"She's magnificent," one of the men said. "And there are no more problems?"

"She is ready," Thora told them. "She is in the best shape she has ever been both physically and mentally. Her brain is able to use the Aegis at full capacity."

As she spoke and pointed to the x-rays on the screen, the Gorgon watched with a sort of detachment. Her gaze wandered to the window and the blue sky beyond. It made her think of a woman, compact and brown-skinned, her eyes dark. Elle Pharell. The reporter. She was waiting for her in Austin. She would have to be careful getting to her. The Gorgon wasn't supposed to have remembered her. She knew this. Thora had tried hard to wash her from her mind. The Gorgon wasn't sure how long Thora had made her sleep. She only knew that it was summer not winter.

She turned her attentions back to Thora. She watched as she spoke to the members of the Pantheon. They all watched her with admiration and respect. The Gorgon could feel it wafting through the room via their pulse.

When the meeting was dismissed, they returned to the car.

"You did well today," Thora said. "I am immensely proud."

She nodded and scooted away so that she could lean over and lay her head on Thora's lap. She felt her hands in her hair and closed her eyes. She played Thora's game, the tamed beast, dangerous yet dependent on her mistress to provide. Thora enjoyed the clinginess. She liked being physically close to the Gorgon. She had come to her every night since her awakening and opened her robe. Without hesitation, the Gorgon would kneel before her and pretend she was making love to Elle.

"Rest," she said. "You deserve it."

"The cold feeling lingers in my head."

Thora made a sympathetic noise. "Nothing you can't handle, my dear, as your brain syncs with the Aegis, it won't be so bad."

The Gorgon closed her eyes. She saw Elle again in her mind's eye. She was smiling. It made her smile to think of it.

"Something amuses you?"

"The Pantheon," she lied. "They were frightened of me."

"Get used to it," Thora said. "We will remake the world, you and I."

She nodded. She would have to be careful. If Thora suspected she remembered Elle she would put her back into the pod and back into a long sleep. She couldn't afford to keep Elle waiting.

A crash jarred the interior of the car. She felt it spin a half circle before the driver brought the car to a full stop. She and Thora ended up on opposite ends of the car, pressed against the window and on the floor. The driver turned to look at them.

"Are you okay?" he asked. His eyes widened when Thora produced a gun from her handbag, checked the chamber, and removed the safety.

"Something is wrong," she said, her usually perfectly coiffed gray hair tousled.

Her words sent the Gorgon into high alert. She lowered herself to the floor and peeked out the window. She saw a large black armored van on the opposite side of the street and men in black tactical gear, the word SWAT written across their chests. Officers in blue cleared the street of pedestrians. Local law enforcement? She looked back to Thora questioningly.

"Get rid of them," she said.

Before she could react, they swarmed the car. A female voice shouted at them from a bullhorn to exit the car, that they were under arrest. Thora handed her a small canister. She opened the door a crack and tossed it into a roll along the ground. Red smoke poured from the object and billowed up in great waves.

She stepped out of the car and grabbed Thora's hand.

She channeled the Aegis and saw the red smoke paint the wave of energy that shot forth and swept away the SWAT team. She grabbed Thora's hand and they fled into the folds of bystanders.

To anyone on the street they looked like bystanders escaping the fray, a mother and daughter, or perhaps colleagues. She heard gunshots close by.

They stopped in front of a café where others had taken refuge. Someone handed them a bottle of water, and she passed it to Thora who drank half before passing it back. They moved toward the back of the café and slipped into the kitchen. Confused workers watched them go but didn't say a word. They went out the back door to a narrow alley.

"What was that?" she asked Thora.

"I don't know," she said and removed what looked to be cell phone from her bag. She pressed a button.

"What the hell is going on?" she asked and listened, her face blanched. "I understand. Strange that they waited until we were away from the others before they moved in. Why would they be after the Gorgon? If I knew the answer to that, I would have never come to the States."

She frowned and ended the connection. She stuffed the phone into her purse and turned to look at her. A small group of people passed in a huddle. They looked lost, but determined to keep moving.

"Well?"

"It's nothing for you to worry about," Thora said. "Olympus has many cowardly enemies who would like to chip away at us rather than take us on. Those were not local law enforcement. Those SWAT uniforms were for the sake of the civilians. Most likely, it was the American government. The clumsy fools."

She moved to the mouth of the alley and waited until a taxi pulled up. When they climbed in, the Gorgon knew that the driver was a wraith. He turned to them.

"Nasty weather," he said.

"Yes, of course," Thora said.

The Gorgon found herself curious of him. She had only met one other wraith. She wondered if he remembered anything after Olympus washed his mind. If he had ever met someone and wanted to turn away from Olympus. She made it a point to make eye contact with him through the rearview mirror. He was African-American, his skin a few shades lighter than Elle's. His hair was a sandy color that nearly matched his skin. His eyes were a mix of brown and green.

They drove down to the harbor, and the driver led the way to a yacht bobbing in the water. They went aboard. Thora went with the wraith to the helm station to give him directions on getting them safely out of the harbor. The engines started, and she watched the New York skyline shrink. It made her ache to think of how close she was to Elle in that moment. She joined Thora in the plush, teak trimmed cabin. There were shorts and a T-shirt waiting for her on a chair.

"You may as well make the best of our impromptu sailing venture," she said with a small smile. She changed below deck and brought Thora a glass of the white wine from the bottle she found.

"How thoughtful," Thora said as she accepted the glass.

The Gorgon went to the helm where the wraith sat in the captain's chair steering the boat.

"Hello," she said.

His eyes wavered from the path ahead to her. He sized her up and checked out her pulse. After Kuwait, she discovered something new about brainwaves that humans emitted: they interacted on their own, bouncing against each other and weaving into complex patterns of sound. She supposed it created bonds, or repelled people from each other. She worked hard to learn to keep her own shielded, but she let the other wraith listen. She wanted to link with him the way Lyles linked with the villagers and Ziggurat people exposed to Cepilon.

"Hello," he replied. "We're sailing up the coast for now."

"What are you called?" she asked.

"I am Jason," he said. "And you are the Gorgon."

She nodded. "You have heard of me?"

"I just knew," he said.

"Have you been in New York for a long time?"

"I have spent my life there," he said, obviously puzzled at her question. "There are a few of us there to watch over the lines."

"Do you know them?" she asked. "The wraiths? Do you speak to them?"

"We stick close. We watch over the Pantheon."

"Do you talk about being wraiths?"

He only stared at her. "What need does that serve?"

She shrugged. "To compare experiences."

"Experiences?"

"What it's like to be us," she said.

Thora appeared, her glass in hand. "He doesn't understand," she said. "It's not his place and neither is it yours."

She looked to Jason who looked back at his course. His jaw was tense, and something had changed in his pulse. She detected anger and fear. Thora walked back through the glass doors and out to the deck. The Gorgon followed.

"I was only curious," she said. "I don't think I've ever met another wraith before."

Thora studied her. "Certain things are put in place for a reason. You need to understand that before we go any further."

"I understand. I didn't mean to displease you."

"I know you would never do anything to disappoint me," she said sternly. "You're innocent in so many ways, I am reluctant to send you out alone."

"I'm ready," she said. "I'm strong."

"Yes, you are, my beautiful Gorgon," she said. "After today's display the council wants to send you on a mission."

She smiled, not expecting the opportunity to leave to come so soon. She would see Elle again and try to convince her to go with her. They could live anyplace they wanted. They would be together.

Thora patted the seat next to her. "Good, come and sit with me and enjoy this day."

She did.

Once they docked the next morning, she found the other wraith in the helm room. He regarded her suspiciously. To him, she was an anomaly. She could feel him feeling her.

She touched his shoulder and looked into his eyes. "Elle Pharell," she said and once again. "Elle Pharell."

She looked up to see Thora on the deck impatient to depart. The Gorgon joined her without another word to the other wraith. She had said all she needed to say.

"I was apologizing for my curiosity," she told Thora.

She laughed. "He is so far beneath you, there is no need."

The Gorgon nodded as if to agree. In truth, she knew what the wraith would do next. He was human, after all, and he would want to know the owner of the name the enigmatic wraith had whispered to him. It would not take him long to find Elle.

CHAPTER TWENTY-THREE

Elle hadn't expected a Tea Party rally to be so festive. A bluegrass band played music on a makeshift stage. People barbequed and showed off their Revolutionary period costumes. Children played between colorful signs warning of socialism and calling to audit the IRS.

Anne and the cameraman, Dave, followed close behind. It had been her idea to cover the rally and to come along. Elle was against the idea. Wandering around a throng of crazies trying to get them to be reasonable was not her idea of a good time. Anne called it guerilla journalism.

The trip to DC was meant to be one of those changes of pace for Elle who had been accused of moping around since her return from Kuwait. The crowd made her nervous. Her mind wandered to Kuwait and the bloodthirsty legion controlled by Lyles.

She watched Anne warm up potential interviewees; they looked at Elle curiously, the only black woman in a sea of white affirmative action bashing, anti-gay, super conservatives. One guy held a Confederate flag in one hand and a Don't Tread On Me flag in the other. She went with them and joined in the chatter.

The Tea Partiers agreed to speak on camera as long as Elle and Anne didn't edit it to suit their liberal agenda.

"We aren't those kind of journalists."

Elle spent the next ten minutes chatting about various hot button topics, and they moved on through the crowd. They received a few jeers as they went. One big-bellied dude stepped in front of her and refused to move even though she said excuse me several times. His face was bright red and on the way to sunburn-ville. He reddened even more as she tried to step past him.

"Please, sir," Anne said, using her Mississippi drawl to deflect his attention. "We're filming for a non-biased report of the rally."

"Like hell you are," he said. His accent was West Texas, and she wasn't sure if it trumped Anne's.

"Come on, man," Dave argued. "Let us pass."

"Or what?" Santa asked. "I'll make you eat that camera."

"Don't be such a fucking pig," Elle said.

Anne groaned. "We're not going to cause a commotion here," she said and then repeated the phrase as if it were some mantra that would keep them from getting into an actual fray. Elle, on the other hand, knew that they were well past the point of no return.

A newcomer joined the scene. He wore a T-shirt with Uncle Sam pointing.

"Let her pass, brother," he said calmly to Santa.

"She doesn't belong here," he shouted, bringing the attention of those nearby. "She's not even a real reporter, just some cunt with Wi-Fi."

"You sonofabitch," Anne said before Elle could speak. She stepped forward, five feet and four inches of pissed off. "You have no right to call her that."

Santa stepped forward, and the newcomer planted a palm in his chest and held him back with little effort. Santa took a swing at the young man who ducked the punch and tackled him to the ground.

"No one wants any trouble," he said. "Just get out of here and leave these women alone."

Santa collected himself gingerly from the grass. He glanced around him to see who had witnessed his defeat.

"Go on," the young man said.

The big man turned and stumbled off.

"Thank you," Anne said to the young man. "Would you mind appearing on camera and saying a few words?"

"No," he said, his eyes on Elle. "I can't believe I'm here talking to you."

Anne looked over her shoulder at her. "It looks like you have a fan in the Tea Party crowd. I hope our demographic isn't changing."

Elle ignored the comment and stepped forward, her hand extended.

"What's your name?"

He stared at her hand and took a step back.

"I came from New York. Someone told me your name, and since then I haven't been able to stop thinking about you. I felt compelled to watch your site and then when I heard you would be here, I came."

"Who told you my name?" Elle asked. "Was it Cassandra Hunt?"

He shook his head.

"The Gorgon," Elle said.

He looked frightened. "How do you know that name?"

Anne looked to Dave. "Go get some footage. Now. We'll be leaving soon."

He did as she asked, knowing best not to argue.

"She told you my name," Elle said to the young man. "Did she say anything else?"

"No," he said. "I'm not supposed to be outside of New York. I wasn't given directive to leave my territory."

Elle put a hand on his shoulder. "Then go back," she said. "Thank you for finding me."

He smiled. "I'm glad to help you."

He reached out his hand cautiously. Elle smiled. "I know about the pulse too," she said. "I know mine sounds strange to you."

She held out her own hand again. "It's okay."

They touched and she smiled. The skin of his palm was dry and comforting.

"How long ago did you see her?" Elle asked.

"Last week in Manhattan."

"Oh shit," Anne hissed. Elle looked to her. "This wouldn't happen to be the same day as that mysterious military terrorist training exercise."

"Yes," he said. "I went to pick them up."

"Who else was with her?" Elle asked. "Was it Thora?"

Anne frowned. "Who the hell is Thora?"

The young man nodded. "I took them to the harbor and we sailed up the coast to Nova Scotia," he said. "It's dangerous for me to be here telling you this."

"I know," Elle said.

"I don't know why," he said. "Why it was so important."

"It was important to me and the Gorgon," she said.

"I have to go," he said. "Thank you for seeing me."

Elle felt out of breath. She walked away from Anne and Dave and stumbled to the edge of the fray. Anne approached with a bothered look on her face.

"She's alive," Elle said. "I should go to Nova Scotia. Oh my God, she was in Manhattan."

"I don't like what this woman is involved in," Anne said. "This happened on American soil for God's sake."

"I don't believe it was really an attack."

"You don't know that," Anne said. "And that man, he seemed like Rob."

"He's a wraith," she said. "He's under someone else's control, but he was able to break free and come here. She sent him."

"I don't think you should be taking off to Nova Scotia of all places," Anne said. "She's probably long gone."

"You're right," Elle said. "She would have given me something more specific if it was time for us to see each other again."

Anne stared at her a moment. "You really have feelings for her."

"Yes," Elle said. "I really do."

"Come on," Anne said. "Let's get out of here before Bubba Claus rounds up some of his friends."

She didn't argue. She glanced over the crowd as they went almost expecting to see Cass hiding out in some ridiculous T-shirt. Cass had sent her a message. She was alive. Elle wished she had more information. It took all of her being not to run to the nearest airport for a ticket to Nova Scotia. But Cass would be long gone.

Elle resolved to be patient. Soon, she would have all the answers she wanted. Soon, she would have Cass with her. She would never let her out of her sight again.

❖

A few days later, as Elle returned home from the studio, her neighbor's Great Dane bounded down the hall and jumped up, putting its giant paws on her shoulders. She stumbled backward as a wet nose grazed her lips and snorted her neck.

"I'm sorry," the lady down the hall said. "I just wanted to give you your package."

"It's fine," Elle said, accepting the box.

"You should get a dog," she said, struggling with the monster at the end of the leash. "Maybe a little Yorkie."

Since Rob and Kuwait, everyone had the habit of mothering her. They all had some idea of how she could bounce back.

"I'm so busy all the time," Elle said as she glanced at the package. The sender was Alexander Mo'moh in Indonesia. She nearly dropped it. She hastily excused herself from her neighbor and entered her apartment.

She cut the tape with scissors and instantly regretted it. What if it were a trap? She cut anyway and opened the box. The sender had filled it with wilting tropical flowers. She smiled and lifted an envelope from inside. She opened it with shaking hands.

Elle,

I know it's unfair of me to ask you to drop everything and come to the other side of the world, but I am. If you can't make it, I understand. Just know that I have missed you even during those moments when I didn't know who I was missing.

She felt a tear at the corner of her eye. She didn't wipe it away, but let it roll down her cheek. There was an airline itinerary with her name on it. There were two flights scheduled for the next day, the final destination Java, Indonesia, with the return two days after the initial landing. She went to her room and dragged her suitcase from the back of the closet and began to pack. She wouldn't tell Anne until she was on the plane.

❖

She landed in Java less than forty hours later. She scanned the people at the gate for Cass. She regretted turning down her airline meal in favor of sipping coffee. She felt almost as she did when she landed in Kuwait, nervous and excited for the unknown.

She passed another gate and then another. She had no way of contacting Cass. There was only the plane ticket and the flowers. She paused at the baggage claim terminal and looked around.

"Hey there."

She turned to see Cass not a foot away from her. She wore cut-off jeans, a Red Stripe tank top, and shades. She looked like an American tourist. That goofy half-grin lit up her face. Elle hurried into her embrace. She smelled of sunshine and sea.

"Hello, beautiful," she said into Elle's ear.

They pulled away only slightly conscious of the people around them. They glanced around them and thought better of kissing. Elle held on to her, though. The rest of the travelers could go to hell. She looked up into warm hazel eyes.

"How are you?" Elle asked. "I mean, are you...good?"

Cass took her hand and led her out of the airport. She took her to a little old Volkswagen. Once inside, they kissed, tugging at each other's clothes touching breasts, legs, and thighs.

"I'm damned good now," Cass said once they parted.

Elle couldn't stifle her smile. "What happened? Where have you been?"

Her eyes steeled a bit. "I returned to Thora. I didn't know what else to do. I wanted to make sure you were safe. She promised not to go after you."

Elle touched her cheek. "She kept her word."

"Thora thinks she washed the memories of you from my mind. I was reprogrammed and given a new assignment."

"What is it?" Elle asked.

"It doesn't matter," Cass said solemnly. "I'm not going through with it. I'm done, Elle. I'm never going back to her again."

Elle embraced her and they ended up kissing again. "I'll go with you."

Cass searched her face. "Do you mean it?"

Elle took her hand and kissed it. "It wouldn't be forever…"

"I don't know," Cass said. "And there's the chance that the people I work for would attack what you love to draw you out of hiding."

Elle sighed. It was a lot to take in. Could she actually sit idly by while people she loved were hurt? While the *Green Patriot* collapsed?

"Don't make a decision just yet," Cass said. "Let's just spend some time together, Elle. I've missed you so much."

She agreed though the question nagged her. Could she really walk away from her life for an undetermined amount of time?

They drove to the northern coast and stopped to explore the sights. They wandered the city hand in hand, settling at a plaza with carnival rides, restaurants, shops, and bars. In between, flowers bloomed and green plants rose up toward the sky. Elle could feel the breeze of the sea though she had yet to see it.

They had dinner at a café. It was easy to fit in with the tourist crowd. Most of them were surfing enthusiasts there for the waves of Western Sumatra.

After eating, they shared some shisha from a hookah pipe while they sipped rum and Coke. The sun set as they watched a group of performers play stringed lute type instruments and flutes. Standing there with Cass, it sounded like the most beautiful music she had ever heard.

As night settled, they strolled through a marketplace. At one stall, she found two beaded bracelets of rough pearls, one for herself and one for Anne, an apology gift for taking off.

"She's probably going to fire me," Elle said.

"I thought you two were partners," Cass said.

"We are, but she's definitely going to fire me," she said. "But it's so worth it to be here with you."

They went to another stall where a round man in a pinkish satin Japanese bomber jacket looked over a selection of masks. He skillfully haggled with the dealer for ten different ones. Elle spotted a silver cuff bracelet with a filigree pattern.

"That's nice," Cass remarked.

"I'm glad you like it, because I'm buying it for you."

She brightened. "A gift? It's not even my birthday."

Triumphant from his purchase, the man in the pink jacket smiled at them good-naturedly. He had heard their conversation and segued in.

"It's best not to question such a lovely present," he said. "Don't accept the asking price."

Elle noticed a hint of a Southern drawl along with the empty sleeve of his jacket. They thanked him and haggled their own deal for the cuff. She presented it to Cass who slipped it on her wrist.

"I'll wear it forever," she said decidedly.

They drove down to the dock, and Cass led the way aboard a small plush yacht with a dark blue hull and a white hardtop. Elle watched in amazement as she piloted them out into the open water of the bay, the lights on land twinkling in the distance.

"It's beautiful," Elle said as they stood on the bow admiring the full moon. "Are you sure this is safe?"

"Of course," Cass said.

Elle smiled. "Good, cause I missed you."

She found herself suddenly shy of Cass and aware of how much of a stranger she was. Sure, they had made love before, but Elle had spent nearly seven months viciously blocking the memory whenever it materialized into her mind.

"Please," Cass said, moving close. "Don't be anxious."

Elle frowned but couldn't help chuckling. "Stop reading me."

"I'm sorry," she said sheepishly. "I couldn't help it."

She guided Elle to the back deck appointed with a lounge area. They sat together and Elle cuddled into Cass's side.

"Have you ever slept out on the sea, under the stars?" she asked.

"I can't say that I have," Elle said.

"I want to see the sun rise with you at my side," Cass said decisively. "I want to make love to you here."

Elle smiled. She sat up to gaze at her face. The only light now fell from the interior of the cockpit. She could only see the bare outline of Cass's face. The rest was vague like a dream. Elle shivered at the thought of waking up in her bed, halfway hung over. She decided to act.

Their first kiss seemed to suffuse her body like some intoxicant. She felt it spread through her blood and belly, over her heart, causing it to flutter. Nothing would do now but to sink into her, to go wherever Cass would take her.

Arms that were more muscular than she remembered enveloped her. Elle had inspected them the entire day and wondered how they would feel around her. She removed her shirt to better feel them.

The hands she knew. They were hungry to touch the curves of her hips as they had in Kuwait. Elle smiled at the memory. She settled in Cass's lap and felt her hands move from her hips and up her flanks. They unclasped her bra and slipped it over her shoulders, and in seconds roved to her breasts testing the heft and firmness like ripe fruit.

"I tried to make myself forget," Elle confessed. "It hurt too much. I feel bad because you went through so much to remember."

"It's okay," Cass said. She rested one hand at Elle's belly; the other she used to hold her chin and guide their lips back together. They made love as if they had all the time in the world. Cass was definitely more muscular than she remembered. Elle let herself abandon her cares and fears. It was just the two of them calling out their passions into the salty air, and holding on to each other for dear life. They moved below deck sometime during the night, Cass guiding the way through the dimly lit cabin. They snuggled deep under the covers of the bed there. Elle slept better than she had in months.

She woke alone. She went up top and found Cass watching the water in the first strains of the sun. Her hair was wet, and she looked particularly appetizing in her black swimsuit. Style wise it was nothing to write home about, but Cass filled it out like an athlete.

"You've started without me," she said.

"I couldn't sleep."

"What is it?" Elle asked.

"None of this will be worth going through with if you're not with me," she said. "I should just stay with Thora."

"Don't say that," Elle said.

They were silent for a moment. "What happened in Manhattan?"

"We went to a meeting and we were attacked afterward."

"By who?" Elle asked.

"They were dressed in SWAT uniforms, but I'm not sure who they were."

"Like a whole SWAT team?" Elle asked. "How did you get out of that?"

"With the Aegis," she said. "It's an implant in my brain—"

"The Aegis?"

She stood, letting the towel around her shoulders fall to the deck. "I should show you."

Elle watched her close her eyes; her drying hair ruffled in the breeze. After a few seconds, Elle felt the air around her seemed to go solid. She could feel it pressing against her skin like a million beads. The surface of the water split as if pounded by a massive fist, and two short waves sprayed up and splashed the water.

Elle turned to Cass. "That didn't just happen."

"It did," she said, and she turned again, making more waves. The boat rocked slightly.

"That's insane." She ran to the railing and looked over the edge. "You can control it?"

She turned back to face Cass. Elle felt a gentle push at her face, her hair stirred.

"What is it?"

"It's sound waves undetectable by anything other than seismic equipment," she explained.

"And it's in your head?" Elle asked. "Isn't that dangerous?"

"Probably if I overuse it," Cass said. "It didn't take much out of me to get me away in Manhattan."

"And what about Prague?"

"Prague?" she asked.

"You robbed a safe deposit box there and killed several other robbers," Elle said.

"I don't remember that I'm afraid," she said. "How did you find out about it?"

"I have a friend," Elle said. "She snooped and hacked footage of the hotel in Kuwait City. She ran your image and description through some databases, and the surveillance video from Prague came up."

"She sounds pretty brilliant."

"Too much for her own good," Elle said. "I convinced her not to make a story out of it. I hope she doesn't connect you to Manhattan."

"Me too," Cass said.

Elle moved close to her and they kissed until they were making love again on the deck in the brightening sun. As she half snoozed in her arms, she wondered about Cass's plan and what it involved. She would have to leave the next morning and had no idea when she would see Cass again. She kept the tears that threatened to herself.

CHAPTER TWENTY-FOUR

Cass hid her own tears as she lay next to Elle. She had never known love before, but that was what she felt for her. Any move she made to get away from Thora and Olympus could end badly not only for her, but also for Elle. Perhaps it was best to let her go. She would have the memories at least. She imagined herself keeping up with Elle over the years, watching her get over the two of them not being able to be together, and meeting someone new. Someone normal who could love her without retribution.

Cass would be noble and take care of both of them, and envy their life together. She would be happy for them though because Elle would be happy. A blast of wind stirred around them. She would have to get up and check the weather. She had been neglectful in her captain's duties. Elle murmured in her sleep, and Cass smiled to herself.

The wind strengthened. A halo of chaos erupted around them. The water suddenly rose all around the boat, spilling over the hardtop and splashing against the cockpit. The boat rocked violently, and she heard Elle scream as the bucking boat pitched her backward over the railing and onto the swim platform at the back of the boat. She managed to catch Elle's arm with one hand and the railing mid-deck to keep them from both spilling over the edge.

She saw the fear in her eyes as the water roiled over them. Cass dragged her through the foam and pulled her shivering body close.

"I've got you," she reassured her.

The boat continued to bob like a toy. The tempest below juxtaposed the calm blue cloudy sky up ahead. Cassandra looked up and saw what looked to be a helicopter without its blades rise out of the water. The thing was sleek and black. It glistened from the sun and spray like some hovering sea mammal. It sprouted wings, and men fell from its belly on dangling black cords. They landed on the deck and struggled to keep their footing.

Cassandra cursed. She didn't know who had sent these men—Thora, Olympus—but she would put them into the sea along with the thing from which they had sprung. She moved Elle's hands to the railing and made sure she wrapped them tight.

"Don't you let that go," she said. "Not for anything."

She nodded. "Be careful."

Cassandra stood and channeled that cold part of her brain where the Aegis resided. She felt the sharp pain, but the release didn't come. The pain that she had learned to tolerate quickly strengthened to an echoing throb. She felt blood trickle from her nose. She tried again, starting a terrible ringing in her ears that momentarily drowned out all sound.

The men advanced cautiously as if they expected the Aegis only to become bold when they saw no evidence of its power.

With no time to try again, she picked up part of a broken fishing rod. One of the black-clad men produced a yoke. It was not of Thora's design or Olympus's. It looked rougher and had jagged teeth on the edges where it locked.

"Come with us," one of the men said, his voice muffled behind the helmet. "And no one will get hurt."

"Who are you?" she asked. "Who sent you?"

"That will be explained to you once you come peacefully."

She flashed a lethal smile. "And my friend?"

"Her safety can be negotiated with your cooperation."

Cassandra shook her head. She gripped the piece of fishing pole in her hand. They came at her. The broken rod connected with one of their shoulders and snapped in half. One of them grabbed her arm, and she heard the click-click of an armed Taser. Another of the assailants grabbed her other arm and twisted. A booted foot slammed over the top of her bare foot. A blow to the side of her neck brought with it 5,000 volts.

Her body seized and she used the momentum to wrest her arms free. With one swift punch, she cracked the black faceplate of the one who had shocked her. He stumbled backward. Two more shocks flared from twin strikes at her flanks. She fell to her knees. She felt the cold press of the collar. She raised her hand to her neck before they could secure it. The device dug into her wrist breaking the skin and drawing blood.

Behind her, Elle screamed. She whirled to her feet. Three of the assailants in black circled her while the fourth struggled with Elle. Just as Cass had instructed, she refused to let go of the railing.

One of the assailants took the opportunity to pounce while Cass was distracted. His fist rocketed forward and she could hear the crackle of electricity. A new toy. A glove capable of delivering a shocking blow.

Cass sidestepped the attack, grabbed the black-clad forearm above the gloved fist, and sent it into the chest of another of the attackers. She ducked the third man's offense and tackled him to the deck.

She grabbed the front of his chest gear and slammed his head in to the deck. His faceplate cracked more. She rammed her fist into the weakened guard and felt it shatter with great satisfaction.

She pried a large shard lose and turned, slicing through the protective fabric and into the arm of one of the men in black. He dropped the collar and it clattered to the deck. She kicked it, and the three of them watched it slide overboard.

The assailants backed off. In the melee, they had switched sides and she stood at the prow while they stood mid-deck, closer to Elle. She held the shard in her hand, ready to tighten it for an attack. Blood dripped from her hand onto her bare feet.

She felt the air behind her grow heavy with a steady thrum. She turned to see the strange craft that had risen from the sea. The air in front of it seemed to take form and ripple like the water. Blue sparks appeared and faded as soon as they had formed. She took a step backward as the air thickened around her, a pressure she knew all too well. She registered what was happening a second before a sudden invisible strike sent her flying backward into the ship's cabin. Upon impact, everything went black.

❖

The glaring sun and the sounds of the sea were the first thing she was aware of. She opened her eyes, expecting to see Elle lying next to her in that bikini. She nearly smiled. Then she saw the dead man in black tactical gear lying prone on the deck, his face slack and cold behind his broken helmet shield.

She scanned the sky for the strange craft. She carefully picked herself up from the deck.

"Elle," she croaked. "Elle."

She picked her way across the deck and looked toward the horizon, for what she didn't know. She had no way of knowing how long she had swam the sea of unconsciousness. She stumbled to the cabin and drank water straight from the tap. Her mouth tasted briny and bloody. She couldn't look straight at her reflection.

She had lost Elle. She had brought her into her hell and the abyss swallowed her up. She turned away from the mirror. She went back on deck. She needed to figure out who sent the men to attack her and take Elle.

If Thora was the culprit, she would want her back into Olympus's fold in exchange for Elle's return. Once she had Cass back in her possession, she would wipe her mind completely. There would be no more Cassandra; there would only be the Gorgon. She would never see Elle again.

An electronic chirp called her from her thoughts. It was coming from the dead man on deck. She went to him and riffled through his gear. In a pocket sewn on to his sleeve was a small black phone. Cass picked it up.

"Hello." A male voice, deep and cultured.

"Where is Elle?" she asked.

"She is safe. On her way back to Austin."

"Who are you?"

"Call me a Good Samaritan."

She ignored his flippant tone. "Who do you work for?"

"An agency like Olympicorp, devoted to the ideals of America's forefathers that have been left by the wayside in the last century," he said. "We protect the interests of the American government and its citizens."

She scoffed. "You seemed real concerned when you kidnapped one of those citizens."

"It's for her own good," he said. "Olympicorp would not have been so kind."

She knew his words were true. "My allegiance is only to Elle."

"I was counting on that, my friend," he said.

"Is that why you took her?" she asked. "So you could strong-arm me into switching sides?"

"I like to see Ms. Pharell as a motivation for you to do what you know is right," he said.

"What do you want from me?"

"Give me one of the Pantheon," he said.

"How do you know about the Pantheon?"

"I'm very good at my job."

"You attacked us in New York," she said. "You're after Thora." He didn't answer.

"You're grasping for straws," she said. "Your little ambush in Manhattan didn't work out so you're going after a wraith."

"We all know that you are more than a wraith," he said.

"And Elle?" she asked. She couldn't hide the emotion in her voice.

"That depends on your cooperation."

Cassandra stared in the distance. Just that morning, she and Elle had huddled under blankets and made love as the light rose. In that moment, she felt suffused by Elle like the sea after a long night. Her life before had been just that, dark, with a few stars but mostly clouded.

She laughed bitterly. "Thora would never turn. She would die first."

"We all have our decisions. Right now you have a very important one to make."

She paced the deck. "You can't hurt Elle."

"I don't plan on it," he said. "Anne Humphries is already sick with worry, as is Elle's mother. Tammy Crockett has your picture. Your little romantic charade will be blown and Thora won't be able to help you."

The bastard knew everything. She was exposed. While she had been busy trying to shield Elle and herself from Olympicorp, a new snake slithered on the scene.

"How do you expect to go about this?" she asked. "They wipe my mind—"

"Didn't they after Kuwait?"

"Yes, but—"

"You remembered Elle," he said sternly. "I bet you remember every detail of what happened in Kuwait."

"What does it all mean?" she asked. "Thora tried several times to erase my memories of Elle, but she couldn't."

"You've bucked the system," he said. "You've popped."

She had heard about wraiths who popped. They were no longer useful to Olympus, as they could no longer be programmed. They were repurposed or killed outright.

"If they find out, they'll kill me," she whispered.

"Or worse."

"If you hurt Elle, Manhattan will look like a picnic."

He laughed. "Open the back of this device. There will be a small capsule. Swallow it with a full bottle of water."

She opened the back of the phone. Nestled in gray foam was the white capsule the man had described. She cradled it in the palm of her hand against the wind. She placed the phone to her ear.

"I have it. What is it?"

"A tracking device," he said. "And an enzyme, the beginning of a treatment that will aid in resisting any further memory wipes."

"Why should I trust you?"

"You could throw the phone in the ocean, clean up the boat, and forget about this whole conversation. It's best that you forget about Elle. She is a lovely woman. Intelligent. Brilliant. Truly unforgettable. She doesn't deserve the pain of a life with you."

"I'd do anything to keep Elle safe," she said. "But then, you already know that."

"You wouldn't have been able to make it out there alone."

"Keep her safe, and you won't have to find out exactly what I am capable of on my own." She swallowed the capsule. Her tears fell freely and so heavily, she doubted she needed a bottle of water to wash down a pill.

"Congratulations, Miss Hunt. You've officially switched sides. Play your cards right, and one day you'll be free of all this."

She looked out at the choppy sea, and pocketed the phone.

About the Author

Tanai started writing strange little novels at the age of fourteen and dreamed of becoming a published author. She is a hard-core musicphile and enjoys everything from Bluegrass to Rap to Metal. She has an extensive collection of digital music files, CDs, and vinyl. Tanai is a total fangirl. The generous space allotted in this biography is not big enough to even begin to list all of her favorite fandoms. She studied graphic design at the Art Institute of Houston and uses what she learned there for her second passion, teaching art to inner city youth. She lives with her hilarious, wonderful girlfriend, Jeanette, and their three dogs, Zeus, Zoey, and Beto.

Tanai can be contacted at: tanaiwalker@yahoo.com
Website: www.imaginarypeople-madeupplaces.com/

Books Available from Bold Strokes Books

The Chameleon by Andrea Bramhall. Two old friends must work through a web of lies and deceit to find themselves again, but in the search they discover far more than they ever went looking for. (978-1-62639-363-9)

Side Effects by VK Powell. Detective Jordan Bishop and Dr. Neela Sahjani must decide if it's easier to trust someone with your heart or you life as they face threatening protestors, corrupt politicians, and their increasing attraction. (978-1-62639-364-6)

Autumn Spring by Shelley Thrasher. Can Bree and Linda, two women in the autumn of their lives, put their hearts first and find the love they've never dared seize? (978-1-62639-365-3)

Warm November by Kathleen Knowles. What do you do if the one woman you want is the only one you can't have? (978-1-62639-366-0)

In Every Cloud by Tina Michele. When she finally leaves her shattered life behind, is Bree strong enough to salvage the remaining pieces of her heart and find the place where it truly fits? (978-1-62639-413-1)

Rise of the Gorgon by Tanai Walker. When independent Internet journalist Elle Pharell goes to Kuwait to investigate a veteran's mysterious suicide, she hires Cassandra Hunt, an interpreter with a covert agenda. (978-1-62639-367-7)

Crossed by Meredith Doench. Agent Luce Hansen returns home to catch a killer and risks everything to revisit the unsolved murder of her first girlfriend and confront the demons of her youth. (978-1-62639-361-5)

Making a Comeback by Julie Blair. Music and love take center stage when jazz pianist Liz Randall tries to make a comeback with the help of her reclusive, blind neighbor, Jac Winters. (978-1-62639-357-8)

Soul Unique by Gun Brooke. Self-proclaimed cynic Greer Landon falls for Hayden Rowe's paintings and the young woman shortly after, but will Hayden, who lives with Asperger syndrome, trust her and reciprocate her feelings? (978-1-62639-358-5)

The Price of Honor by Radclyffe. Honor and duty are not always black and white—and when self-styled patriots take up arms against the government, the price of honor may be a life. (978-1-62639-359-2)

Mounting Evidence by Karis Walsh. Lieutenant Abigail Hargrove and her mounted police unit need to solve a murder and protect wetland biologist Kira Lovell during the Washington State Fair. (978-1-62639-343-1)

Threads of the Heart by Jeannie Levig. Maggie and Addison Rae-McInnis share a love and a life, but are the threads that bind them together strong enough to withstand Addison's restlessness and the seductive Victoria Fontaine? (978-1-62639-410-0)

Sheltered Love by MJ Williamz. Boone Fairway and Grey Dawson—two women touched by abuse—overcome their pasts to find happiness in each other. (978-1-62639-362-2)

Asher's Out by Elizabeth Wheeler. Asher Price's candid photographs capture the truth, but when his success requires exposing an enemy, Asher discovers his only shot at happiness involves revealing secrets of his own. (978-1-62639-411-7)

The Ground Beneath by Missouri Vaun. An improbable barter deal involving a hope chest and dinners for a month places lovely Jessica

Walker distractingly in the way of Sam Casey's bachelor lifestyle. (978-1-62639-606-7)

Hardwired by C.P. Rowlands. Award-winning teacher Clary Stone, and Leefe Ellis, manager of the homeless shelter for small children, stand together in a part of Clary's hometown that she never knew existed. (978-1-62639-351-6)

No Good Reason by Cari Hunter. A violent kidnapping in a Peak District village pushes Detective Sanne Jensen and lifelong friend Dr. Meg Fielding closer, just as it threatens to tear everything apart. (978-1-62639-352-3)

Romance by the Book by Jo Victor. If Cam didn't keep disrupting her life, maybe Alex could uncover the secret of a century-old love story, and solve the greatest mystery of all—her own heart. (978-1-62639-353-0)

Death's Doorway by Crin Claxton. Helping the dead can be deadly: Tony may be listening to the dead, but she needs to learn to listen to the living. (978-1-62639-354-7)

Searching for Celia by Elizabeth Ridley. As American spy novelist Dayle Salvesen investigates the mysterious disappearance of her ex-lover, Celia, in London, she begins questioning how well she knew Celia—and how well she knows herself. (978-1-62639-356-1)

The 45th Parallel by Lisa Girolami. Burying her mother isn't the worst thing that can happen to Val Montague when she returns to the woodsy but peculiar town of Hemlock, Oregon. (978-1-62639-342-4)

A Royal Romance by Jenny Frame. In a country where class still divides, can love topple the last social taboo and allow Queen Georgina and Beatrice Elliot, a working class girl, their happy ever after? (978-1-62639-360-8)

Bouncing by Jaime Maddox. Basketball Coach Alex Dalton has been bouncing from woman to woman, because no one ever held her interest, until she meets her new assistant, Britain Dodge. (978-1-62639-344-8)

Same Time Next Week by Emily Smith. A chance encounter between Alex Harris and the beautiful Michelle Masters leads to a whirlwind friendship, and causes Alex to question everything she's ever known—including her own marriage. (978-1-62639-345-5)

All Things Rise by Missouri Vaun. Cole rescues a striking pilot who crash-lands near her family's farm, setting in motion a chain of events that will forever alter the course of her life. (978-1-62639-346-2)

Riding Passion by D. Jackson Leigh. Mount up for the ride through a sizzling anthology of chance encounters, buried desires, romantic surprises, and blazing passion. (978-1-62639-349-3)

Love's Bounty by Yolanda Wallace. Lobster boat captain Jake Myers stopped living the day she cheated death, but meeting greenhorn Shy Silva stirs her back to life. (978-1-62639-334-9)

Just Three Words by Melissa Brayden. Sometimes the one you want is the one you least suspect. Accountant Samantha Ennis has her ordered life disrupted when heartbreaker Hunter Blair moves into her trendy Soho loft. (978-1-62639-335-6)

Lay Down the Law by Carsen Taite. Attorney Peyton Davis returns to her Texas roots to take on big oil and the Mexican Mafia, but will her investigation thwart her chance at true love? (978-1-62639-336-3)

Playing in Shadow by Lesley Davis. Survivor's guilt threatens to keep Bryce trapped in her nightmare world unless Scarlet's love can pull her out of the darkness back into the light. (978-1-62639-337-0)

Soul Selecta by Gill McKnight. Soul mates are hell to work with. (978-1-62639-338-7)

The Revelation of Beatrice Darby by Jean Copeland. Adolescence is complicated, but Beatrice Darby is about to discover how impossible it can seem to a lesbian coming of age in conservative 1950s New England. (978-1-62639-339-4)

Twice Lucky by Mardi Alexander. For firefighter Mackenzie James and Dr. Sarah Macarthur, there's suddenly a whole lot more in life to understand, to consider, to risk…someone will need to fight for her life. (978-1-62639-325-7)

Shadow Hunt by L.L. Raand. With young to raise and her Pack under attack, Sylvan, Alpha of the wolf Weres, takes on her greatest challenge when she determines to uncover the faceless enemies known as the Shadow Lords. A Midnight Hunters novel. (978-1-62639-326-4)

Heart of the Game by Rachel Spangler. A baseball writer falls for a single mom, but can she ever love anything as much as she loves the game? (978-1-62639-327-1)

Getting Lost by Michelle Grubb. Twenty-eight days, thirteen European countries, a tour manager fighting attraction, and an accused murderer: Stella and Phoebe's journey of a lifetime begins here. (978-1-62639-328-8)

Prayer of the Handmaiden by Merry Shannon. Celibate priestess Kadrian must defend the kingdom of Ithyria from a dangerous enemy and ultimately choose between her duty to the Goddess and the love of her childhood sweetheart, Erinda. (978-1-62639-329-5)

The Witch of Stalingrad by Justine Saracen. A Soviet "night witch" pilot and American journalist meet on the Eastern Front in WW II and struggle through carnage, conflicting politics, and the deadly Russian winter. (978-1-62639-330-1)

Pedal to the Metal by Jesse J. Thoma. When unreformed thief Dubs Williams is released from prison to help Max Winters bust a car theft ring, Max learns that to catch a thief, get in bed with one. (978-1-62639-239-7)

Dragon Horse War by D. Jackson Leigh. A priestess of peace and a fiery warrior must defeat a vicious uprising that entwines their destinies and ultimately their hearts. (978-1-62639-240-3)

For the Love of Cake by Erin Dutton. When everything is on the line, and one taste can break a heart, will pastry chefs Maya and Shannon take a chance on reality? (978-1-62639-241-0)

Betting on Love by Alyssa Linn Palmer. A quiet country-girl-at-heart and a live-life-to-the-fullest biker take a risk at offering each other their hearts. (978-1-62639-242-7)

The Deadening by Yvonne Heidt. The lines between good and evil, right and wrong, have always been blurry for Shade. When Raven's actions force her to choose, which side will she come out on? (978-1-62639-243-4)

Ordinary Mayhem by Victoria A. Brownworth. Faye Blakemore has been taking photographs since she was ten, but those same photographs threaten to destroy everything she knows and everything she loves. (978-1-62639-315-8)

One Last Thing by Kim Baldwin & Xenia Alexiou. Blood is thicker than pride. The final book in the Elite Operative Series brings together foes, family, and friends to start a new order. (978-1-62639-230-4)

Songs Unfinished by Holly Stratimore. Two aspiring rock stars learn that falling in love while pursuing their dreams can be harmonious—if they can only keep their pasts from throwing them out of tune. (978-1-62639-231-1)

Beyond the Ridge by L.T. Marie. Will a contractor and a horse rancher overcome their family differences and find common ground to build a life together? (978-1-62639-232-8)

Swordfish by Andrea Bramhall. Four women battle the demons from their pasts. Will they learn to let go, or will happiness be forever beyond their grasp? (978-1-62639-233-5)

The Fiend Queen by Barbara Ann Wright. Princess Katya and her consort Starbride must turn evil against evil in order to banish Fiendish power from their kingdom, and only love will pull them back from the brink. (978-1-62639-234-2)

Up the Ante by PJ Trebelhorn. When Jordan Stryker and Ashley Noble meet again fifteen years after a short-lived affair, are either of them prepared to gamble on a chance at love? (978-1-62639-237-3)